The Orange Room

ROSIE PRICE

Harvill
Secker

1 3 5 7 9 10 8 6 4 2

Harvill Secker, an imprint of Vintage, is part of the Penguin Random House group of companies whose addresses can be found at global.penguinrandomhouse.com

First published by Harvill Secker in 2024

penguin.co.uk/vintage

Typeset in 10.8 /14.8 pt Calluna by Jouve (UK), Milton Keynes
Printed and bound in Great Britain by Clays Ltd, Elcograf S.p.A.

The authorised representative in the EEA is Penguin Random House Ireland, Morrison Chambers, 32 Nassau Street, Dublin D02 YH68

A CIP catalogue record for this book is available from the British Library

HB ISBN 9781787304093
TPB ISBN 9781787304109

The Orange Room

I

That summer she drove every morning across the common. The light was hazy, and her wheels kicked dust into their arches as she turned off towards the hotel. She pulled up, yanked the handbrake with both hands. Rhododendrons spilled pollen from their large, purple heads and ivy grew thick around the side of the building, pressing the rear windows shut. At this time, the hotel was still and quiet. She propped open the back door, flipped on the light.

Rhianne pulled her hair up into a ponytail. She had two thick, peroxide skunk stripes that ran from the base of her skull, and she wore matte foundation beneath a streak of bronze powder whose pigments showed up in a thick shimmer. Around her eyes, neon eyeliner, bold and geometric. This was the kind of make-up whose purpose was to draw attention rather than conceal. She liked the colour, liked knowing she could open up her compact and let out the little pieces of light contained in that dense palette. *Warpaint*, Alexander used to call it. 'Ready for battle,' he'd tell her, whenever her face was fully made. 'Always,' Rhianne had said, spreading her elbows wide in her chair. She felt, then, the closest she ever had to power. In the bar, she stripped back the curtains on their rails, pushed her pen into her ponytail.

The White Hart was a low, limestone building set just back from the common and sinking into the edge of the valley. At its front entrance it appeared compact, almost residential, but its south face was open and sun-drenched, giving on to a jumble of converted outhouses and walled, dense gardens. There was the bar and the kitchen, guest rooms upstairs, and the kind of menu that brought clientele from London in Porsches and gun-metal S-Types. The kinds of people, Alexander would have explained, in the evening quiet of his top-floor office, who didn't know there was a difference between wealth and good taste. 'Not like us, Rhianne. We understand. That's us. Renaissance rich, cash poor.'

In the restaurant, breakfast had been set out the night before: napkins laid on scarred wooden tables with bright, unmatched crockery; cereal bowls and juice glasses put out on the side. Rhianne tore the clingfilm from the bowls and pushed through the door to the kitchen. The atmospheric shift constituted noise and light, Kiss Radio over the sound of spitting fat. There was Callum – just his torso – on the other side of the hotplate. Callum was quiet, serious. Always his head bowed, the back of his neck exposed, his hair soft, buzzed short. During service, he would work quickly, pausing to run his cloth around the edge of each dish he plated, calling serv-*ice* in a tone that was low, commanding, which made him seem older than Rhianne's twenty-three.

It had been this way every morning for a month. There was a kind of arrogance to Callum's containment, his ease in this place – the way he pulled his knife from its block without looking at it, the way he flicked his dishcloth back over his shoulder when he was finished with it – which gave her a sense of her own impermanence. He might nod, or perhaps he would ask how she was as he came to stand by the still to fill his big two-handled pan with hot water. His disinterest suited Rhianne because – despite the colours, the skunk stripes – she did not particularly want to be seen. They were midway through June. If she had not left, if she had stayed in London, today would have been the final day of her degree show.

Callum did not look up as she went up the back steps. She

crossed the courtyard to the walk-in fridge and took the butter block and an industrial tub of yogurt down from the shelf, back to the kitchen. She laid out the block and he came, stood next to her, filling his pan from the still. She could feel him watching her. Her knife was old and blunt, and she pressed down on it with both hands, aiming for a clean cut, but the butter was thick and cold, and it crumbled straight away on the blade.

'Hold on,' he said. Callum filled a metal jug with hot water and, drawing a bigger, heavy-handled knife from its block, dropped it into the water. He stood, shoulder to shoulder with Rhianne. The mirrored blade steamed up.

'What's that for?'

'Nothing, really.' Callum pulled out the knife, touched its blade with his fingertips. 'It's just in case you wanted to keep all your fingers.'

'Well, maybe I don't.'

'No?' Callum dunked the knife back in the water. 'Because I heard you were an artist, so, probably you need them.' He picked up his pan, didn't wait for her to reply. 'Maybe just give it a minute,' he said, 'and then try.'

Rhianne blinked. So, he had heard about her. She took the blade out of the water. It melted the butter as she pressed it through the block, sinking easily in a smooth, straight line.

'Better?' Callum didn't look up from the hotplate.

'Better,' Rhianne conceded.

She cut the rest of the block quickly, her palms slippery, grateful for the distraction of fast-filling tables, the smell of perfume and expensive soap in the restaurant, plates coming out from the kitchen, which was full now with bodies and noise: mixers, the dishwasher, the ovens pumping out heat. Rhianne, invisible, marking quietly the passing of time by the filling of the restaurant, the accumulation of checks up on the board. She wrote her next check, passed it to Callum. She shouted, 'Check on.'

'Rhianne.' Callum ducked down so that he could see her through the little gap in the shelves between the pass and the kitchen, held up the check. 'The fuck's this supposed to say?'

'It says eggs.'

She met his expression and saw that there was a smile, tugging there, behind his features. His cheekbones glistened in the heat. She took the check back, smoothed it onto the hotplate and drew one neat, round ring, and another, larger, surrounding it: one egg, fried, sunny side up. She handed back the check. 'Better?'

Callum studied it. 'A lot better.'

Rhianne pushed the pen back into her hair. 'You heard it. I'm an artist.'

'I'm going to need you to sign that. For when you're famous.'

Callum sparked the grill. Rhianne headed for the crockery, pulled a stack of plates towards her. Maria, the pot-wash, shuffled up the steps with a fresh stack. Annabel was hovering, cleaning the sugar bowls. 'Serv-*ice*,' Callum said, spinning the dish towards Annabel. 'Full English. Egg,' he said, loud enough for Rhianne to hear, 'sunny side. Don't drop the plate.'

'Would I?' Annabel pinched the rim of the plate in her napkin, and she smiled, a flush travelling from her jaw to her cheeks. Rhianne watched as she pushed through to the restaurant. Her ponytail was tied high on the crown of her head, and it bounced as she walked. Rhianne's hands were dry, and they smelt of vinegar.

2

Rhianne, when Melissa asked how her day had been, answered that everybody was fucking. 'Or about to fuck.' It was morning, and Rhianne was sitting at the kitchen table with her spoon in the peanut butter. 'But I guess that's adult life for you.'

Melissa glanced up at the clock, at Rhianne, in her pyjama shorts.

'The guests? The staff? Who?'

She shrugged. 'Just. Everyone.'

Melissa did not acknowledge Rhianne's deliberate double use of that word, a neat little bomb at the breakfast table, loaded with the new and freshly destructive energy Rhianne had been wielding in the weeks since she had moved back home. It was a Friday and the first clear-skied morning in weeks. Melissa was slotting a Curly Wurly into her shoulder bag and here Rhianne was in the kitchen in her pyjama shorts talking about fucking or about-to-be fucking.

'I don't know,' Melissa said, 'I'd say adulthood is much more administration. Taxes, bills. Mould management. Work.' She was assessing her reflection in the mirror next to the door, pulling her frizzy blonde halo of hair back into the clip she kept attached to the hem of her coat, putting on her glasses. Transition lenses, kept on a string of beads around her neck, which, cruelly, Rhianne said made her look like a conspiracy theorist. Rhianne's laptop was open on the table, and Melissa could just make out the screen, greasy and finger-marked in the sunlight that fell through the open patio doors. She brushed her fringe, muddy roots, so that it sat more evenly across her forehead. 'You're not working until two?'

'And then until ten.'

'Good, so you can do it today.'

'Yuh-huh.' Rhianne nodded, put the peanut butter spoon back in her mouth. She stood, deposited her plate and cup in the dishwasher. Her top rode up over her little round belly, which, lately, was less little than round. Through the fleece material of her shorts, it was possible to make out the outline of a thong, sitting high on her hips. She'd gained weight in the weeks since she'd returned, and Melissa knew the cause. The peanut butter, partially. The picking, too. Standing in front of the cupboard, just as Dominic did, scooping great handfuls of granola out of the packet and shovelling them straight into her mouth, leaving, always, a scattering of cereal crumbs just beneath.

'Sooner rather than later. The form. Wasn't the show today?'

'It finished yesterday.'

Rhianne took the spoon out of her mouth and dropped that in the dishwasher, too.

'Do you want me to look at it with you again?'

Rhianne kicked the dishwasher shut. Inside, crockery clattered. Her voice, which had been deliberately steady, now broke. 'I don't want to fill in the form because I don't want to talk about it and I don't want to think about it.'

Melissa sniffed. 'Oh, so you'd rather ruin your life than have a conversation?'

'I don't want to fill in the form.'

The two women stood, staring at each other. Melissa was the first to blink. She had seen the form, the university's lettering across the top. Name. Date. Incident.

'It was quite a complicated form,' she said. And then, as if she hadn't been the one to bring it up, 'It's not the right time to talk about it. We can do that later.'

'I'm not here later.'

'You're not ruining your life . . .' Melissa paused. 'But you're not here for dinner?'

'Nope.'

'You're working.'

'Yep.'

Melissa scooped her car keys from the table, throwing another glance at Rhianne's laptop. Her emails were open, as were half a dozen tabs. The laptop's battery, she saw, was on red. 'Shut the door if you go anywhere,' she said.

'Not like I've got anywhere else to be,' said Rhianne. 'But yeah, I'll shut it.'

Melissa bent at the top of the garden steps to pull dry leaves from the stems of her dahlias, and took them down to the compost by the gate. Rhianne's car was parked up next to hers, its left front wheel halfway up the bank, its underside caked in mud. Car-flinging, Melissa called it, not parking. The house was on the west side of the common, and here, at the far edge, the great expanse of green valley turned into a patchwork, down into which Melissa's Burgundy Saab 900 now nosed.

Rhianne was and was not Melissa's daughter, had been her not-daughter since just after she'd turned six. At the time Melissa met Dominic – her not-husband – she'd had no children of her own. It had been three years since Dominic's wife had died, three years since Dominic had sat Rhianne down and told her that Josephine hadn't gone because she was still there, in his chest. Foolish, Melissa had thought, but also credible: it seemed entirely possible that Dominic, the sheer bulk and force of him, could contain two people. The size of his ribcage, Melissa used to think, had enough room for two sets of lungs, two whole hearts.

Melissa slowed at the chicane. Rhianne wouldn't fill in the form. Probably, she'd eat the rest of the peanut butter and maybe do some unpacking. She had, at least, moved the boxes from the corridor and into her bedroom. Melissa flipped the indicator left, took the bypass past Merrywalks. They'd talk about it again tomorrow.

'A drink,' Melissa had repeated, the first and only time she heard the story in full. 'He said it was just a drink?'

'Obviously he didn't say anything else,' Rhianne said, 'he's a sexual predator, not an idiot. Not that the two are mutually exclusive.'

'You can be both,' Melissa said.

Rhianne had blinked at her. Said nothing.

That was it. Rhianne had brought her anger – justifiable, legitimate – home with her, and with it, or beneath it, this disturbing counter-current Melissa could not quite qualify. There was a charge that had not been there before. Small things, unexpected things. The way she'd started doing her make-up – bolder – and those nails, that she painted up in her room. Blue, with bright orange dots in the centre of each cuticle. And the clothes she wore now, baggy-fitting and loose, and yet somehow all the more revealing. The car, which Dominic had bought her for her birthday, already dusty and unkempt. And those words, which sat with Melissa now as she drove down Cainscross, took the right just after Budgens. *They're all fucking,* Rhianne had said, *or about to fuck.* Recklessness. Something about it was reckless.

The surgery was an old building with a parquet floor and an institutionalised smell about it, the automated door heavy on its hinge. She pulled up in her spot, closest to the door. There was polish on the floors, and on the high reception desk, applied by contract cleaners over layers of disinfectant. It was the kind of cleanliness that made Melissa's skin dry, the back of her throat itch. The receptionist, Christine, had become obsessive about handwashing, so that often she had red bumps on her knuckles, the skin chapped even in summer.

'Have you still not asked Dr Taschimowitz for the hydrocortisone?' Melissa said. She swept today's cases up out of her tray. 'You may as well not be washing them so much because your skin will crack and then you're dealing with impetigo as well as eczema.'

When Rhianne was thirteen she'd had eczema on her face, the sensitive area around her nose. She'd scratched it so much the skin cracked and bled, and she'd had to take steroids. Rhianne hadn't missed a day of school, had gone in, determinedly, with a great yellow scab on the side of her face. She'd cried when she got home, and Melissa had told her how proud she was, told her that she would go back the next day and the one after, until the other girls got bored of laughing and the scab would be gone. Christine, though, was not so bold.

'I don't know if he can do that,' she said.

Melissa crossed her arms over the paperwork she was holding, bit back her sarcasm.

'A doctor? Write a prescription?'

'Will they mind if it's not my doctor?'

Melissa leaned over the counter and snatched up the keys to Dr Taschimowitz's office. 'Leave it with me,' she said. 'I'll do it. Just so you can see how easy it is to get things if you ask properly.'

It was the kind of backed-up day that would have caused a younger, less experienced practitioner anxiety, but which, for Melissa, was manageable, familiar. She took the blood pressure of a fifty-three-year-old who had lied to her about his salt intake, measured the lung capacity of a teacher down at Rhianne's secondary school who was complaining of a tight chest. A quarter-hour with Gerald, who lived out the other side of Selsley and who only ate roadkill. All of them anxious. A challenging enough day – she slipped logo-less condoms into a brown paper bag, passed them across her desk – that her mind was absorbed. She'd tell Dominic about it later; she looked forward to that. The way the night would hold still as she spoke, the conspiracy spun in those quiet hours, and within it, her brief authority. Her last patient today was a medical student, a twenty-three-year-old about to take her elective, who had told Melissa that she would need Hep A, Tetanus and Typhoid, probably also Diphtheria. She most likely still believed – mistakenly – that a successful medical career was about knowing diseases and diagnosing them and not about cultivating loyalty. Melissa had put condoms into a brown paper bag for her, too, told her she should take them for her holiday.

Melissa took her phone and the Curly Wurly out of her bag. She checked Dominic's location. The dot blinked down at Ebley Mill and she wiped chocolate flakes from the screen. Melissa's office window opened onto the footpath that ran alongside the school playing fields. The vertical blinds swung slightly in the breeze, weighted by their little chains, and she saw that the fields were full. Sports Day. Squealing, whistles blown. There were the days, years ago, in the holidays, when Melissa used to bring Rhianne into work. Normally Dominic would have her at the mill, lifting her up in one arm onto his shoulders and taking her out to his car, but when he was back-to-back or on site Rhianne would be stationed behind the surgery reception desk with a paper and coloured pens and one of those juice bottles with a straw that helter-skeltered around the outside.

Rhianne had developed a habit, around then, of chewing her bottom lip. Not the cutesy chew of a pretty, put-together child, but a gummy kind of hoovering whereby she sucked the whole of her bottom lip into her mouth and kept it there until Melissa pinched her cheeks between her thumb and forefinger, waiting for the lip to be ejected, before wiping the girl's mouth with a tissue. 'She's got such energy,' the receptionist used to say.

Melissa knew precisely what she meant. The first time they met, Dominic had shown her a photograph of Rhianne, smiling and toothless, her face tilted up towards the camera, her eyes wide and full of expectation. Hope. 'She's a handful,' Dominic said. 'She gets that from me.' He pulled his chair closer, then, and his knee collided with the leg of the rickety metal table, knocking the water bottle sideways. He caught it before it fell. 'A handful,' he said again. He clarified. 'But a good handful. One you want to hang on to.'

On one of those days at the surgery, Rhianne had wandered out into the waiting area and towards a man wearing no shirt and with a large, open sore on the side of his face. She'd been standing looking up at him when the receptionist realised and snatched her up by the wrist. On the way home, Rhianne had sat on her booster seat sucking her bottom lip while Melissa lectured her on respecting the privacy of their patients. 'Particularly,' she had said, 'the ones who have come in with open wounds and should probably be in a rehabilitation centre.' Melissa had glanced sideways at Rhianne, who seemed unmoved by the reprimand. Rhianne had let the lip go, then, and asked Melissa what a rehabilitation centre was.

'For people with addictions,' Melissa said. 'To things that hurt them.'

'So do they get better?' Rhianne said.

'Sometimes,' Melissa said. 'Sometimes they get worse again.'

'What about Jonathan?'

'Who's Jonathan?'

'In the surgery.'

Melissa had bitten back her next question, the realisation arriving that Rhianne had stood talking to the man for somewhat longer than the receptionist had implied.

'Jonathan,' Melissa said, 'needs to take care of Jonathan. And you know who Rhianne needs to take care of?'

She could remember, still, Rhianne's big, open face. Her expression so large that Melissa had the impression, then, as she'd had many times since, that the girl felt things that could not be contained. 'Who?' Rhianne had said.

'Rhianne. Rhianne needs to take care of Rhianne.'

Turning from her office window, Melissa finished her chocolate bar and went out into the corridor. She knocked on the door two down from hers and let herself in. She laid the prescription on Dr Taschimowitz's desk, and put a sticky-note on top of it, asking him to please sign it and leave it at the front for Christine. Melissa saw that her handwriting was very round, like a child's. She tore off the note, rewrote it, neater this time.

3

The shifts broke up the day awkwardly, so that there were early mornings and late nights and, if they were splits, an expanse of dead time between. Most days, she went home, opened her laptop at the kitchen table. She would sit in front of the form, the auto-complete boxes swimming across her vision. First name, Rhianne, and surname, Colvin. Not so difficult. Miss. Degree course, level, year of enrolment, year of expected graduation. Straightforward enough. The problem came with the longer bits. 'I need you,' she said, propping Jess up next to her on speakerphone. 'I have to explain our relationship.'

'OK,' Jess said. 'That's simple. You were a student. He—'

Rhianne interrupted. 'There's five lines.'

'Just say you were his student and he was your tutor.'

'Do I have to fill all of the lines?'

'Ignore the lines. Say you were his student.'

'OK,' Rhianne said. She sat closer to the screen. 'I was his student.' She typed, tongue pinched between her teeth, sat back. 'OK. Witnesses.'

'OK, so,' Jess said, 'we agreed. There don't need to have been witnesses.'

This was as far as they'd got before, but the problem with the form was that if it wasn't submitted right away its contents emptied from their little boxes so that next time she had to start all over again.

'Copy and paste it,' Jess had said, the last time they'd got to this point. 'In case.'

Jess wouldn't have had to copy and paste because for Jess, words were easy. Jess knew how to change the order of a sentence so that it sat in perfect balance, the cadence speaking to a higher kind of competence, a fluency that Rhianne had never found in language. For Rhianne, with every sentence, her thoughts seemed to calcify, her fingertips stuttering over the same few keys before backspacing, retyping, backspacing again.

And there, each time she sat down with the form, stood Alexander. Just as he had been as she worked, scraping thick layers of paint from her canvas, dried flakes falling on her feet and on the floor. The insides of her palms aching from the force with which she held her putty scraper, the image – a woman's face – visible only in flesh-tone contour, distorted. Alexander leaned close, folded his arms, straightened. 'Not what I expected,' he said.

Rhianne shifted in her seat, pressed the screen of the laptop back. 'OK. So, I have to describe the incident.' She bit at her thumbnail. 'They've given me five lines for that bit.'

'Yep,' Jess said. 'Five lines. It's cool. We can do five lines.'

'It was a Tuesday in May,' said Rhianne. She backspaced, tried again. 'It was a sunny Tuesday in May.'

Jess was hesitant. 'Do you need the sun?'

'I should set the scene a bit, shouldn't I? You know,' Rhianne frowned at the screen, 'so they know it's real.'

'OK,' Jess said. 'OK. A sunny Tuesday.'

'Yeah,' Rhianne said. 'We can check the weather, maybe. I'm sure it was sunny.'

Rhianne typed. Backspaced, typed.

After her shift that evening, she walked through the hotel, flipping off light switches, pulling the curtains on their rails. Brendan, who owned the hotel, was away that weekend. As Rhianne was locking his office at the back of the building, she heard from the other side of the door, loud, clear: 'Check on.' She unlocked the door, opened it. Callum, leaning back in Brendan's chair. In darkness, except for the desk lamp, a pool of light. He had a big hardback notebook resting on his belly. 'You trying to lock me in?'

'I thought everyone was gone.'

'You thought wrong.' Callum tipped back a little further, reached with his fingertips for the edge of the desk. He looked precarious suddenly, younger. Swinging on a chair: that was a thing that teenagers did. He was wearing an oversized T-shirt patterned with bright splashes of colour, flecked like paint.

Rhianne stood in the doorway. 'Why did you say check on?'

'That's all you ever have to say to me.'

'Maybe I've got nothing else to say.'

'I don't believe that.'

Rhianne folded her arms.

Callum laughed, pulled himself forward, landed on all four wheels.

'Come,' he said, pulling up a second chair. 'Sit. Tell me how you are.'

'I'm fine.' She became aware, then, that the muscle just under her left eye was twitching. She'd already seen, in the reflection of the mirror behind the bar, that there were dark sweeps beneath both her eyes. Callum turned the desk lamp towards her, held it there – an inspection.

'You don't look fine,' he said.

'I'm fine,' Rhianne said again. But she sat, this time, in the chair he'd nudged towards her. Callum dragged the chair and her in it closer to him, leaned his weight on its arm so that she pitched, just a little, towards him. 'Just tired.'

'All right,' Callum said. On the desk, Rhianne saw now that there was a framed picture of Callum with a little girl Rhianne recognised to be a niece or a goddaughter of Brendan's. In it,

Callum's hair was longer and his face less defined, and he was smiling an oversized smile, all dimples and teeth, the girl collapsing in giggles in his arms. Rhianne stared at it, the question – how long had Callum known Brendan's family? – forming, unasked. Callum picked the order book back up, put it into her hands. 'Well, you can help me with the orders. How many seabass do we need?'

Rhianne looked down at the book. 'Thirty?'

'Sure,' Callum said, 'thirty seabass. Let's add some sharks in there, too. Start an aquarium?'

At that moment, his humour was too sharp for Rhianne.

'I don't know,' she said. 'It's not my job.'

'Twelve,' he said. Softly, he placed a pen in her hand. 'Put twelve.'

In the little box next to the seabass, she wrote the number twelve. Below, the bream.

'Six,' Callum said. 'People don't like bream as much as bass. Which is dumb, because it's actually nicer. They just don't know it.'

'Six,' Rhianne said. She wrote a six in the box.

'And crab,' Callum continued. 'Five kilos for crab.'

'I like crab.'

'You like crab. Let's put six kilos.'

'OK. Six kilos.'

Callum pulled the office phone towards him, dialled. 'You don't have to go, right?' he said. 'You can read these out to me.' He picked up the receiver. 'You ready?'

Rhianne read from the paper. With every item, every time she spoke, Callum's weight on the arm next to her grew heavier, then lighter again. The chair was buoyant, bowing to him as he leaned closer, coiling back every time he went to glance at his menu – bright on the screen of Brendan's computer – repeating the order into the phone. Rhianne had woken at six thirty that morning, worked a split without managing to nap in-between, but her awareness sharpened, calibrating around the movements of the chair, gently rocking, the sound of his voice, reciting the order. Numbers, quantities, kilos. Pen markings on a thick, crinkled piece of paper. At the bottom of the page, she stopped, turned it. The back was blank, the indents of her writing visible on the underside. Callum hung up the phone. She asked him, 'So why are you still awake?'

'Why do you think?' Callum flipped the front page of his clipboard. 'Working. Doing three people's jobs. Welcome to hospitality.'

He looked past her, to the CCTV feed up in the corner of the office, which flickered, switching between cameras. In the top-left corner, the waste-bin behind the hotel, and the car park, on the far edge of which was the entrance to the staff house, a small converted barn where there were two rooms for live-in staff: Callum and, for the time she was here on placement, Annabel. Rhianne watched. A figure appeared on the screen. She recognised him: a guest, here alone, who had slung himself over the bar for the second half of the evening, and was now stumbling up the path towards the staff house. He was thick-set, broad shouldered, the top buttons of his shirt undone; at the bar, he'd asked Rhianne how old she was.

'Isn't Annabel in there?' Rhianne said, suddenly panicked.

Wearily, Callum pinned the order sheet up on the board. 'I think he's lost.' He unhooked the master key from its peg. 'Come on, Rhi-Rhi. Let's go help.'

She followed him out of the office and out the back, up to the top of the path. In the car park, Rhianne touched Callum's arm, pointed towards the staff house. The door was open, and one of the lower lights lit. She spoke quietly. 'What should we do?'

Callum looked down at her, his face grave. 'I think,' he said, 'we should probably get you one of those eye pillows. A facemask, once a week. Just to reduce the puffiness.'

Rhianne swore, more loudly than she meant to. 'Can you stop with the insults?'

'Or,' he continued, 'maybe you could ice a teaspoon.' He covered each of her eyes with his palms. 'It'll do wonders for your complexion.'

Rhianne snatched his hands from her face. Laughing, now. Callum hushed her. 'You'll disturb him,' he said. 'He's trying to break and enter and you're ruining it.' Callum closed his fingers around her wrist, tugged briefly. Let it go.

'I'll deal with it,' he said.

'All right,' Rhianne said. 'He's in Dragonfly Suite, by the way.'

'Yeah?'

'He made sure to tell me,' Rhianne said, 'when I was pouring his drinks.'

Callum nodded. In his jaw, a flicker of something; in Rhianne, a guilty satisfaction. 'All right,' he said.

'You want some help? Carrying him?'

'No,' said Callum, 'better I don't have witnesses, Rhianne.' He looked at her, serious for a second, then broke into a smile. 'Go on,' he said. 'Fuck off. It's late. Bedtime.'

She got in her car, checked her mirror as she pulled away, thinking, half-hoping, that he would be standing, waiting. The reflection, though, was empty.

4

A drink, that was it. An evening in May. Sunshine, electricity. Really, though, it was not so much the drink as everything that had come before it. For example, there had been her obvious talent. Without that talent of hers, there never would have been an Alexander. Rhianne knew this about herself. She'd always had that rare privilege of knowing that whenever she picked up her pen and started to work, the image in her mind would be the one that would then begin to appear on the page before her. It was a particular power, to capture a person's essence in shape, colour. The subtle tilt of a chin revealing their curiosity, the curl at the corner of their mouth their assuredness, there, marked out in ink or in graphite. This power had seen her with ease through school, her art foundation, the first years of her degree, and it had drawn him – Alexander – to her corner of the studio.

At first, he'd said nothing. He'd stand, watch, then walk away. She had signed up to his studio hours knowing that he had a reputation for breaking his students down, building them back up again. Galleries and exhibitions across London had begun to fill with Alexander's protégés. It was the kind of unmaking that Rhianne was hungry for. But the whole of that first term she was in his class, he'd ignored her. September through December he hadn't once looked at her, and Rhianne had begun to think that maybe the rumours were overblown, or that he had not noticed her, until, in the last session of that first autumn term, he stepped forwards, blocked her path as she was leaving. She did not know that he knew her name.

'Rhianne,' he said quietly, 'you're a superstar.'

Over the break, she left all her materials in the studio, including the photograph around which she was designing her final year project. A few days before Christmas she rolled over in bed, looked up at the wall and panicked to see a blank space where the photograph had always hung. There were other photographs of her mother up on the wall, but this one was her favourite. Josephine was looking straight into the camera. She wasn't smiling; she was in the middle of speaking, her hair whipping across her face and one hand drawn up to the edge of her mouth, the three bands of her Russian wedding ring – the ring Rhianne still wore – loose around her little finger. In the photograph, the sun was low, and Josephine, standing before it, was bathed in warm, orange light. Rhianne felt sick; she didn't sleep that night, thought instead of the photograph lying in the corner of that darkened, empty studio in King's Cross. She only had one copy. 'Dinner,' her father had said, gruffly, when Rhianne asked what they'd been arguing about when he'd taken the photo. 'She wanted to know what was for dinner.'

Rhianne went back as early as possible on New Year's Day, straight to the studio, swiped her card at the door. The light sensor switched, and she knelt down in front of her station, opened the folder, spreading the pages out across the floor until she found what she had been looking for. She picked it up, swore. 'Fuck. Fuck, fuck.' She sat back. She didn't realise how heavy her breathing was until – he had been there, behind the desk, the whole time – she heard him.

'Happy Fucking New Year,' said Alexander.

He sat with her for a short while that evening. He told her he had seen what she was doing, and that he liked it. He glanced at the photograph, told her that great art came from great pain. The lenses of his tortoiseshell glasses gleamed blue in the light. Then, he got to his feet, asked her if she was staying tonight to work, and she told him that she was.

That year Rhianne had lived with two of her classmates in King's Cross. Music came through the walls of the attic room, and Rhianne, ignited, watched herself slide back the mirrored door of her wardrobe, pulling clothes from their hangers. She understood that a decision was being made. Today, because of him, she was wearing the neon eyeliner that lifted the corners of her eyes, that the scoop of her neckline was lower, because she wanted him to see how she radiated. And, despite knowing that she was putting herself in danger's path, she felt as unable to alter this course as she would have the arrangement of stars cycling home on a cold, clear night after an evening in his rooms spent working late. 'Stay,' he would say, and she, favouring excitement over familiarity, cancelled dinner, cancelled drinks, stayed.

He helped her apply for her Master's, wrote and submitted her references. The offer – contingent on her finishing her degree, getting the grade Alexander predicted – came within weeks. The more confident she grew, the more he gravitated to her. Sometimes he would sit with her, they would talk. Rhianne was at an age where it was possible to misinterpret his lack of depth as mystery, and so, as far as she understood it, he taught in a university because the wisdom he had to impart was too profound for a commercial setting, not because he had been fired from three consecutive posts. The end of his marriage had been a tragedy, a painful tearing asunder, not because he'd charged an OnlyFans subscription to his wife's credit card while she worked twelve-hour shifts in the university's mental health student services. When he fell silent, looked at her across the tops of his tortoiseshell glasses, it was because he was deep in reflection, not because he had nothing to say.

The studio was in a converted granary just above the canal basin. The windows were large, panoramic. In the winter, heat escaped them; in spring, light began to gather through them, intensifying. The backs of her knees itched. She awaited the precarious kind of pleasure she felt when he moved through the room, passed her station. The project was taking form: a thick, acrylic painting of that photograph of her mother, the stripe of orange light across her face, which she had scraped and then repainted. Ten times, then twenty, she had scraped off the paint to reveal the wrinkled canvas beneath it, added layers, sometimes squeezing paint straight from the tube, smearing it with a palette knife across the canvas.

'It's about memory,' she told Alexander one night, as the studio darkened. Both of them were standing, looking at the painting. 'The more you try to remember something, the more you try to grasp it, the further away from you it moves.'

Alexander was quiet for a moment, and in that moment Rhianne felt sure that he had been stunned by her insight, her ingenuity. But instead, he appeared irritated.

'You're thinking like a student,' he said. 'A student writing a shitty evaluative essay. If you want to be an artist, you have to think like one. You have to think in form, not ideas.'

She was stung, but she persisted. Worked harder. Spent less time with other students, more time in front of her canvas. She'd seen Auerbach: paintings inches thick because of the layers, the textured, messy bursts of colour blending to brown and then overlaid, again, with fresh colour. She had a vision in mind, and she was determined to bring it to her canvas.

She had thought that in staying, moving into Alexander's orbit, she was moving towards her power. She did not know that instead, she was relinquishing it. She did not know, but every night, a small piece at a time, she was succumbing to the base chemistry of attention and reward. She'd worn the skirt, the eyeliner, felt the look that had slid down to her waist, lower; known that this was not what she wanted. And the harder she worked, the closer her deadline drew, the more critical he became.

'I told you,' he said, 'you're over-editing. Doubting yourself. You need to commit.'

He was right. She had scraped the canvas too many times, layered on so much paint that the painting now was heavy. Her mother started to look less like her mother, nor did she look like a piece of art. Instead, her features grew messier, ill-defined. Her deadline was less than a week away and she had mixed, blended, too many times: the painting had begun to turn, the play between dark and light flattening, weighted, dull. That day in the studio, thick bands of paint had started to peel away from the canvas, and Rhianne had stuck her scraper behind them, tearing one, and then another, to the floor. The painting was ruined. She wedged the scraper just above the left ear of Josephine who was no longer Josephine but a muddy, amorphous splodge. The canvas was thin, wet, and giving way to the impact, it tore. Rhianne stood, shaking.

Alexander took a hold of her elbow, firm. 'Come,' he told her. 'Come, come.'

He led her out of the studio, back down the corridor to his office. He sat her down, propped himself against his desk, opposite, folded his arms. She didn't know what she was expecting: reprimands, probably. The advice to learn to control her emotions. 'I think,' Alexander said, 'what you need is a little distraction.' He was studying her softly, kindly. She thought that she would have preferred anger. 'What about this evening?'

She knew what it was, and she went anyway. Dalston, just off the Kingsland Road. Alexander was waiting for her in a corner booth, elbow slung over the seat. She stood in front of him, her thumb hooked through the strap of her bag. At first, she kept both hands on her drink. She had ordered something with whiskey. The rim of the glass was rolled in brown sugar, a slice of caramelised orange peel suspended in amber liquid. The bartender had set fire to the orange peel as he delivered the drink. Alexander had ordered a martini, which stood tall and slick, next to her squat, sugared drink. She took a sip. 'Better?' Alexander asked her.

She put down the drink.

'You said art comes from pain,' she said. 'That night. New Year's Day.'

'Pain,' he said, nodding slowly. 'But not pain alone. Pain on its own is ugly, meaningless. It has to be transformed. Alchemised.'

'Alchemised.' She liked this word. She sipped her drink. Alexander was relaxed, open. A drink was what she needed. To take things more lightly.

'You,' Alexander said, casual, 'you're an alchemist.'

Rhianne flushed.

'You disagree?'

'I don't know,' she said.

'You think I don't know talent when I see it?'

She drank her drink, and another. She felt light. She started to giggle, showed him how she'd re-stitched the button on her jeans, torn them just above the knees herself.

'They're distressed,' she said.

He leaned closer. 'And why are they distressed?'

Rhianne put her straw to her mouth. 'Wouldn't you be? If you looked that good?'

He called a taxi because it was late, and they were adults. In the back seat of the car, he put a hand on her knee. Electricity shot up the inside of her thigh. The hand stayed there; she didn't move it, she stayed perfectly still, paralysed by the force of those two opposite instincts: desire and, beneath it, repulsion.

Excitement stirred, and fear. His fingertips pressed more firmly, and then a little less firm, shifted further up her thigh. The car had been moving slowly, through backed-up traffic, but now the lights rushed past. They were coming fast down Caledonian Road. At the turning, he shifted closer to her, tilted his face. His breath was hot and it smelt of liquor.

'But wait,' she said, 'the deadline is next week. What are we going to do? About the painting?'

Alexander smiled, leaned closer. His teeth were pointed, stained.

'Give a fuck,' he said, 'it's not like I'm not going to pass you.'

She sat straighter. 'I tore a hole in the canvas.'

'That's modernity for you,' Alexander said. 'You could take a shit on the floor of the studio and call it art for all I care.' The hand on the thigh squeezed tighter, and an image appeared to her, as involuntary as it was vivid: her, with her make-up fully done and her trousers around her ankles, squatting on a desk in front of Alexander, and him, leaning back in his office chair, swirling a martini. She recoiled, and he, sensing, straight away stiffened. They had arrived at the lights at the bottom of the hill. He stayed for a moment, where he was. Rhianne turned her face away from his, looked out of the window. Everything shifted.

Alexander withdrew the hand and shuffled to the front of his seat, speaking to the driver. 'Right,' he said, 'then second left.' They pulled up outside the station. Rhianne's thigh pulsed. She sat, waiting for him to speak, but instead, he took his phone out of his pocket, swiped.

'Thank you for the drinks,' said Rhianne. 'I had a good time.' She waited, open. 'So we can talk next week,' she said. 'About what to do with the project.'

He looked at her, suddenly weary. 'I told you,' he said, 'you should have left it as it was, weeks ago. There might be something we can do.' He checked the date on his phone. 'There might be some kind of dispensation available.'

Rhianne was numb. 'You mean, not finish?'

'Natalie can advise,' said Alexander. 'Dr Kendall. She deals with problem cases.' The phone, again, and the scrolling. He glanced up at her. 'She's a dear friend. I'll put you in touch.'

Rhianne did not speak to Alexander's friend, and nor did she submit her project. The next time she went to the studio, Alexander was absent, and she stood numbly across from her ruined canvas, unable to comprehend the magnitude of her failure. She stayed in her room for a week before she called her father in tears. He came to collect her. They carried her boxes one by one, and in the car, she slept, and when they were home, she went straight out to the garden. That day, the sky had been clear, and from here, it was possible to see all the way past the valley to the Severn and the bridge above it, its steel cables suspended between its two towers. Slowly, she watched the sky turn orange. The knot in her chest loosened.

Her father came, later, to find her, sat down on the swing whose seat hung at a diagonal and low to the ground so that his legs were folded in on themselves, the ropes cutting into his shoulders. He was a tall man, large and sandy-haired, and the swing-set these days looked as though it had been dropped from a great height, embedded at an awkward angle into the grass that grew up around its rusted legs. He extended his legs, pushing himself back, swung forwards.

'I told you,' Rhianne said, when he asked for the third time whether she couldn't just ask for an extension. 'And anyway, I put a spatula through Mum's eye.'

'Melissa said that I should say that if he did something that he shouldn't have done' – Dominic dug the heels of his shoes into the dry ground, shuffled himself forwards a little on the swing. He wasn't looking at Rhianne, but down at the shoes, their dusty heels – 'then you ought to tell us.'

Rhianne nodded. 'If I tell you,' she said, 'you have to not be weird.'

Dominic's brow grew heavier. 'I won't be weird.'

'Or angry.'

'I might be angry.'

'Promise. Please.'

Dominic heaved a breath. 'I won't be weird or angry.'

'OK. Then I'll tell you. But later.'

'When Melissa's here,' Dominic said. Fleetingly, he appeared relieved; almost hopeful. 'Melissa will be a good person to talk to.'

Rhianne told them both over dinner. The mentoring, the project. The slow erosion of her confidence. And then, when she got to the part about her showing up at the bar in Dalston, Dominic voided a bottle of tomato ketchup onto his rice. Rhianne, watching her father, edited. She left out the second drink, and the third. She left out, too, the taxi, the thigh. The way that the memory of it was still alight in her body. 'So,' she said, 'I left. Pretended I had to go and see my boyfriend. Cycled home.' The kitchen lights were bright over their dinner plates.

'They might let me on the MA anyway,' she said. 'I have to ask for dispensation. I can apply, apparently.'

Melissa asked Rhianne whether she had spoken to any of her friends at the university about what had happened.

'Don't have any,' Rhianne said. She leaned across the table, took a piece of garlic bread and tore it in two, deposited half on the edge of Melissa's plate, put the rest in her mouth. 'Don't worry.' Her mouth was still full. 'I'll make new ones. I'm really nice.'

It was good, Dominic told Melissa later, that they were all able to talk about it. The bed sagged as he sat down on its edge. 'It's good for her,' he said, 'and probably for us, too. We need to talk about this stuff. Sunlight is the best disinfectant.'

Melissa reached for the light. 'Really? I thought it was bleach.'

5

Dominic and Melissa had first met seventeen years ago in a wine bar in Clifton. The bar was dark, candlelit, and his glasses had steamed up as soon as he stepped inside. By the door, he'd surveyed the available tables with the help of the waitress. The tables were low, small, and he knew that he was wearing too many clothes. His underarms prickled. Dominic did not like to sit in discomfort, and he liked even less the thought of inflicting it on others. Solutions, for Dominic, were the language of love.

'These are too small,' he said, 'our knees will be touching.' The waitress, who could have been no older than twenty-one, giggled. 'Not that I don't want them to be touching,' Dominic said, 'but maybe these will be better.' As he turned towards the high seats by the window he saw her, stepping across the road from the bus stop, her long coat wrapped around her body, her dry hair bright and blonde. She was wearing on her lips that mulberry shade of L'Oréal which, she would later tell him, really did something for her in winter. Dominic took off his glasses, which had steamed up again, replaced them.

'Because of the heat,' Melissa said, stepping in through the open door. She kept the coat around her, did not move closer.

'Because,' Dominic agreed, 'of the heat.'

In the end, they sat outside at a metal table. Too small, and the pavement was narrow, but at least it was cooler out here. It was an October night, and every ten minutes, the heater timed out and

Dominic stood to reset it. Melissa ordered a bottle of wine without looking up at the waitress. Dominic, wanting her attention, asked her how she felt, dating somebody who had a child, who'd already been married.

'Good,' Melissa said. Only then did she smile. 'Straight to the meaty questions.'

'And?'

'Who says I haven't been married?' Melissa said. 'That's a joke,' she said, catching Dominic's expression. She radiated assurance. 'No marriages,' she told him a little later. 'Near misses, though. One or two miracles.'

They made their way through most of the bottle. Melissa leaned closer to him, asked him about his eye. The right one, the pupil of which was permanently dilated behind his glasses.

'I got punched,' Dominic said. He took off his glasses, rubbed the eye. 'The muscles around the pupil, if they tear fully then they never repair.'

'Punched,' Melissa said.

Dominic put the glasses back on, smiled.

'Bar fight. It was a wayward few years. Wrong crowd.'

'And now?'

'Less wayward,' he said. He smiled. 'And the crowd, well. She's six and you wouldn't mess with her.'

'No bar fights?'

'Not so far,' said Dominic. 'We'll see.'

When Melissa went inside to the bathroom, she handed Dominic her bag. He took it, held it dutifully with both hands as though she had handed him a crystal vase and not her Donna Karan clutch. He liked it, that she had entrusted her bag to him. He leaned forwards, squeezed it gently, and smelt the same saccharine bubble-gum fragrance he had noticed when Melissa had stepped in through the door. It intrigued him, the sweetness, because Melissa was brittle, uneasy with softness. Josephine never carried a bag. She always put things in her pockets, and she was always losing things or asking other people to carry things. Dominic had liked that: being asked to carry things. Melissa came back out; she swept her bag up off his lap and for a moment he thought she was going to leave. But then, abruptly, she sat.

Still, with the bag on her shoulder. 'It's a long time since I did this sort of thing.'

'And? How is it?'

'It seems fine so far.'

She looked up at the heater, which had timed out again.

'You're cold,' Dominic said. He stood, pressed the heater back on. Then he sat, and he took both her hands in his, and rubbed the backs of her hands with his palms. Her hands were cold. He had not wanted to let go.

He'd decided, even before meeting, that he liked the brittleness. He'd liked it in the weeks they'd spent having conversations on the phone after he'd put Rhianne to bed. It was Melissa who'd suggested the phone calls. 'It would make sense to have a conversation,' she had written, 'if we're going to meet.' Dominic had replied that yes, he would like to have a conversation, and he'd phoned Melissa on her landline at the time she'd told him she'd be free. They'd spoken for half an hour before Melissa had interrupted him. 'I'm going to go now,' she'd said, before she hung up. She ended all her calls like this, abruptly and without explanation. Before long, in Melissa's little one-bed, Rhianne staying with her granny, Dominic would learn that Melissa ended nights like this, too. Dominic, halfway through a chapter of his book, would be plunged into darkness by Melissa, who had finished getting ready for bed and usually had to wake early the next morning. 'Lights out, is it?' Dominic said, on the third such occasion.

Melissa turned, peered at him in the darkness. 'Were you not finished?'

'No, no,' Dominic said. 'Lights out, guv. Lights out means lights out.'

She sat now, switched the light back on, blinding Dominic. 'You want them on?'

Dominic shielded his eyes. 'Guv,' he protested, rolling onto his side, burying his face under the pillow. 'Lights out, lights out.'

He had thought, feared, that the chaos of his life would be too much for Melissa, and for a time he kept it hidden. He called frequently, drew her into his life, which was rich and full, made sure she understood that there was space being made for her. It felt good. And the time he had to cancel dinner because Rhianne's head had been split open with a sharpened bamboo cane, he called Melissa from the waiting room. 'They'll glue it,' she'd said. He could hear her eating an apple on the other end of the phone. Melissa ate apples whole, seeds included, and he would find stalks, sometimes, left at the desk where she worked late, finishing her admin. 'A bit of blue glue and an Ibuprofen. It'll be like nothing ever happened.'

Other disasters followed. Fixable things: leaks, asbestos. And then the death of Josephine's mother, who had never got over the grief of losing her daughter and whose sadness Dominic had never been able to face. More dinners were cancelled, and Dominic could no longer pretend that he was not scattered, unreliable, that he did not have a magnetic relation to chaos, and he would slip, without meaning to, off-radar. Then, when at last he called Melissa, after he had put Rhianne to bed, when the house was still, he was sure he could sense that she was there, on the other end of the line, watching the phone, unwilling to pick it up. This, more than anything, made him certain that she cared, and he did not fight the impulse, when she finally answered, to flood her with affection.

'I just wanted to hear your voice,' he said. 'It makes me calm.'

'Don't do that,' she said.

31

'Do what?'

Silence for a moment.

'Don't tell me you love me and then cause me pain.'

There had been a crack that had opened in her voice that day, and for the first time he'd understood what lay beneath. A whole history of hurt, which, now, he wanted to hold, knew that he could hold.

Rhianne had been hardly three when Josephine died. Dominic was not unaware of the seismic effect Melissa's arrival would have on his daughter, and – Melissa would never know this – he contemplated ending things more than once for this exact reason. But in the moments when he was not occupied, in those times when he tried to distance himself, turn his attention solely to Rhianne, he was confronted by the memory of her mother, retching over the toilet bowl, bones in her back. Chrysanthemums on her bedside table. The chart next to them, the language of it alien to him. How helpless they both had been, and she, in her pain, unreachable.

Here, in Melissa, was somebody new, somebody without context. Here was a place of safety, a place he could hide. He would not be made to feel things he did not want to feel. He would not, for example, be made to feel loss. And he made a choice, the day that he packed Rhianne up into the car and told her they were going to meet a new friend of his for ice-cream, that he would stay here, in this place, where he was protected. 'That seems weird,' Rhianne had said, when Dominic tried to tell her they'd met at the surgery.

Melissa, in the passenger seat, shot a sharp, sideways glance, but Dominic was looking in the rear-view mirror. Rhianne's eyes – her mother's eyes – usually so full and trusting, narrowed.

'Grown-ups are weird,' Dominic said. He looked away.

Later that day Dominic logged onto his computer, opened the

page through which he had met Melissa. His profile, the picture of him in a high-vis vest and a hard hat, and the job description – *builder*, the modesty of which belied his success. His reddish hair still full in that picture, but soon it would start to thin and his waist would thicken. He imagined himself as his daughter would if ever she found this page: wanting to be wanted, and he had felt a spike of shame which, almost immediately, he buried in the same place he had his grief. He deleted the page, resolved that he would never again make himself so vulnerable.

For the first month after the ice-cream, Rhianne remained suspicious. But then, one night, when Melissa was staying at the little house in Cashes Green, Rhianne came downstairs with her blue plastic suitcase. She perched on the edge of the sofa next to Melissa, waiting patiently to be asked what was inside, at which point she climbed up onto the seat behind Melissa and unclipped the suitcase, laying it open on the cushion. Melissa eyed its contents. Butterfly clips, little elastic bands, a whole rainbow of glitter tubes. Rhianne selected a short, fat tube, filled with a transparent kind of gloop.

'What's that for?' Melissa asked.

Rhianne dug her elbows into Melissa's shoulders and began pulling clumps of Melissa's hair back into her sticky little hands, knotting the hair which, Dominic knew, Melissa had washed only that morning. 'Hair glue,' Rhianne said. She sniffed.

'Hair glue, Melissa,' Dominic said helpfully. 'Just like regular glue. But for your hair.'

Dominic flickered between channels on the television, settling on *Spirited Away*. In the darkness between the full-coloured shots he saw Melissa's reflection, the little stumps of hair that Rhianne was gathering in her fists and smothering with glitter: thick, sticky, her fingers pressing it right into her scalp. Melissa took off her glasses, rubbed her eyes. He saw Rhianne's smallness, climbing Melissa like a mountain, the discomfort on Melissa's face, which was slack, leaning just a little away from Rhianne and her busy hands, her heavy breaths as she tied tight little knots, pushed butterfly clips along Melissa's scalp. On the television, the robed, faceless figure filled the screen.

'Green, royal green,' Rhianne chattered, 'suits your colouring, darling, suits that lovely pale skin.'

Dominic watched as Melissa closed her eyes, irritable, and he willed her to soften, feared that she would not. And then, Melissa shifted in her seat, opened her eyes. On the screen the figure receded, the reflection of woman and girl, woman and daughter, replaced with scenes of woodland, a bright, clear sky, a blue-crested dragon flying into the distance, with it, Dominic's fear. When Rhianne was finished, Melissa looked sort of like a swamp monster, with her hair in short, green-glittered stumps. 'You look nice,' Dominic said. He had hoped for a smile, which Melissa only half-conjured on her way out of the living room and to the bathroom. Rhianne sat on the sofa, organising and reorganising her suitcase, pushing her glitter tubes back into the box. In the walls, Dominic heard the sounds of the taps running, the pipes deep in the house. When Melissa emerged, twenty minutes later, her hair was wrapped in a towel. She sat down beside Rhianne. 'What?' Melissa said, when Dominic asked her, gently, what happened to her hair. 'I liked it,' she said. 'I did.'

That night, Melissa moved on top of him in the dark. Every time he reached for her, fingertips sinking into her thighs, she pushed his hands away. Firmly, but gently, pinned his hands back on the pillows behind him, kissed him, deeply.

6

Rhianne had forgotten this feeling. How it was to have purpose, to belong. Every time she took that journey across to the hotel, followed the dusty track to the back entrance, she felt content. Locked her car, entered to find there was order, repetition, familiarity. Summer was wedding season, every weekend drunk on romance. On Fridays, guests would arrive, Rhianne heaved suitcases onto her hip, followed Sophia, the restaurant manager, up the back stairs. The hotel filled with silk, colour. Bottles popped at the entrance and the bride stepped into the sun, gathered her dress up around her knees. Inside, heels skidded on the waxed wooden floor. Then, service called, and they flew out the kitchen doors, arms filled with plates that grew heavier, hotter, more elaborate.

The music started. Rhianne stacked empties into the glass machine, wired at the end of a twelve-hour shift. One of the groomsmen tried to climb headfirst into the glass recycling bin and Callum pulled him out by the back of his belt. At a certain point, somebody was always on the edge of fighting someone, or staggering upstairs to the wrong room, or back out of the hotel and onto the driveway. She stood with Annabel behind the bar, they worked their way through trays of glasses, twisting the base, running a softened cloth around the bowl so that every glass gleamed when it was held up to the bar lights, glittering in the mirror.

Weekdays were quieter: married couples, babymoons. 'That couple,' Sophia told her, fingertips on her elbow, looking towards the far corner of the restaurant. 'Swingers.' Secrets spilled; and Rhianne thought how wrong she'd been to think that life had been there in a classroom, a studio, flattened onto a canvas. That had all been artificial. This, here, was life.

In the afternoons, Rhianne changed the flowers because if they were left for too long there would be a stench like rotting bodies when the water, jelly-like, got poured out down the drain. She stood in the heat of the kitchen, the full purple heads she had cut spread across the draining board, petals spilling, and she was aware of Callum, head bowed over a chopping board, shoulders broad. The boxes of muddied groceries he carried in from out the back, which he washed, scrubbed, sliced open to reveal flesh that was bright, dewy. She was aware, too, of Maria in her striped apron and her flesh-coloured stockings. Maria had worked at the Hart since before it was the Hart, and as she hauled herself from the sink to the dishwasher, arms filled with Tupperware, there was the uncomfortable knowledge that her breadth and her bulk put Rhianne in easy contrast.

Rhianne always told the guests that she'd picked the flowers herself because that made them tip better. It was a part of the appeal of the place: provenance, according to Brendan. 'People are disconnected,' he told Rhianne, 'they want to know where it comes from, before they put it in their bodies.' That lamb you had for dinner last night, those sheep were reared in the farm at the bottom of the valley. And the carrots, those were picked by our gardener yesterday.

'How am I supposed to remember where all of this stuff comes from?' she asked Callum.

'Who's checking?' Callum said. 'Make it up.'

'The parsley,' said Rhianne, 'I shat it out just this morning.'

*

June turned to July. In the middle of service, Callum pushed a plate towards her, asked her what time she was on her break. 'Come knock,' he said. 'First door.' His voice indiscernible to anybody except her beneath the whirr of the oven fan. When the first half of her split was over, instead of getting in her car and driving home as she usually did, Rhianne crossed the courtyard and entered the staff house. It was the first time she had been inside. The staff house had once been a stable and through the entrance, fire doors either side, there was a musty kind of feel to it: rattan carpet, beige.

Right, to the kitchen, left through to the living room and up the stairs to the bedrooms. The door to the stairway swung shut behind her and it was dark. The lights out, only the fire exit illuminated. He didn't answer her knock straight away and she waited for him, standing back against the wall in the dark. Callum, in joggers and a crisp T-shirt, there in the doorway, curtains drawn behind him. Rhianne knew, if she looked down, that she would see the outline of his penis. He rubbed his face. 'Sorry,' Rhianne said. 'I woke you up. I'll let you sleep.'

'No,' Callum said. 'I need to not be sleeping. Wait.'

She stood in the doorway while he opened his curtains, remade his bed. From where she stood, she could see only a slice of the room: his bed, reflected in the mirror. Narrow for a double, pushed up against the wall. 'Your room is nice,' she said, a reflex: explicitly, it was not.

Callum shut the door behind him. Leaning close as he tested the handle.

'You know your face?'

'What about it?'

'It's unbelievably readable.'

Rhianne neutralised her expression, the look of judgement that had crossed it.

'Too late,' he said. 'I know you're lying.'

'OK. The room is horrible.'

'There we go,' Callum said. 'You don't need to lie to me.'

She followed him down the darkened stairway. 'I know you can't help that it doesn't have much light and it's kind of cramped, but, you know. You could at least have a lamp in there or something.'

'A lamp.'

'At least. Just for a bit more light. It's like a cave. I'm surprised; I thought you had good taste, being a chef. You know?'

He stopped at the bottom step, searching for the door handle. 'It sounds like you're the one with good taste.' He opened the door, followed Rhianne through to the living room, which was fitted with furniture that was too worn or broken for the guests to use. Callum propped open the door with a dumb-bell sitting on the floor next to the sofa. There was a faded, nineties feel to this room: two beige sofas and a pine coffee table lacquered with rings of Polish vodka and orange squash, Golden Virginia tobacco spilling out of its pouch. There was dust suspended in the shaft of sunlight that shone through the single-glazed window.

Callum picked up the television remote, flicked through the channels. A level of calm had settled over him, deeper than that which emanated from him in the kitchen, that which she had experienced the night they'd stood out in the car park. Rhianne stood close to the doorway, trying to configure whether her presence here was superfluous. She felt that if she left, he would perhaps not notice. But still, he had asked her to knock. She did not leave; instead, she sat down, took off her shoes and pulled her legs up onto the sofa.

'You hungry?'

'Not yet,' Rhianne said. 'I will be.'

'You didn't eat staff lunch.'

She knew this about him: he was observant. She kept her eyes on the screen.

'I'm selective. I only have staff lunch if my favourite chef is on.'

'Is that right?' Callum said. He looked sideways at her now. Not a smile, but appraisal. Rhianne sank back into the sofa's cushions, wondered whether anybody had ever died sitting here. It had that kind of energy about it: off-white, a fuzzy layer of dirt she could skim with her fingernail.

'Pasta and sauce,' Rhianne said. 'In case you were wondering.'

'Really? That's your request?'

'Yep.'

'It's a bit basic, no? Seems like your standards have slipped.'

'Nothing wrong with being basic.'

'You would know?'

'I would,' Rhianne said, 'and they're not slipping.'

Flirting, but generic. She wanted more. There was the sound of music playing upstairs. Callum's eyes flicked up.

Rhianne tried her best to remain casual. 'Is that Annabel?'

'Yep,' he said. And she was glad that he looked irritated. 'And Taylor Swift. I wouldn't mind,' he said, 'if her taste was actually good.' He turned up the TV volume. 'She'll be gone soon. Those placements are always short.' Rhianne's foot was resting close enough to him to feel the heat of his body, and she felt the sudden urge to press its sole into the flesh of his thigh. Instead, she sank back further, pulled her hair back up into a high ponytail. 'So,' said Callum, 'what about you?'

She was looking at the screen rather than at him, and her chest, minutely, tightened.

'What about me?'

'What are you doing here? You're some kind of artistic prodigy. Shouldn't you be in London or Amsterdam or New York or somewhere?'

'I'm on sabbatical,' she said. 'Don't rush me.'

'OK.'

Rhianne shifted in her seat, glanced at him.

'I needed a break. For various reasons.' Slowly, Callum nodded. She was unsure how much to give away, but at the same time aware of how fully his attention had calibrated around her. 'Which I might tell you. Depending.'

He took her outstretched foot in his hand, pressed the arch, kneading it with his knuckle; a place she'd never been touched before. Face-down on the table, her phone vibrated. 'Depending,' he said, 'on what?'

She looked at him, steady. 'On whether I like you enough.'

'Oh,' Callum said. He stopped kneading, pressed harder. 'So, the jury's out?'

'I think it has to be.' She smiled. The phone vibrated again. He was pressing right into the bone. She pulled her foot away from him. 'Ow,' she said.

'All right, all right. You're cautious. I get it.' His eyes slid to her phone. 'Aren't you going to check that?'

Rhianne picked the phone up off the table. 'It's Jess,' she said. 'My friend.'

'Wants to know what you're up to. Who you're spending all your time with.'

'Something like that.'

Callum reached for her foot again, but Rhianne snatched it away from him. The episode ended; its xylophonic soundtrack jarred in the silence between them.

'There's nothing wrong with being cautious,' Rhianne said.

Callum settled back. 'Not everyone's like him, you know.' Rhianne said nothing, kept watching the screen. 'Whoever it was that hurt you.' It flickered to black, a pause, in which neither of them reached for the remote. The next episode began to play.

7

Melissa pulled out against the end-of-day traffic and turned down towards Ebley, towards the mill. She parked by the water, and, opening the car door, she stuck her legs out onto the gravel and stretched. Melissa's legs had been aching, the veins that were roped down the insides of her thighs especially painful today. From her bag, she took the napkin-wrapped pastry she had been keeping there since this morning, tore off a chunk. Half past six, Dominic had said, which meant most likely seven. She looked over towards Dominic's office window.

The mill had always been impressive to Melissa. The first time she'd pulled up to see the scrubbed limestone walls, the frosted-glass doors, she'd known for sure that Dominic had played down his success. She was not, of course, intimidated. Melissa, who knew how to unblock an airway and jumpstart a heart, would not be made to feel that there could be anything taking place here that might be beyond or above her. But her work was different from this. Hers was not a concrete legacy but rather one of touch: a private bequest of care, administered behind synthetic curtains and self-locking fire doors. Even after all these years, there was something about the curvature of that ceiling in the atrium, the framed and mounted blueprints, those bronze plaques, which, whenever she stepped into Dominic's building, made Melissa pull her lanyard out from under the strap of her bag and rest it where it was visible on top of her jacket.

When they were first together, she would stop by on her way back from the surgery, picking out the caramels from the chocolate box in the kitchen, making small talk with Roberta, the young woman who did Dominic's administration. She had told Dominic that Roberta was pregnant before Roberta knew herself. When Roberta came back from her year off, Melissa had brought Ludo, who was a puppy then, to play with the baby, and Roberta had laughed at the little jacket Melissa had put Ludo in and asked her if she was trying to pretend that the dog was a human.

'Idiots, everywhere,' Melissa said, when Dominic, enveloping her into his chest, smelling of sawdust, asked her what had put her in such a mood. The hug: safety. They had been trying for a baby for six months now. There was the appearance of a sticky hand, nestling into Melissa's palm, tugging on her arm, Rhianne's voice, around belly-height.

Melissa kept on going to the office, and she kept on bringing Ludo, moved him, when he was big enough, up into a full-grown dog jacket. She told Roberta she needed to turn the string-of-hearts plant up on the shelf behind her, that she needed to turn it every fortnight. Melissa could tell that Roberta was neglecting the plant. It didn't die, but nor did it grow, so Melissa would wait until she'd gone to fill the kettle or collect a package, and she turned it herself, relaying its tendrils over the edge of the shelf.

Just after Rhianne turned eight, they bought the Minchinhampton house, began the renovations. Halfway through the work, Melissa bled on the floor of the shower, doubled over with cramps that knifed her lower belly.

Afterwards, the veins on her legs which, for years, had existed as faint blue traces beneath the surface of her skin burst into thick, hot ropes running down to her calves. Melissa knew her own body, and the veins she understood to be its protest against those long days spent on her feet with her circulation constricted, and the life that had briefly grown. Not again, she told Dominic,

42

when he saw her new prescription, the twenty-eight round pills in their rectangular packet. She couldn't. Not a third time. Still she turned the string-of-hearts about every two weeks, and the plant flourished unnoticed, a little secret between Melissa and Ludo, whose ears twitched every time Melissa dragged the chair over to that high shelf and stood up on it.

Probably, right about now, the plant needed turning. It also needed some company. Melissa had been thinking about a monstera, those big Edam leaves, but she didn't trust Roberta with it, not now she was a part-timer. Melissa finished her pastry and she shifted in her seat, brushing the crumbs into a small, localised patch in her lap and out onto the gravel. Slowly, she got out of the car. Her legs pulsed. She didn't much feel like going inside. Dominic had been putting her on edge lately. He'd been excitable, puppy-like, doing odd things like making dinner reservations, asking too many questions about her rota. Melissa feared he was going to do something reckless like plan a holiday.

Melissa never knew quite how to explain to him the resistance her body offered when faced with the prospect of pleasure which, over the years, had become less comfortable to her than life measured in bloods, mapped in graphs. Human contact mediated through a pair of disposable gloves or the polypropylene shield of a fitted facemask. The presence, always, of death. She leaned back against the exterior of her car, the sun on her face, waiting until the door to the mill slid open and Dominic emerged. She had been right, he was nervous about something.

'I thought we'd go to the brewery.' He sat in the back of the Range Rover, pulled on his walking boots. 'Down the river.'

Melissa was suspicious. She watched Dominic wipe his forehead.

'Air con,' he said, 'broke again.'

'I don't know how you stand that synthetic air.'

They walked, and Melissa loosened. Ludo nosed ahead. The sky was clear today, and blue. The path grew earthier as they approached the river, the hedgerows full and thick. Herb robert, the dog rose. The ferns, which only a few weeks earlier curled in on themselves like green-shelled snails, were now springing up, unfurled, quivering above the hedgerows.

'What is that?' Dominic said. Behind her, he wheezed. 'Smells like cum.'

'Castanea sativa,' said Melissa, 'it's the sweet chestnut.'

'Every year, the same.'

Melissa walked ahead. 'It's European.'

The shaded path opened out onto the bank, the river wide, glittering. Dominic was right about the smell: cloying, sticky pollen at the back of the throat. Melissa, despite herself, giggled. They had half a mile or so before they got back into the town, to where the brewery decked just over the river's edge. The pain in her legs had dissipated, and she felt teenage, silly.

Dominic grinned at her. 'What's got into you?'

'Don't start that,' she said, 'you're the one who's hiding something.'

'Hiding what?' Dominic said. They were walking side by side now, the sky just beginning to lose its heat. Mosquitoes, this close to the water, likely ticks, too. There was a flash of irritation towards Dominic for not having thought of such practicalities, but today, it quickly dissolved. Something about that slant of light had caught her.

'I always know,' Melissa said. She was keeping him on edge on purpose. She would never actually reveal what it was that she knew: the contents of his emails, for example, which she read with an unhealthy regularity. The password to his Facebook account, which she used to log in and, periodically, delete any friends – female, usually – she didn't like the look of.

'You didn't see,' Dominic said. 'Don't tell me you saw.' He had his right hand stuffed funnily in the pocket of his shorts. Melissa slowed her pace. It was important that Dominic assumed her to be omniscient, but not, in this moment, quite as important as him telling her what he was fondling in his pocket.

She skewered him with her gaze. 'Depends what.'

'So you don't know,' Dominic said. He'd stopped walking completely now, paused by the turnstile at the end of the path. Ludo's tail wagged. 'I suppose I'd better tell you.'

He didn't kneel, but sat inelegantly on the step of the turnstile, lowering himself down with one hand, and with the other reaching for the little box in his pocket. He pulled it out.

'Jesus,' Melissa said. 'Oh, what is this?'

'Melissa,' Dominic began.

'Are you dying?'

'No,' he said. 'I'm not dying. Not yet.'

'You're having an affair. You're guilty, I can tell. I knew you'd been acting funny.'

'I'm not having an affair.'

She couldn't help it: involuntarily she glanced over her shoulder, towards the woodlands, then back at him. The corners of Dominic's mouth twitched.

'There aren't any hidden cameras,' he said, 'if that's what you were wondering.'

'I wasn't,' Melissa said. She looked back at him, waved vaguely in the direction of the woodland. 'I thought you might have organised something. As a surprise. I've seen them on the internet.'

'Melissa, I love you,' Dominic said. 'Please stop panicking.'

'I know,' said Melissa. And she did know.

At the brewery they sat out on the deck, and Dominic had his pint and half of hers. There was too much gas even in this flat, local-brewed ale, and Melissa declined when Dominic went back for a second. They'd have to ask Rhianne to come and collect them, probably sit in the back of the car like teenagers. Even after all this time, she wasn't used to it. Love that refused, somehow, to die. 'When we were younger,' he said, 'it was because of Rhianne, you know? But she's an adult now. I think she can cope. And, anyway, there are tax breaks.'

'You think she's used to me by now? Just about.'

'Just about,' Dominic scratched his face, 'but let's wait a little bit.'

'Wait?'

'To tell her, I mean. That's if you're saying yes, obviously.' He watched her. Smiled, lopsided. 'What? What is it?'

'I'm saying yes,' Melissa said, 'in a minute.' She drew her jacket around her. 'It's a funny time for it, don't you think? What with, well. Rhianne. Homecoming.'

Dominic grew serious. 'I disagree,' he said. 'Joy is thin on the ground lately, and we could do with some more of it. Something good in amongst all of that, you know?' He stopped, then resettled on the same refrain. 'She's an adult now.'

The sun had dipped, the sky bleeding pink. Melissa watched for a moment. Marriage was for young people. Young people starting families. The inner seams of her thighs ached. 'Maybe I need some time to think about it.'

'Time? Fifteen years not long enough?'

'Seventeen.'

'Since we met,' Dominic said, 'but I wasn't sure about you, the first two.'

'No?'

'Thought it might be a fling.'

Melissa slapped his forearm. 'Sorry,' she muttered. 'Mosquito.' She reached for his beer, took a long sip. 'All right,' she said. 'To tax breaks. And joy.'

'To joy,' Dominic said, 'spread nice and thick.'

8

On the underside of the long pinewood table was a single pro-
truding nail, its head hammered so that it bent back on itself and
dug into the joint. The nail was on the kitchen side, where Callum
sat twice a day to eat. Today, sausages and mash. Callum pushed
his half-finished plate away. An islet of oil shuddered on the surface of his gravy, separated in two. Callum leaned back so that he
could see under the table, feeling for the edges of that rounded-
off nail.

Opposite him, Kieran, the weekend pot-wash, was hungry.
He always sat hunched over, with his fork in one hand and the
other hand cupping the outer edge of his plate, his little finger
pressing down into the table to keep the hand steady, as though
somebody was about to snatch his food away from him. He ate
frantically, gulping in air, his spine bowed like a weighted branch.
Then, there would be gas: whole-body-jolting belches that jerked
him straight again. 'Sorry,' he said, only now registering Callum's
presence.

'Better out than in,' Callum said, watching.

Kieran swallowed another belch. Callum wiped his hands
clean, pinched the nail beneath the table, and started to tug. It
was firmly wedged. Kieran was sitting back in his chair, watching Callum. He put a self-conscious hand to his belly, swallowing
another belch.

'Easy,' Callum said.

'Sorry,' said Kieran again.

Callum pushed his half-empty plate closer to Kieran. 'You should eat,' he said, 'it's free.'

Kieran took the plate.

'You like the food?' said Callum.

'Yeah, I like it.'

Callum could remember that feeling. Good, hot food; free food. Brendan, the first time Callum had sat across from him at this same table, around Kieran's age or older, had sent him back for seconds. All the while he ate, Callum's phone had been ringing. Callum had ignored it, until eventually Brendan asked Callum if he wasn't going to answer, and Callum, calmly, without picking the phone up off the table, connected the call, put it on speaker. A torrent of expletives filled the room. Callum paused, listening, then went back to his food. The expletives kept coming. Brendan cut the line.

'So, you didn't tell him you were coming here?'

'Nope,' Callum said.

Brendan nodded. 'Not all blood is family,' he said.

The calls had kept coming until Callum blocked the number. He was unfazed. This was a skill of his; he knew – had known since childhood – how to be at peace in chaos. 'You have to hold on to that,' Brendan had told him, the first time they'd met, back when Callum was working as a barman in Bristol. 'In this industry, but also in life.' Brendan had been out for dinner with his partner that night, chancing a bar at the rough end of town when a fight had broken out. It had been Callum who'd broken it up, and Brendan who insisted he come back with them. Jack, after so many years with Brendan, was used to such impulses. He stood Callum next to the sink, cleaning up the cut that had landed just above his eye. Brendan, after, offered him a pot-washing job, lodgings at the new place he was opening. And something more. Three hot meals. Belonging. The next weekend, the sous chef hadn't shown up and Brendan moved Callum from pot-wash to starters. The following month he'd signed Callum up for training, with the promise, if he showed up to all his classes, of chef's work on the other side.

Callum was good at his job. Where others floundered under the pressure, it had always been easy for him to step back, hold himself with focus, ease. In Brendan there was a turbulence that erupted, at times, into full-blown rage. These eruptions did not bother Callum, and rarely was he the subject, because they were prompted by mistakes that Callum would never make. Burning beignets, scouring Teflon with a wire sponge. Loading the logs in the fireplace so high that the flames licked the flue. Brendan's unpredictability never bothered Callum; in fact, the drama was a source of comfort. Every time Brendan blew up in Callum's presence, he would stand back, behind the hotplate, eyes down, hands busy, wearing a quiet smile, knowing that later there would be a hand on his shoulder. Brendan, with a squat, amber bottle.

'Leave that,' he would say, 'I need your young tastebuds.'

Callum would follow him through the back of the hotel, here, to the laundry, where Brendan would put two tumblers down on the table. First, he would vent. And then, when he was calmer, he would pour, and he would insist that Callum give him his honest opinion on this particular cask: body, depth, finish. Callum was a fast learner. The language of the tastings came to him quickly, and he found it easy, even under Brendan's watchful gaze, to shake off any assumptions or expectations his new employer might have of him, any attachments to a particular cask, and to give his honest opinion. He would close his eyes, run the amber liquid through his teeth, the roof of his mouth, savouring.

'What do you like to drink?' said Callum now, to Kieran.

'Squash, usually,' said Kieran.

'Squash? That just on the weekends or weeknights too?'

The sarcasm sailed past. 'Just depends if Mum bought it, really.'

The door kicked open, and Callum, seeing Rhianne enter, sat straighter. 'Careful, Rhianne,' he said, 'Kieran's on a sugar high. Anything could happen.'

He couldn't help it. And anyway, she was here early, before her shift. Her make-up was bright today; he could see the shimmer around her eyes where she hadn't quite rubbed it in. Callum imagined her, leaning close to her mirror, adding an extra layer. Rhianne slid her bag to the floor, tied her apron. She pulled it tight around her waist. Callum watched.

'Yeah? What's for dinner?'

'Sausages and mash,' Callum said. 'Average, but Kieran liked it, didn't you, Ke-ke? Ate mine as well as yours.'

Rhianne smiled at Kieran. 'It's OK,' she said. 'I'm not hungry.'

Last night, she'd come up to the staff house again, and this time she'd brought a small, blank sketchbook. They'd sat together with the television flickering. He liked how, if he edged closer to her, she would shut her book, keeping her thumb in the page. 'You're not gonna show me,' he said.

'Not yet.' She flipped open the back cover, started to shade the corner of the page with the flat edge of her pencil-tip, like a schoolgirl. Desire flared in Callum. Her nails were always a different colour, and today they were patterned with bright blue dots. She picked up the conversation where they had left it, before time had slipped. 'You speak to him, still? Your dad?'

'So that's how this works? I tell you my life story and you give me nothing?'

She shrugged. 'You don't have to tell me anything you don't want to.'

'All right, then.'

'I'll tell you,' she said. 'Just don't rush me.'

But she'd stayed until long after it got dark, until after the auto-play had timed out, and now, today, in the laundry, Rhianne pulled her hair up into its band, the peroxide stripes bright, and she smiled at him straight across the room. The ice machine clunked.

'I'll see you later,' she said, to both of them, but speaking really to Callum. Her skin looked soft today, dewy.

'See you later,' said Callum.

The door swung shut.

'See you later,' said Kieran quietly, mimicking Callum's voice.

'Oh, he speaks,' said Callum. He was vicious, excitable. He leaned across the table, snatched Kieran's fork up off his plate, wiped it on the boy's chef's whites. He sat back, jammed the fork into the nail, and pushed, levering hard, and untoothed it from the wood.

9

The next morning, Rhianne orbited the kitchen. Loitered around the sugar bowls, the jam pots, even helped Maria with the washing-up because it put her over on Callum's side of the hotplate. Every night that week, in the staff house after work, she pressed her foot against his thigh. They were letting the episodes run, and slowly, at last, she felt comfortable enough to begin talking. She watched their reflection in the screen of the television as she spoke, the glint of the silver chain Callum wore around his neck. Gently, he pressed her, softening her with teasing, taking a hold of her foot. He left long silences, and she fell into them.

She had been nervous, but there was something about his openness that made her want to talk, and she told it in full, included her desires, her confusion. She told him how she had started to feel anxious, her moods and her confidence low. It was Callum who put a name to it. 'Depression,' he said, nodding, and she knew from his tone that she didn't have to say more. She told him about those long nights in Alexander's office. And then, that moment, in the taxi, when she had seen the colour of his teeth, the film of plaque that coated them.

'That's it,' he said, 'all it took was teeth?'

'I mean, no, but also,' Rhianne grimaced, 'maybe yes?'

Callum pressed his mouth closed.

'OK.' He spoke through tightly shut lips. 'No teeth. Got it.'

'Not you,' she said, 'that doesn't apply to you.'

Callum, his mouth still shut, said something incomprehensible.

'Can't hear.' She giggled, climbed closer, pressed her hand over his mouth, covering it. 'Try again.'

'I said,' Callum spoke into her palm, 'that the jury's still out on me.' He put his hand on hers, suddenly serious. Slowly, he pulled the hand away. 'I mean it,' he said, 'thank you for telling me all of this. About what happened to you. It means a lot to me. That you can trust me.'

'I do trust you,' Rhianne said.

'Good,' said Callum. 'You should.' The air dense. His fingers slid up into her hair, and gently, he tugged, so she fell in towards him. A kiss. Soft, electric.

That night she drove home with all the windows down, and the following morning, she burnt her hands plunging them into hot water because quite suddenly she seemed to have too many limbs. She watched her wrists turn pink, considered the possibility that what she had felt had only been imagined. All through service, when she turned to look at him, his eyes were down, busily working. Then, at last, when the last table had gone, he came and stood by her, where she was standing at the still. He snapped the tap open, and she smelt his moisturiser, soap, cutting clean through the fried remnants of the breakfast service, as he stood waiting for the pan to fill.

'Something wrong?'

In the noise of the kitchen, his voice was lost to everybody except her.

Rhianne shook her head.

'Good,' said Callum. He lifted the pan in both hands. His smile tugged there at his mouth. Rhianne stacked up the tubs of fruit, yogurt, compote, and took them out to the walk-in fridge. She imagined, every time she came out here, that the door would be off the latch and that she would be locked in. It was more like a vault than a larder. Behind her, Callum caught the door. The smile was gone, and instead there was concern, a softness in his expression. 'How are you feeling,' he said, 'about last night?' He stepped inside the fridge. The door swung slowly shut, bumping against the open latch.

'I feel fine,' Rhianne said.

'Fine?' He was looking at her steadily, and in that look was a rising heat which seemed suddenly to speak for them both. 'Maybe,' she said, 'definitely.'

'Good,' Callum said, 'because I'm good. I'm really good.' He took the tubs out of her hands and put them up on the shelf. He kissed her, there, once. Paused. 'So, you're fine?'

Rhianne shook her head. 'Better than fine.'

July grew hotter. There were nightly phone calls; hourly collisions in the hotel. She drove home, boy-racers firing past her. The cows migrated across the common. She swiped at her phone, searching with her fingers for the imprint of him – the letters of his name sliding every half-hour onto her screen – held there in her hand, slipped into her pocket. Except there was no need to pocket him, because here he was, in the flesh. They sought each other out. In the walk-in fridge, up against the dairy shelf, huge slabs of cheese and industrial-sized tubs of mayonnaise behind them; in the laundry cupboard, which smelt of vinegar and starched napkins.

With the heat came wasps. They'd nested under the eaves of the hotel, and they were landing on the lips of jam pots, drowning in afternoon cocktails. Brendan announced that the hotel would have to be fumigated, closed for twenty-four hours so the nest could be filled with toxic gas by men in hazmat suits.

Callum and Rhianne shut themselves in his room with the window closed, an acrid smell coming in under the invisible crack between the window and its frame, and he kissed the insides of her thighs and her pussy and told her she tasted good, and then kissed her full on the mouth so she could taste herself too. It hurt, a little bit. Sharpness, an intake of breath, his mouth speaking into hers, asking her if she wanted to stop. In the room next door, Annabel's cupboard door clicked shut, and they fell into whispers, conspiratorial. It was the middle of the afternoon, and the fact that it was light outside and that it was a still, warm day made Rhianne feel unafraid of the pain. When he fell, breath heavy, on top of her, she wanted him to stay there so they could do it all again, and again.

His face was illuminated by the light that slanted through the narrow gap between the drawn curtains. Bare, soft. On his body, she mapped his biography. A tattoo, his mother's birthday, on his arm. Kitchen burns on his wrists, and a white ribbon, where he'd sliced his wrist open on a shattered wine glass. Bristol's Old Market, he told her. It was in that bar that he'd met Brendan, where Brendan had rescued him. The scar on his forehead where his father had slammed him head-first into a radiator.

Rhianne rested the side of her face on his chest, felt his ribcage expand, shuddering. Questions rose up. About his history, his hurt. The ribcage, beneath her, sank, and there was the sudden, sticky awareness of a whole life lived, to which she had no access. Then Annabel's music starting up again. 'Fuck,' Callum said. He banged on the wall with his fist. The music quietened. 'Every night,' he said. He rolled onto his back, reached for his phone, closed one eye at the screen. Rhianne sat up, the intimacy interrupted, got up out of bed, feeling suddenly that she had overstayed her welcome. She searched for her underwear, her trousers. Callum was lying there on the bed, his phone held above his head, tapping the screen with his thumbs. Rhianne dressed, pulled her top on over her head, stood.

Callum put his phone down. 'You in some kind of a hurry?'

'Don't you have to go and help Brendan?'

'Can't wait to leave,' he said. 'All right, I get it.'

'I thought—'

'Don't worry about it,' he said.

'All right.' Rhianne went to open the door. She felt oddly tight-chested.

'Wait.' Callum sat up. He was laughing at her now. He caught her by the wrist. 'Don't go. I'm not ready for you to leave.'

Afterwards, they went outside, walked down through the vegetable patch and past the little shed where Brendan would hang flanks of pork and whole salmon and smoke them over coals. They went up to the smallest outhouse, hidden behind the walled garden, a disused barn with its front wall collapsed and dandelions growing through the cracks in the cobblestones. There was an unplumbed copper bathtub just outside, which Callum had helped Brendan drag out from the back kitchen years ago, when they were first renovating the hotel. Callum slid down inside it, grabbed hold of her waist and pulled her on top of him. She thought, briefly, of Alexander. He seemed old to her now; distant and grotesque. From here, there was an afternoon breeze, the back of the hotel and the valley unfolding below. She sank into Callum, the anticipation of many more such moments now, too, unfolding.

'The lighting,' she said, holding out her thumb and her forefinger in an L, framing the scene. Her nails today were cornflower blue, and her jewellery glinted. 'It would be perfect here. I might come up here.'

'Oh yeah,' Callum said. The hand on the wrist pinched. 'Because you're what, an artist? I don't think you mentioned it.'

Rhianne dropped the hand, playing along. 'Yeah, well. I try not to make a thing of it.'

'Smart.' He let go of her wrist. 'You wouldn't want anybody feeling inferior.'

The air got colder. Rhianne took off the sweatshirt she was

wearing, his bright purple one with the white Nike tick on the chest, and wrapped it around him, told him she still had to go. She began to pull herself up out of the tub. He pulled her back in towards him. Her phone started to ring. Callum snatched it from her hand.

'I need to go home.' She unwrapped his wrist from her arm, lifted herself up away from him. She held out her hand for the phone, which Callum did not hand over. 'Come on. It's family.'

'Oh,' Callum said. He smiled. 'Fuck your family, though.'

Rhianne tugged at the hand. 'I never did like them.'

'Right?'

She leaned back over. Kissed him, her hands on both sides of his face. 'Right,' she said back. Callum held the sweatshirt out for her. 'Keep it,' he said. 'I've got more.'

It was true: Callum's wardrobe, which she'd opened while he was in the shower, was filled with neat stacks of sweatshirts, T-shirts, matching tracksuits in bold patterns. To Rhianne, those clothes – the quality of them, the vibrancy – were a clear indication of an expressive soul. She had noticed, at the back of the cupboard, a poster-roll, something bright, unframed. She did not look further – there would be time for this later. She imagined this now, too: him, unfurling the posters for her on the floor of his bedroom, and her, tracing the lines with her fingers.

She wriggled back into the sweatshirt. A gift: a promised reunion.

'Wait,' Callum said. He pushed her phone into the front pocket of her jeans. 'Wait. What are you doing later?'

'I'm having dinner.'

'Later, later.'

Nothing, she told him.

'Perfect,' Callum said. 'Let's go somewhere. Let's go for a drive. Somewhere not here. I'll message you.'

10

That evening, after leaving him, she was wired. Her car kicked up dust and the thistles on the roadside were purple, hazy. The air smelt of honeysuckle. There was a dull pain between her legs, but it was not unwelcome. This pain was presence, a new-born awareness. And her body, too, was newly hers, its sensations now arriving to her in a long-unspoken language – one she had forgotten, one that moved, somehow, in waves. In Callum's bedroom, her make-up had bled; smudged into his chest as she buried her face in it. Dissolved in heat. She removed the last of it in the shower, lay on her bed upstairs in her room, Callum's sweatshirt laid across her bare shoulders. She had come straight up here, knowing that she was already late, conscious of bringing sweat and sex into the house on her skin. She thought of his body, alight.

They were eating outside this evening. She could hear the plates being carried out and the table laid. She stayed there on her bed, not moving, hoping that they would start dinner without her. Only when she heard the conversation quiet behind the clatter of cutlery did she lift herself up onto her elbows, crawl to the end of her bed, leaning over the stack of cardboard boxes and towards the window. She could see the tops of their heads, her father's, hair thinning, Melissa's copper roots, her platinum-dyed halo; between them, on the table, big bowls of fresh vegetables, potatoes, breaded fish. They were leaning close, unaware of her presence, up here. Rhianne closed the window, drew back out of sight. On the bed, beneath her bare thigh, her phone vibrated. Callum, making plans. Callum: here, concrete.

She reached for her phone. When she looked at the screen, she saw that the message was not Callum, though, but an email notification from a sustainable fashion brand. Sustainability, kindly, could fuck itself. She swiped through her phone, wrote a message to Jess. *You remember the guy I told you about*, she wrote. She read back the message, unsent, deleted it.

She didn't start to get worried until she was dry, deodorised, dressed. She did not reapply her make-up – something stopped her. She went downstairs, ate dinner in the living room. She sent Callum a message. *Be done soon. Where shall I meet you?* Below his icon, she saw that he was online. She wrote, sent, another message. *Miss you.* He hovered, online. Disappeared without responding. A brief spike of anxiety, silence quelled by the memory, still now embodied, of his hand on her wrist, pulling her back in towards him. She finished her food, stared blankly at the television screen, picking at the corners of her nails. Then, a vibration. This time, his name on the screen. She opened the message, in her mind calculating times; the distance she would need to travel, whether she needed to fill up the tank. She thought of the music she would play. The message, though, was not a meeting place, or a time. *Sorry.* For a while, nothing. And then, another message. *Something happening. Can't talk.*

Hours passed. It grew dark. She went back up to her room, lay on her bed with the window open, wings beating in her chest. Dust, grease, on the mirror where she'd propped it up earlier that evening, ready to apply the make-up she was no longer sure she needed. In thirty-minute interludes, explanations, half-formed, arrived. Something was happening. She waited for him to say that they were having a drink, or that they weren't, before she understood that their plans had been subsumed by the drama of whatever it was that had taken place. Something to do with the hotel, with a family member. Scenarios emerged. She waited. At last, he was online again, and she couldn't wait any more. She called him and when he answered, his voice was flat. 'Hey.'

'Hello?'

Silence, for a moment. 'Why do you sound so worried?' Callum said.

'Something's wrong,' Rhianne said. 'What's going on?'

'Yeah,' Callum said. 'You know what's wrong?'

She held her breath. She felt sick.

'Petrol pumps,' Callum said. 'You know? The ones that have short hoses, as if I'm supposed to know which side of the car the petrol tank is.'

'Callum—'

'No, I'm serious. They're fucking with me, those pumps. Trying to make me hop out of my car all excited thinking I'm getting my petrol and then, oh, look. The hose is too short and the tank is on the other side to where I thought it was the last time I filled up.'

Rhianne stayed silent.

'Sorry,' he said. 'I just needed to get that off my chest.'

'OK. You said something happened.' In the hours that had intervened, in among his silence, a fear within Rhianne, one she did not know had existed, had taken root. 'What is it?'

'I'll tell you,' Callum said. 'Just not on the phone. Look, what are you doing tonight?'

'Nothing,' Rhianne said. She bit down on the confusion that now, after hours of waiting, she was being asked to reconfirm her availability. 'I'm doing nothing.'

His voice softened. 'OK,' he said. 'It's late, but maybe we should see each other. You want to come here?'

She drove the lanes in the dark, the windows down. Her face was bright. She'd run her eyeliner quickly around the edges of her eyes, placed a dot in each corner, one on the inside, one on the outside, lined up like dominos. She was glad, at least, to be moving – away from uncertainty, towards his presence, in which she was confident she could alleviate doubt, fear. The car park was quiet when she pulled up; the staff house was dark, except for his room, whose window was edged with warm light.

'I'll leave the door open,' Callum had told her. 'Just come up.'

He was sitting on the floor. Rhianne stood in the doorway, breathless from the steps. He was wearing the same clothes as before, but his body seemed to have crumpled within them. He held his hand up to her. She took it. His touch pulsed. He pulled her down towards him.

'What is it? What's going on?'

Callum shook his head, rubbed his eyes. 'My ex.'

'Your ex?'

He tried to pull her close, but she resisted. 'Yeah,' he said. 'Grace.'

Grace. Rhianne hadn't heard the name before. Her head swam. 'She was here?'

'Fuck, no. She wouldn't dare. Just, she was calling Sophia.'

'Grace knows Sophia?'

'Yeah. I mean, they were always mates.'

The realisation dawning. 'She used to work here?'

'That's how we met.'

Rhianne nodded. She felt sick. 'What did she want?'

'Grace,' Callum said, 'it's complicated. She . . .' He started to speak, then stopped. He looked tired, run out. 'Please. Can we talk about it later?'

Rhianne was hungry for information. But here he was, in pain, and she: a balm, or a salve. She put her hand on his arm. What she felt – a mixture of fear, anxiety, relief – all of it was subsumed by that need, now fulfilled, for touch. She felt the muscles of his forearm tensing and then giving way beneath her hand. Then he took her hand in his, inspecting her nails.

'What did you do?'

'They're just chipped,' she said. She pulled way her hand, but he held on to it.

'Were you nervous?'

'Forget it,' she said, 'let's talk about it later.'

He stood then and he lifted her up into bed with him, pulled her clothes from her body. He drew her hair up into a ponytail, kissed the base of her neck, where her hair was platinum, and she fell into him. She was in pain, a little, from before, but she wanted him, and as he started to move inside her the pain lessened, gave way to warmth, pleasure. She closed her eyes, pulling his shoulders in towards her, and he was getting close: she could feel it, the rhythm of him, and she could not move for the weight of his chest, but he was moving faster, deep, and her attention, suddenly, was not on him, but just behind him, on the spot on the wall. Something she had seen before, but never fully registered. In among the photographs that were tacked there – of Sophia, two of the chefs she recognised, Brendan – there was one, half-focused. Callum, with his arm around a woman Rhianne didn't know, planting a kiss on her cheek. 'Callum,' she said. And she pushed him, harder than she meant to, on both shoulders. He recoiled, kneeling at the back of the bed. 'Is that her?'

'What?'

Rhianne pointed. 'That's Grace?'

He looked at the photograph, then at Rhianne. 'Yeah,' he said, 'that's her.' He shrugged. He was still hard, glistening. The scene was suddenly ridiculous. 'But you know that's not actually her, right? That's, like, a visual representation of a person, not an actual tiny person.'

She kicked him; he snatched up her foot.

'Obviously I know that. But why is the photo there?'

He was holding the foot tightly. 'I put it up,' Callum said, 'three years ago, when we were first together. Before everything went to shit. Before,' he hesitated. Rhianne braced herself. 'Before I found out she was fucking someone else.'

Rhianne tugged her foot from his hands, harder than she meant, sat up against the wall. She pulled the covers up over her. 'That's horrible,' she said, 'but . . .' She was looking at the photo, perturbed by its presence. The fact that it must have been there that first time they had slept together. 'Surely take the photo down by now.'

She could not hide her feelings, and she knew that he could see them. She was jealous, contracted. Minutely, Callum nodded. He knelt, pulled the photo from the wall, tore it into two, four, eight pieces, threw it over his shoulder. 'I didn't even bother. I didn't want to waste the energy. Not any more than I already had.'

She was waiting for the fluttering in her chest to settle. Then, slowly, she leaned over the edge of the bed, looked down at the torn-up remnants, now scattered on the floor.

'I didn't even get to see it.'

'It's been there the whole time.'

'Well, I didn't look at it properly.'

He moved closer to her. She was coiled up, ready.

'Maybe,' and the corners of his mouth twitched, 'you were distracted.'

'Distracted by what?'

He was kneeling in front of her now. Shoulders rounded, supplicatory. He put his fingers to her chin. 'Can I kiss you,' he said, 'or are you going to kick me again?'

Rhianne turned her head to the side.

'No? I can't kiss you?'

'You can.'

He leaned closer. 'But. Do you want me to kiss you?'

She nodded. Sulking. But the fingers were still there, firm.

'What's that?'

'I want you to kiss me,' she said.

'What's that?'

She turned back towards him, pulled him in. The kiss, sweeter than before.

He spoke into her mouth. 'So, I can kiss you.'

'You didn't have to tear up the photo.'

'I did,' he said. She could feel how hard his heart was beating, that his arms were trembling. 'I needed to do it for me. And for you.'

He held her. Rhianne spoke into his chest. 'Who was it?'

His chest rose, settled. 'Someone in the kitchen.'

'He's still there?'

'No,' he said. He was blunt. 'No. Both of them left.'

Callum was quiet. They slid down into the bed together. Her fear ebbing, falling through the floor beneath them. He traced circles on her hip. She closed her eyes. Lying there in the security of his touch, knowing that he would stay awake until she slept.

'Rhianne,' he said. 'Rannie.'

She turned her face, blinked up at him.

'Do you want to go away somewhere?'

'With you?'

'No, not with me. With Kieran.'

She had become childish, sulky. 'No.'

'Yes, with me. The last weekend of August. The bank holiday, I hate bank holidays.'

'Where?'

'Anywhere. I don't care. As long as you're there.'

'Yeah,' she said. 'OK.' She closed her eyes. She slept deeply, his arm heavy across her chest. In the morning the sun fell brightly across the courtyard. On the gravel, as she walked out to her car, there were dead and dying insects.

11

There was a small patch of light on the ceiling: its source the lone streetlight that stood at the end of the Colvins' empty lane. Dominic, lying in bed looking up at that light, was sleepless, and he was irritated by his sleeplessness. All of this, here, the house he himself had rebuilt, the woman next to him, whose love had emerged in the aftermath of his greatest grief. Their marriage, next spring, and a grown daughter, talented, kind, with an almost degree from a prestigious university. Not all of it perfect, but he had built, kept on building. Performed miracles, acts of creation: the sinking of steel into wet concrete; triumphs of architecture over gravity; life, even. He should, at least, have been content enough to sleep.

'The primal urge,' Melissa used to say, when they first bought the house on Minchinhampton Common. Dominic had stood in the kitchen and looked up at the hole in the ceiling, from which a slice of sky was visible. 'You could get rained on in here,' he'd said, and he'd been delighted by the scale of the project. Josephine had been dead five years. Melissa walked across planks laid out on the torn-up floor. Her hands had hovered just below her belly button. No, it had not been painless, their journey. Pain necessarily was part of it, and losses: large and unspeakable.

They shopped at Waitrose now, and when Melissa tried to claim that it was because they had the good mayonnaise there, the kind you couldn't get even at Big Tesco, Dominic told her they all knew it was the widened aisles she liked, and the café with its view of the car park and the basement toilets with the air conditioning. Organics, essentials, farm sourced. Soft-edged lettering, lower case so as not to be confrontational. Earlier today, Dominic had stood in the milk aisle, watched Rhianne reach for the shelf and pick out the gold-top like it was nothing.

A natural progression, and he could understand the logic. They used to have the full-fat on a Sunday, but now they were richer and there was new milk, more fatted than full-fat, with that thick coin of cream that sat just beneath the foil. It was sold in a bottle that resembled the kind that would have come from a milkman years ago, but jumbo-sized and made of quality plastic and with a cardboard choker detailing provenance, the name and star-sign of the cow that had provided it. Such details were condescending, indulgent, and the milk was almost twice as expensive as the one they usually bought. You have to earn milk like this, Dominic wanted to say, but he stopped himself. Not today.

'They have it at the hotel,' Rhianne told him, handing him the bottle.

Dominic put the milk in the trolley. She walked away, and, watching, he felt the void that sat just behind his ribcage crack open. The void, he was sure, had something to do with fear: Rhianne's failures; his own. She had good taste, though; she got that from her mother. The lone bottle rolled. Dominic added another, and pushed off.

She could have the fancy milk. Today was Josephine's birthday. He watched the till ring up, handed over his card, Rhianne inspecting the magazine rack, waiting. In the car on the way home she started to blast her playlist and Dominic turned the music right down, told her he'd found a job that she might want to apply for. A design studio, one that would accept her without the full degree. 'Reception work,' he said, 'but you have to start somewhere.' In the passenger seat, Rhianne was quiet. Dominic adjusted the volume back up. 'The deadline's next week.'

Dominic pulled back the covers. It was the right thing to do: to try to help, even if his timing had been off. Melissa, beside him, stirred. Quietly, he rose, and went downstairs. In the kitchen, he stood in front of the open fridge, looked at the milk. He allowed the memories to surge up. Josephine, so many years ago. The scent and feel of almond oil on warm, sun-spotted skin. Cheap, gold-plated jewellery that left green marks on her earlobes and at the base of her throat, leaning up against the kitchen doorframe, which had been etched over the years with Rhianne's height, laughing at Dominic when, again, he suggested baked beans for dinner. The Post-it Notes and coloured paper plastered across the walls of their bedroom where she had set up her office, Blu-tac picking chunks of paint off the wall. The sound of her, insistent, picking her nails while she worked. The fridge alarm started to beep. Upstairs, he heard a door closing.

It was Rhianne. She stood now in the doorway in an oversized T-shirt. 'You're up as well,' she said. She rubbed her eyes, and he felt guilty about earlier, turning down her music. Guilty that she was awake because of him.

'Cortisol, probably,' Dominic said. 'I read that it spikes between three and four a.m.'

It was cowardly to blame chemistry, but Rhianne was looking at the sweet peas he'd bought on the way home from the shops. Rhianne had waited in the car at the garden centre, said nothing when he got back in, silently deposited the bouquet on the back seat. The only time of year he bought flowers and the only time of year he felt justified buying flowers – Josephine's flowers – because the garden was already so full, and Melissa spent all year tending to it.

'Could also be the date,' said Rhianne.

'It could also be the date,' Dominic said. 'What about you?'

Rhianne shrugged. She looked sad, and this was unbearable.

'Cortisol, you think?' Gruff, but smiling.

'Cortisol,' she said. She was smiling now, too. 'Seems like it's got a lot to answer for.'

'Fifty-seven,' said Dominic. He gripped the countertop. 'She would have liked fifty-seven, don't you think?' He pulled the granola out of the cupboard, leaning up against the worktop with the packet open and picking. Whenever he couldn't sleep, he ate. He always left a trail of crumbs, and Rhianne always noticed, always asked him about it in the morning. Denial had been Dominic's automatic response, until Rhianne had suggested that they call the council to deal with the giant insomniac mouse that had started raiding their cupboards. 'Medium-sized,' Dominic had said, holding his belly protectively. 'Maybe extra medium.'

He poured the cereal into its bowl, peeled the lid off the gold-top and poured, so that the cream slid out of the bottle. He sat, eating with his shoulders hunched, his face close to the bowl.

'Do you remember,' Rhianne said, 'the pears and custard?'

'I do remember the pears and custard.'

'When she forgot about them and put them back in the cupboard.' Rhianne was reciting. She had been too young to remember; it was a story he had told her. Dominic spooned cereal into his mouth. 'And they were there for a whole week.'

'I do remember,' Dominic said again.

'They would have been there longer.'

'Much longer. Fossilised.'

Dominic carried on eating. He couldn't tell if the silence between them was reflective or uncomfortable. He pushed the bowl away, leaned back. Rhianne rubbed her eyes. On her T-shirt, the University of the Arts London's logo. The T-shirt was spattered in something, paint or glue. 'It doesn't bother you,' he said abruptly.

'What?'

'Wearing that,' Dominic said. 'With that logo.'

Rhianne was blank. 'Why would it?'

'He's still there,' Dominic said.

'I know he's still there. What's it got to do with anything?'

'I checked,' Dominic said.

'Why?' Rhianne said. The T-shirt swamped her.

'Because I wanted to know,' said Dominic, more forcefully than he meant. 'What father wouldn't?'

Rhianne picked at her thumb. 'I know I haven't done the form . . .'

Dominic softened. 'I know,' he said. 'That's not what I meant. That's why I want you to apply for this job. Put all of that behind you. Move on. It shouldn't be for you to deal with people like him.'

Rhianne took a big, shuddering inhale, nodded. Her eyes were shining.

'Go on,' he said, 'what is it?'

'If I don't,' Rhianne said, 'he's just there.'

'People like that. They get what's coming to them. One way or another.'

'You really think so?'

'I do think so,' Dominic said. Forceful again. 'I know so.'

Rhianne was quiet. She sat there in the dark. She looked at the sweet peas, spilling flimsily from their vase over by the fridge. He hadn't trimmed them, and Melissa would do it, probably, in the morning. 'I'll do it,' she said. 'I'll do the application tomorrow.'

She left him there, at the table, and Dominic sat in the dark, waiting for the sound of her bedroom door to close before he poured himself another bowl.

12

Through July and into August, they'd sat out on the driveway with the engine running, the sound of it white noise to Melissa. There and not there. 'Bring him in next time,' she shouted, when eventually the front door slammed. Rhianne swept past the door of the kitchen, up the stairs to her room, a trail of hairspray and deodorant. The car stayed there a while, engine idling, before it pulled away. Melissa didn't know why it was necessary for him to drive her, when Rhianne loved her little car. Two weeks of this, maybe three, until, one day, the engine cut, the sound of both doors closing, one after the other. Melissa took a second pack of chicken out of the refrigerator, caught a glance of herself in the glass panel above the stove. Her big blonde fringe was frazzled, and her cheeks had that pink flush across them, the one that went diagonal, in the opposite direction to how blusher was supposed to go. She could hear Rhianne out in the hallway. 'You don't have to take them off.'

'On your beautiful floor? No, I'll take them off.'

Callum, when he appeared in the doorway, was holding his trainers. Melissa took in the brightly socked feet, the thick-shouldered sweatshirt, the face. Nice eyes, eyebrows that appeared groomed in the way they were these days. She thought that this was a bootlicking kind of a thing to say about someone's floor, even if it was true that the wood was spotless and the shoes were muddy. Callum put the trainers down in the corridor, wiped his hands on his jeans. 'I'm Callum.'

'I'm covered in onion,' Melissa said, eyeing his outstretched hand. She picked up the chopping board and scraped the onion peel into the bin. 'I know about you,' she said. 'You're one of the cooks.'

'Chef,' Rhianne corrected, 'cooking is what you do.'

'It's all creativity, isn't it?' Callum said.

Melissa stuck her knife into the plastic seal of the chicken packet. 'The only thing I create is a mess.' She skimmed the fat from the meat and threw it into the pan, where it landed with a thick slap: the oil wasn't hot enough. 'You're staying for dinner, are you?'

Callum glanced at the worktop, the stack of ingredients. 'If there's enough.'

'There's plenty,' said Melissa. 'There are beers. Rhianne, help yourself to some beers.'

Rhianne popped the cap from two bottles and she and Callum stood next to each other but not touching, leaning uncomfortably against the counter, the two of them looking suddenly more like teenagers than young adults. Melissa realised that they were intending to stand there and watch her cook. 'Go outside,' she said. 'You can set the table.'

Dominic was out in the garden, and Melissa watched as he and Callum did that stiff, forward-leaning handshake that men did. Dominic, heavy-footed, came in, Ludo scuttling under the table in front of him. He took a beer from the fridge, opened it.

'How do you like your new friend?' said Melissa.

'What friend?'

Melissa glanced outside. Callum was touching the camellia. 'Monty Don over there.'

'That's Gordon.' Dominic opened the lower cupboard, closed it, then opened the door above it. 'Gordon Ramsay.'

Melissa stirred. 'What are you looking for?'

Dominic shook his head, closed the door. She knew what he

was looking for: the big box of flapjacks he had bought a few days earlier, which he wasn't supposed to have bought because he was supposed to be eating less sugar to help with his sleep. Melissa had emptied them into a lined Tupperware and taken them to work. Dominic was standing close to her, and for a moment, Melissa feared that he was about to try to stir something.

'I think,' Dominic said, 'tonight. Don't you?'

Melissa moved closer to the stove, protective.

'Tonight what?'

Dominic sipped his beer.

'I think we should tell her. I think it'll be a good night to tell her.'

Melissa glanced out to the garden. Saw the logic. 'All right,' she said, 'tonight.'

They ate out in the garden. Dinner was not good. The oil had been too cold and the chicken had turned greasy and then dry, and they all knew it, because Rhianne was pushing her food around her plate, glancing at Callum's, next to her, and even Dominic, who usually inhaled his food, had to take a second to chew. But Callum had finished his portion, asked – too polite – if he could serve himself seconds.

'Is that miso,' he said, 'there's something earthy. In the sauce.'

'Miso,' Melissa conceded, 'and a bit of cane sugar.'

'To balance the lime.'

To balance the lime, that had been exactly it.

'That's where the richness comes from,' Callum said, spooning more onto his plate, onto Rhianne's. 'I've been trying to teach Rhianne, but . . .'

'Why do I need to cook,' Rhianne said, shrugging. 'I've got you, haven't I?'

'For now,' Callum said.

He was smiling, and the lights out here were twinkling, and

72

Melissa felt suddenly glad that he was here; happy that Rhianne was happy. She didn't know whether Dominic could feel it too. He was looming over his plate at the other end of the table, and when he spoke, it was abrupt, directed at nobody in particular. 'What about the food, then,' he said, 'at your place?'

'It's good,' Callum said, 'obviously it's good.'

'But, you know,' Dominic persisted, and Melissa saw, too late, where he was very clumsily heading, 'for larger groups. Bigger groups and celebrations.'

'Funerals,' Melissa supplemented.

'Funerals,' said Dominic, 'you know, and weddings.'

'Yeah,' said Callum slowly. 'Yeah. There's a menu. It's a good menu.' He glanced sideways at Rhianne, and Melissa saw how he shifted a little closer to her, moved his arm around her, protective. 'It's not like some of the bigger places where the quality dips the more people you add. We do what we can handle, and we do it well.'

'Rhianne,' said Melissa, 'what he means is—'

'She said yes,' Dominic said. He cracked a smile, large, beaming. 'For the record. Before she tries to tell you any different.'

For a moment, everybody was waiting for Rhianne to say something. She was sitting, glassy-eyed, stunned. The fairy lights twinkled. It was still out here. Then, Rhianne pressed herself back into Callum's arm, pouted.

'Took you long enough,' she said, 'fifteen years.'

'Seventeen,' Dominic corrected.

'Seventeen years,' said Melissa, 'it's true. I did say yes. Eventually.'

Rhianne couldn't quite make eye contact with her father, or with Melissa; she was looking, instead, somewhere in the middle of the table, the bravado in her voice disguising her obvious shock. 'Well,' she said, 'if you do it at The White Hart at least the food will be good.'

Callum tightened his arm around her shoulders.

'Good,' he said, 'you hear that? The food is *good*.'

'Maybe check the rota,' Rhianne said, dropping her voice. 'Do it on a day when Callum isn't working.'

'You see?' Callum said. 'You see?' But he was smiling, and now, because he was smiling, so too was Rhianne. Noise, again. Crockery, dishes passed: seconds, even of that dry chicken. Relief. More beers hissing open, and Dominic, compensating, steering the subject towards Rhianne; her brilliance. He was insisting, now, that Rhianne show Callum her paintings, because she was talented, he said, really very talented.

'He likes to pretend he knows,' said Rhianne to Callum. 'He doesn't know.'

'I do know,' Dominic said.

'You don't know,' Rhianne said, 'you thought Frida Kahlo was a man.'

Melissa remembered: Rhianne had jammed Dominic's printer by blowing up the portrait of a thick-browed face in a halo of flowers. 'He looks miserable,' Dominic had said, when they'd managed to fix the printer, Rhianne smoothing the torn-up print out onto the kitchen table, 'and that was even before you tore his face in half.'

'He?' Rhianne had said, full of pity, contempt. 'It's Frida Kahlo.'

'Frida Kahlo's a woman,' said Dominic now. 'Everybody knows that.'

'Yeah, everybody knows that,' Callum said, and there were those dimples again.

'You know even less than he does,' said Rhianne.

All confidence, there on the surface. Quietly, though, she was picking at the skin around her thumbnail again, and there was the sound of it, in the brief silence that had settled now that the extractor fan had timed out inside. Melissa looked at Rhianne's hands, the raw redness around that thick shellac. Then Callum shifted, lowered his gaze, and Rhianne, not looking but conscious of his stare, dropped her hands down beneath the table. Melissa looked at Callum. He tugged Rhianne's hand into his, kissed her knuckles.

'It's the monobrow,' said Melissa. She looked away. 'People are stupid. They get very easily confused by that sort of thing.'

'Exactly!' Callum squeezed Rhianne and kissed her on the side of her head. 'I really think you should start painting again.'

In the kitchen, Melissa put the lights on. Voices carried. Then, the popping of the patio doors and Callum came in with the rest of the dishes, stood next to her at the sink. She glanced back out to the patio, to where they had left Rhianne and Dominic. They had stood, both of them, and Dominic was holding her, her cheek resting on his shoulder. Callum rolled up his sleeves and Melissa saw that there were marbled patches of skin on the underside of his arms.

'Pan handle,' he said, and turned the soft skin of his arm towards her, showing a scar just below the inside of his wrist. He dried his hands, showed her the other arm: here, a scar a little pinker than the other. 'Griddle.' He squeezed his fist, the veins of his forearm stood up.

'You've got some good veins there,' Melissa said. Callum had seen her looking back out to the patio. She moved past him. 'They'll tell you, should you ever need cannulating. Nice easy job.'

13

On the calendar pinned up on the wall of her room she drew a square around the three last days of August, from the Friday to the end of the Bank Holiday weekend. A firm, quiet delineation, there in pen, which she had requested two weeks ago. Brendan had flipped forwards in his diary. 'Same days as Callum,' he'd said.

Answering, Rhianne had been vague. 'Are they?'

'He's guessed,' she told Callum, 'definitely.'

He closed the boot, her suitcase in it. 'Let him guess.'

Things had been good, these last weeks, since the dinner, since Melissa had brought that oversized sapphire out of its blue velvet box. That night, they hadn't spoken about it, but Callum had held her, and she knew that he understood, because he had suffered his own betrayals, the marks of which were borne by his body. Marks of violence, of heartbreak. Different, but the same. She could see, now, how neatly his wounds mapped on to hers. They pulled down onto the slip road, into the traffic, watched the seat belt strain and then loosen across his chest. 'So, they booked it? For April?'

'The hotel? Yeah. For April.'

They were close to Bristol now, three lanes deep, inching towards the city.

Callum nodded. 'How are you feeling about it?'

'What, about the hotel?'

'Not about the hotel,' Callum said. He checked the mirrors. His expression was serious. 'About your dad. His new girlfriend.'

Rhianne laughed. 'She's not exactly new.'

'No, but,' said Callum, 'this is new territory, and she's not your mum. You're allowed to feel a way.'

Rhianne nodded. Loyalty tugged at her. Beyond it, desire.

'I want them to be happy,' she said.

'Sweetness and light,' Callum said, 'the three of you in perfect harmony.'

'Not for much longer,' she said. 'I've actually got a job interview when we get back.' She'd been waiting to tell him about the email. It had come earlier that week and she had spent the last few days preparing. 'In London.'

Callum was quiet, just for a second, moving back up into the fast lane.

'For a design agency,' Rhianne said. She didn't add the bit about her dad, how he'd found the agency, told her to apply. 'It's entry level. Nothing impressive. But they want to interview me.'

'Of course they do,' Callum said, 'why wouldn't they?'

They passed the city, drove against the traffic. This is how she always felt with Callum – that they were making their own way. Free, the road open, down towards the coast. They were staying in South Sands, an Airbnb right on the beach. It had a webcam attached to its front and Rhianne had watched it, had seen how the sea came right up to its window when the tide was high.

The shack was small, vulnerable-looking on the shore. The main room was as nice as it had looked in the pictures – a newly fitted kitchen and a view right across to the other side of the coast – but the bedroom, at the back of the shack, and the bathroom, were both cramped. Rhianne was disappointed by the smell of damp. 'I think it's been freshly painted,' she said. Callum edged his way around the far side of the bed – there was hardly room for his thighs between the bedframe and the wall, and Rhianne felt suddenly panicked. He ran his hand along the inside of the window, the bent metal blind, cracked it open.

'Probably to cover the mould,' he said.

'Is it mouldy?' Rhianne said. 'Are you sure?'

Callum shrugged. He pushed on the window, testing to see if it would go further, but it would not. 'I mean,' he said, 'obviously that's what happens, if you book somewhere that's basically underwater half the time.' Rhianne, when booking, had been especially excited about the way the tide came right up to the shack. The understanding was crushing, that of course this was the source of that waterlogged stench. Callum edged his way back towards her. He put his hand to Rhianne's face, dragging down the corners of her mouth. 'What are you sad about?'

'This place is mouldy, and it's not as good as it looked.'

'Like you, then,' Callum said.

He squeezed her cheeks together with his hand, kissed her on the mouth.

They crossed the sand, and the sky was oppressive and wide, clouds that kept in the late-August warmth but kept out the light. Callum, at the shoreline, hesitated. Rhianne stripped down to her swimsuit, walked straight towards the water. It was cold, needle-like, but she did not react, kept on walking, as if it were nothing, until she was up to her thighs, aware that Callum was somewhere, there, behind her. 'It's moments like this,' Callum said, gasping, 'that remind me you will never understand what it means to have a penis.'

Rhianne dived into the water, surfaced, looked back for him over her shoulder. For a moment, she thought he had turned back. Then, the surface of the water broke; he was there, beside her. He gasped for breath. She wrapped her legs around him. Kissed him. Her body, his. Warmth. She kissed him on the mouth. His lips tasted of salt. 'How do you feel?'

He kissed her back, a hand on her face.

'Happy,' he said.

They walked back to the shack barefooted, trailing sand and salt water through the living room to the bathroom, where they showered, steam rising. They got into bed, naked, her hair wrapped in a towel, skin smelling of soap. It was the middle of the afternoon, but they had nowhere to be, and it always tired her out, cold water swimming. Something to do with the energy expended staying warm. She fell asleep with her head on Callum's shoulder, her arm heavy across his chest.

It was almost dark when she woke. Early-evening light coming in through the little window, sort of pink, sort of blue. Waves, they must have been up against the window by now. He was awake: she realised that it was the movement of his body against hers that had woken her, his leg, heavy on hers, him shifting his weight on top of her. The duvet covers a cavern around them. Him, gently, pushing her thighs apart. She put her arms around his neck, brought his mouth to her. He was hard, his whole body awake in a way that hers wasn't yet, and he pushed himself inside of her, and it was his heat, his presence, that woke her fully.

'I was sleeping,' she said. She went to kiss him back, but his hand was there on her throat. A place it had been before, squeezing, gently, in a way she'd liked. In the half-light she couldn't quite make out his expression. She was surrounded by his heat: his breath, the movement of his body.

'I have to make the most of you,' Callum said, 'before you leave me.'

'I'm not leaving you.'

'You are,' he said, 'you're leaving me for Maria. You're moving to Amberley and adopting cats together.'

Rhianne laughed, but it was half a laugh, because her breath – with his hand there – was more than a little constricted. 'London,' she said, 'not fucking Amberley.'

She put her hand to his wrist, pulled it, hard. In the dim light, the bed bowed as he pressed himself up. As he stood, she felt the heat of his body receding from hers. He walked out of the room, into the living room. Rhianne called his name, confused. There was the sound, out in the living room, of the fridge opening. A few moments later, he reappeared with a bottle of champagne. He stood in the doorway, peeling the foil from around the top.

'You brought that?'

Callum nodded. He sat on the side of the bed, unscrewing the little cage around the cork. He popped it, handed Rhianne the bottle. 'Just in case,' he said. 'I brought it in case you did something amazing, you know, like you always do.'

'What's it for?'

'Your interview,' Callum said, 'or did you forget already?'

He watched her as she took a sip.

There was something about the way he was moving – the abruptness of his speech – that prevented her from asking him to go and get glasses. Her sip was more of a swig. The bottle, presumably, had been shaken in the car ride down, so the liquid, cold, surged up her nose and she handed it back to him, sitting up and choking just a little.

'Congratulations,' Callum said. He took a swig, still sitting there on the side of the bed. Rhianne wished he had not got up. She wanted him to come back to her. 'Come here,' she said. In the few minutes he'd been out of the bed, his skin had grown cold. She wrapped her thighs around him, pulled him close, kissed him. But Callum was restless. He pulled himself from her grip, stripping back the covers, and he took another sip from the bottle. He shifted onto his side so that he was lying next to her, the duvet tangled at their feet. He put his hand on her waist. 'So,' he said. His hand slid down to her hip. There, his fingertips pinched. 'Rhianne. What are your weaknesses?'

'What?'

'You need to prepare, right? Your interview. What are your weaknesses? You want this job. Tell me what your weaknesses are.'

His face was only an inch or so from hers, and she started to laugh, embarrassed by the performance. His expression did not change, though. He lifted himself up onto his elbow. He released her hip, drew two fingers to his mouth, inhaling, like he was smoking a cigarette. The imaginary smoke, he blew into her face.

'You sure you want this job?'

'Why are you smoking if this is a job interview?'

'So, you don't want the job.'

'I do,' she said. 'I don't have any weaknesses.'

'Everybody has weaknesses.'

'All right,' she said. 'Chefs. Those are my weaknesses.'

'Chefs?' Callum said. 'OK.'

'Chef,' she corrected. 'One very particular chef.'

'All right,' Callum said. 'Good answer.'

She turned, leaned closer, wanting to stop his next question. Her body was alive to his presence, his proximity: she was willing to play the game, but wanting, prematurely, the reward. But before her lips reached his, he put his hand on her throat. 'Next question,' he said. 'Tell me about a time that you faced a challenge at work.'

'This colleague,' she said, 'kept sticking around after his shift to do orders. Kept bumping into him late at night, around the bar, you know? In the office.'

'Mm,' Callum said. 'Sounds tricky. So, what did you do?'

'I slept with him,' she said.

'Sensible,' Callum said. Consulted an imaginary document. 'All right. And that's not the first time you fucked someone you worked with? Or, you know, studied with?'

'Callum,' she said. She tried to move closer, but the hand was pressing, holding her away from him. His expression was blank, and in the half-darkness, his hand pulsed. 'What do you mean?'

The room small, low-ceilinged. The covers were pulled back and she wished that they were under them, that she was not naked. She wished for weight, heat, protection. Past him, she could just about make out the source of the mould – there in the top corner of the room, where it had spored, the smell of it now filling her nostrils. The hand squeezed.

'You want me to repeat the question?' Callum said. 'Because if you have a habit of fucking your colleagues, probably it's something we should know.'

Rhianne froze. It was an imaginary question in an imaginary game, and asking him to repeat it would make it real. It would make this interrogation real, this betrayal. And it would make the grip of his hand on her no longer a joke, part of a role, but a real hand of bones, tendons, a pulse – pressing, more tightly now, into her too real flesh.

'You don't want to answer.'

'Callum,' she said again. Her voice rasped.

His name, a spell. He let go. Rolled onto his back, drew those two fingers to his mouth again, inhaled, an exaggerated exhale of his pretend cigarette. Now, no part of his body in contact with hers. 'Shame,' he said. 'She was a good candidate.'

Then he reached over, without looking at her, took a final swig from the bottle on the bedside. She lay there next to him, unable to move, not wanting to speak.

14

When she woke, he was gone. It was bright in the bedroom – they hadn't closed the blinds the night before – and she had rolled into the middle of the bed. She gathered the duvet around her, a shield against the memory of last night. Her heart, suddenly, was hurting. She called his name, quietly at first, then louder. He did not reply. She stood, wrapped herself in the duvet, went into the living room. The air was cooler out here, fresher. Empty. She scanned the room. His car keys were still here, and his phone, so he had not gone far.

Rhianne stood at the window, adjusting to the light. She could see her reflection: hazy, a large, ridiculous shape wrapped in a quilt. And there, in the distance, Callum, walking across the sand. He was carrying a plastic bag, and she could see the white flesh of fish, wet, heavy against the inside of the bag. She leaned nearer to the window, studying her reflection more closely. On her throat were raw, pink marks, tinged already with the green of a fresh bruise. Rhianne retreated. In the bedroom, she peeled the duvet from her body, got dressed. By the time she re-emerged, Callum was there, standing over the counter, the fish in its bag on the chopping board in front of him. He was looking at something on his phone. She stood in the doorway until he looked up, saw her.

'You're up early,' said Rhianne.

'Mackerel,' Callum said, 'you wouldn't believe how fresh it is.'

She watched as he washed his hands, dried them. He unpacked

the fish onto the chopping board, gutted it into the sink. The smell was a shock to her, but it shouldn't have been. She was used to working in a professional kitchen by now, but somehow, this morning, her sensitivities were heightened. Merely the fact of a different knife – blunter than Callum's own – was enough to change the way the blade cut into the flesh. Tugging, rather than slicing, so that he had to tear the fish's belly.

All the while he worked, he did not look up at her. He had left the door open, and her bare feet were cold on the tiled floor. She stood there on the other side of the counter, waiting for him to speak, to acknowledge what had passed between them the previous night. Waiting, even, for him to notice the marks on her neck. His questions, his interrogation. The hand on her throat. 'Callum,' she said.

He looked up, sharp, his expression serious, just as it had been the night before. He rested the knife, blade flat, on the chopping board. 'Rhianne,' he said, 'there's something wrong.'

Here it was. Breath tangled in her chest.

'Coffee,' Callum said. 'We don't have coffee. Can you find the coffee?'

'Coffee,' she said. 'I saw it. In the cupboard.'

Callum held up his hands, which were covered in mackerel, suppliant. He smiled. The smile was wide. Rhianne could not help but marvel at its symmetry. 'Can you,' he said, 'Rannie? Please?'

She nodded. Slowly, she moved to his side of the kitchen. Into his orbit. She knelt, started to rummage beneath the counter where she had seen the coffee. She opened the packet. The smell of it, like the fish, overwhelming to her, and this packet just on the wrong side of fresh. She heaped a spoon into the cafetière that sat on the counter, boiled the kettle. All the while, Callum continued with his mackerel, cleaning it with a meticulousness she had not seen before. She sat the coffee pot, full and steaming, on the worktop, understanding that Callum was not going to acknowledge what had happened last night. That if she wanted to talk about it, she would have to raise it herself. But it was an ugly thing, difficult to approach in words.

'You can plunge it,' Callum said, looking at the coffee.

An order. Rhianne bristled. She stepped closer to the pot. With one hand on the pump, another on the lid, she began, slowly, to press. The granules stirred beneath the pressure of the filter as it descended. She leaned her weight forwards. 'Just to be clear,' she said, 'I don't like it. So you know, for next time.'

'Don't like what?' Callum did not look up, continued with his fish.

'Being choked,' Rhianne said. She boldened. She was standing right in front of him, only the counter between them, and the cafetière, half-plunged. 'During sex.'

'All right,' Callum said. He looked up, but it was only a glance. The briefest acknowledgement, before he looked back down at what he was doing. 'We didn't have sex.'

'What?'

'We weren't having sex,' Callum said.

'OK. In sex, out of sex. I don't like it.'

She pushed the plunger the whole way down, poured the coffee.

'OK,' Callum said, 'but I was hardly touching you.'

Rhianne laughed. Later, she would tell herself that the laugh had been a mistake. That if she hadn't laughed, if she had just stopped there, it would be enough. He, too, would have stopped. But she couldn't stop. She was angry. She stepped towards him, pulling her hair back from her neck, revealing her throat, the marks she knew were there.

'So what are these?' she said.

Callum paused, and he looked at her. His eyes slid down to her neck.

'It's a friction mark,' he said.

85

He had finished with the fish. He picked it up, carefully, wrapped it in foil. He put the chopping board, the knife, in the sink, began to run hot water. Steam rising up into the fan above the sink, and he still wasn't looking at her. A single, knotted string, a fuzz of grey mould settled across its vents. Callum left the tap on full.

'Yeah,' she said. 'A friction mark. Which you put there,' and then, because he was ignoring her, because he would not react, she pushed. 'When you strangled me.'

Callum hardened.

'Strangled you?'

Rhianne stood her ground. 'Choking. I don't know, whatever that was. Hurting me.'

'If I was hurting you, you should have said something.'

She hesitated. It wasn't even about the bruise, or strangling, choking, whatever it had been. It was about the questions, the betrayal. Something in the way the atmosphere had shifted. But she had this: the bruise. Something concrete, something she could touch, a way for her to show him how he had hurt her.

'Maybe I didn't want to say anything,' she said, 'because I was scared of you.'

What warmth remained vanished. In its place, contempt.

'You're scared of me. OK.'

'Last night. Just for a second, I don't know. I thought—'

'Don't worry. I get it.' He looked away, the little muscle in his jaw twitching. 'I didn't know that's what you thought of me. Because, you know, why would you be with someone you're scared of?'

Rhianne's voice was quiet. 'I'm not.'

'It's OK,' he said. He continued washing, stacking dishes up onto the draining board. He could not look at her. He turned the tap off. Somewhere inside the hollow walls of the building, a valve squeaked. 'I didn't know,' he said. 'But now I do.'

'Callum.' Her voice pleading. 'That's not what I think.'

He looked at her now, straight.

'But you said it.'

She shook her head. 'I didn't mean it.'

'I thought you would understand,' he said. 'After everything I told you. What I've been through.' His eyes were glittering. 'I'm trying so hard to be a good person.'

'You are,' Rhianne said. 'You are a good person. Please. Let's talk about it.'

He stacked the board, the knife on the draining board. She did not want to speak again. In his mouth, her words were turning against her. They stood. A cavern of space between them, neither of them moving, until at last, Callum reached across, picked up the foil package he had placed there on the side. 'I'm hungry,' he said. His voice was flat. 'Let's eat.'

They smoked the fish outside, both sitting in the doorway to the shack. It was cold enough for them to wear jackets, and they sat close to the heat of the smoker. There was the sound, in the distance, of waves pulling back, rushing away from the shore on the strength of the tide. The rustling of Callum's puffer, thick around his neck. Those bright paint flecks of colour across the quilt of his jacket. Callum ate with his hands, stacking the fish up onto pieces of toasted bread, sprinkling salt, pressing it down with his fingers, licking them, wiping them. The food was rich, full of flavour. The silence between them thick, sickening.

As they sat, accusations rose to the surface of Rhianne's thoughts. As soon as they found clarity, they sank, muddied by her fear of Callum's silence, his anger. This wounded look of his that persisted as he finished his meal. Callum screwed up the foil his fish had been wrapped in, and looked down at hers, of which she had only eaten a mouthful.

'I'm not hungry,' Rhianne said eventually.

'OK,' Callum said.

She stood, went back inside. In the kitchen she filled a glass of water, drank it there, slowly, waiting for him to come inside, to finish what he'd started. To do something, anything. In the reflection of the glass, she could see him there, still, head bowed, on the back doorstep. She retreated. In the bedroom, she took her swimming costume from the radiator, where she had left it drying the night before, a towel from the bathroom. She left her phone, her keys, walked out through the open door and crossed the beach.

It felt good, to walk. It was still early. In the distance she could see tankers on the horizon, their lights little constellations in the mist. The tide had begun to draw away and the sand beneath it was compact, shimmering. She threw down her towel, back in the same spot they had swum the day before, stripped off her clothes. The swimming costume was still damp, its material clinging to her skin. She did not look back at the shack, but walked across the heavy sand, barefoot, straight into the sea.

The water hit her stomach and she inhaled sharply, tripping forward. This was the moment: she plunged herself fully into the water. Came up, inhaled. The second or third breath after coming up was always the deepest. She needed this. She needed to have the air shocked out of her lungs to remember how to breathe. There was the curious feeling of having the hair on her arms stand up on end even though she was underwater, feeling as though warm, solid things – hands, fingertips, lips – were not real things, that they could not exist, because there now was only ice and salt.

She swam. Dipping her head every few breaths and tasting salt, heading out to the orange buoy in the distance. This was a fishing beach, and the area where they were swimming was cordoned off by buoys and ropes to keep swimmers away from the boats that they'd seen come in every twenty minutes or so. There was a tarpaulin path, staked down into the sand, that ran from the jetty up to the unloading bay, boats beached either side of the path. The waves and the currents were playing tricks, bringing the buoy up in her eyeline, making her feel as though it was only a few metres away, before pulling it back down again and bringing it far from her reach.

Once there, she held on to the base: it was large and slippery, kelp and seaweed wrapped around the chain that kept it anchored. It was impossible to feel fear when she was thinking only of survival, but as soon as she stopped and the heat her body generated began to dissipate, she grew cold again. She felt the salt crystals hardening in her hair, and she felt, too, the sting of regret, and the urge, suddenly, to go back to him, to undo what had been done. She thought of how he had stood there, across from her, this morning before she had spoken. Open arms, a smile. Breakfast. Before she had turned it on him, before she had made him feel what he must now be feeling. She thought, too, how they had been encased in warmth: the covers', their bodies' heat, his thigh across her waist.

The tide still tugged out but she swam as fast as she could back into shore. She did not dress but wrapped herself in the towel she had left. Walked, ran, across the shore back to the shack. Ready, now, to repent. Ready to reconcile. The door was open, the cafetière, their two undrunk coffees, still there on the side. Callum, though, was gone.

15

It had been a morning of handing out contraceptives and inoculations; of dressings and irrigations. Her last patient was here to have her smear, but she wanted the full works, she told Melissa. Melissa, who recognised most of the young women who came through her door, hadn't seen her before. She was a jumpy thing, but there was a kind of assertiveness about her, the way she sat, dumped her backpack on the floor between her legs, spread her knees wide.

'I hate this stuff,' she said. 'So can we get it all done? Checkup, HPV?'

'Fine,' Melissa said. 'Fine.'

The girl waited for her in the consulting room. Stripped off her jeans, underwear. She leaned forward as she sat, legs swinging under the bed, clearly not wanting to lie back for a minute longer than was necessary. Melissa kept her back to the girl, snapping her gloves over her wrists, as she told her to lie back. 'Move your bottom up,' she said. She was tense. Melissa could tell that as soon as she turned around: the way she moved her legs up into the stirrups: stiff, unpliant, her hands balled into fists at her sides.

Bodies, to Melissa, were endlessly readable. It was the reason, perhaps, she herself did not rely upon language to do the talking for her. Language muddied things, it brought in confusion – words always saying things that didn't want to be said – brought you from your feet on the floor up into your head which, when you were lying naked from the waist down on a spot-lit surgical bed, was the last place you needed to be. She put a hand, gently, on the girl's ankle. 'Bum back,' she said, 'towards me.' She shifted and beneath her the tissue paper stuck and tore. But now she had come closer, her legs had bent a little, she had relaxed. Melissa switched on the lamp, swivelled it so it shone directly between the girl's legs. 'Woman,' Rhianne would have said. 'She's twenty-nine. Stop calling her a girl.'

Melissa talked the girl-woman through everything she was doing. She warned her of the sensations – cold, slimy, uncomfortable – she was about to experience. Perhaps a little painful, because it mattered to tell a person about pain. 'And if it's too much, you tell me to stop.'

She didn't have to tell Melissa to stop, though. The speculum inside her, her whole body straight away tensed, a piece of elastic, taut. There were two things she could do in this situation: keep trying, hoping the speculum would ease further in, or stop and talk. She paused for a moment, feeling the resistance of the girl's body against the foreign object inside her. Carefully, she withdrew the speculum. 'Give me a second, love,' Melissa said. She looked at the girl's face. Tears had begun to form in the corners of her eyes. Melissa went to the cupboard, brought her a box of tissues. 'What's going on here?' she said.

The girl took a tissue, held it in her hand rather than wiping her eyes. She eased herself up to sitting. 'This is difficult for me.' She had gathered herself with immense speed, Melissa thought. Her nostrils were flaring with the effort it took not to cry; it was no wonder her whole body was strung like a guitar.

'Do you want to talk about it?' Melissa said.

The girl looked at her, breathed in deeply, exhaled. A loud, forced-out breath. Melissa held up the speculum. 'Is there some-body *else* you'd like me to insert this into? I'm taking requests.'

The girl blinked, taking a second to understand what Melissa was saying. And then she let out something between a sob and a laugh, a horrified kind of a-*ha* sound.

'I'm serious,' Melissa said, snapping the spring. 'I've got a list.'

'One or two,' the girl said. Now she was really laughing. She took another tissue. Melissa waited until she had stopped, and she told her she could go home, they could do this another day if she wanted. She could bring somebody with her, they could listen to some music or watch something to make it easier. 'But you should have it,' Melissa said.

It was this, more than anything, that made the girl lie back on the bed again. Somehow Melissa had known that she would. This time, the speculum slid inside, still with resistance, but more easily than it had before. She put in the swab, circled it gently but firmly. 'You OK?' she said, as she went. The girl nodded. She was holding her breath again, but it didn't matter now, soon it would be over. 'Nearly done,' Melissa said.

Afterwards, she left the girl to get dressed, went and sat behind her desk in the next room. There was a barrier there, now. Clothes, the computer screen. The girl sat across from her. 'You live here?' Melissa said.

The girl shook her head. 'I'm visiting,' she said. 'Down to stay with my mum for a couple of weeks.'

'Oh,' Melissa said. 'She'll like that.'

'I'm helping her to paint her shed. It needs repainting.'

The girl waited as Melissa brought up her records.

'Don't tell me,' Melissa said.

'Quaile. Like the bird. Will I have to come back?'

'I knew it was something. With an *e*?' Melissa typed, the screen loaded.

'With an *e*.'

'In three years, yes. But at least your mother will be glad. You'll need another test.'

'But not sooner?'

'Not unless you have HPV. And that won't be for a year.'

The girl slumped in her seat. 'Is that likely?'

'Incredibly, yes,' Melissa said. 'Four out of five women by the time they're fifty.'

Melissa looked across at the girl, aware she may have spoken too sharply.

'But it'll be fine,' she said. 'The same thing again.'

'Will it be you who does it?'

'Unless I drop dead,' Melissa said. She reached for her bag. 'And next time,' she pulled out her purse, 'we can have some treats. For our troubles.' From her purse, she extracted three pound coins and a fifty-pence piece, held them out to the girl, woman, woman-girl. 'There's a Tesco, just up the hill. If you get here early enough, there's *pains aux raisins* in the baked goods section. One pound seventy-five each.'

The girl looked at Melissa's hand, confused.

'And if I don't have HPV?'

'Then you'll have two *pains aux raisins*,' Melissa said. She dropped the money into her open hand. 'Go on,' Melissa said. 'Go on.'

It always took Melissa a few minutes to type up the notes. She was slow with the keyboard, so she had already started as the girl left, typing with just two fingers, the letters always seeming to evade her. What she really needed was a secretary. The heavy door swung closed, the handle slowly latching into place. Melissa thought again of Rhianne: that she should message, remind her to get her screening. Rhianne was still only twenty-three, she wouldn't even be invited for her first screening for another few years. But, nonetheless, a flash-forward, years in the future: Rhianne, undergoing chemotherapy for cervical cancer because Melissa had not reminded her to have her smear.

Melissa finished typing and packed up her things. The letter would come to the mother's house; Melissa had forgotten to mention this in the appointment. She should have told her to tell her mother about the letter, to let her know it was coming. She'd like that, the mother, and it made Melissa feel good, the thought of this woman she did not know receiving the envelope with her daughter's name on it. The daughter who didn't visit a whole lot these days, who couldn't quite bear the weight of memories that did nothing for her, served no purpose except to put a wedge, there, between home and her. The letter a thread between the two of them. She stopped in the doorway to Taschimowitz's office, pulled out the Tupperware into which she'd emptied Dominic's flapjacks.

'That's very kind of you.' Taschimowitz pushed back his chair.

'Go on,' she handed him a piece of kitchen towel, 'take one. I made too many.'

Dr Taschimowitz smiled at her. His sleeves were rolled up, wrists delicate and bare. He didn't usually work Saturdays, but it was a bank holiday, and they were short of staff at the moment. Rats, sinking ship. They'd talked about it at length during those long shifts in the winter. They'd stayed after work, neither of them wanting to go home because normality felt to them both to be a fiction, the performance a drain on their resources which, at this point, were meagre. They used to play Bananagrams; Melissa always lost, but she never minded because she didn't expect to be more intelligent than somebody with so many letters after their name. He'd rest his chin on his palm, his fingertip resting on his temple, drumming the table. Once, Melissa had stolen *aborts* from him to make *albatross* and she'd almost told Dominic about it when she got home but decided not to.

'I put that prescription on repeat for you,' Dr Taschimowitz said, taking a flapjack. 'Hydrocortisone. You know she can ask me herself, if she needs. We can register her here.'

'She's shy,' Melissa said. 'Not her fault.' She hesitated. It was now or never. 'And the other thing?'

Taschimowitz looked at her blankly, put the flapjack in his mouth.

'The veins,' she said. She had hoped that Taschimowitz would not make her say it. If she had to, though, she'd roll up the hem of her scrubs, plant her socked foot on his desk, show him the inside of her leg. 'The big ones. In my legs.'

'Oh. I need to check. Don't let me forget.'

Taschimowitz wiped his hands on his jacket, mouth full. Melissa closed the Tupperware. 'I won't,' she said.

In the car park there was just her car left, and Christine's. The girl with the smear had gone. The camellia was gathering green-yellow buds. Melissa looked up at the sky, the lenses of her glasses turning from see-through to tinted. The inner seams of her legs ached. Dr Taschimowitz's friend was a vascular surgeon, this was her area. This wasn't something Melissa particularly wanted to do, lie back on an adjustable bed and take down her trousers so she could reveal to this friend of Dr Taschimowitz the full, matronly ugliness of her. But she was embarrassed by her secret, so much so that she hadn't even told Dominic about it. Her secret – closely held, hot and shame-filled – that she didn't want this feeling any more. She didn't want to feel that her body was ugly.

In her car, Melissa took her phone from her bag, looked over the tops of her glasses so that she could see the notifications that slid onto the screen. Missed calls – six – from Rhianne, and a series of messages. When Melissa called back, she picked up on the first ring.

16

That first year Melissa and Dominic were together, they had gone on holiday, the three of them, driven Melissa's Saab to the ferry, then all the way across France with a trailer tent strapped on the back. There was a heatwave that summer, and the car's chassis cracked on the drive out. They stopped every few hours to buy iced tea and pastries and Rhianne peeled herself out of the back seat of the car onto the oil-slicked concrete of the petrol station. Melissa went with Rhianne to the toilets, held her by the under-arms as she squatted over the porcelain hole-in-the-ground.

In those days, there was little money. Dominic was still graft-ing, and Melissa on a National Health wage. The company he'd set up when he and Josephine first met hadn't yet secured those big contracts – taking projects at local schools, building the bridge that crossed over from the main road to the mill at the bottom of Horsley. That would come. For now, though, they were holiday-ing in their trailer tent, whose wings folded out into a double bed where Melissa and Dominic slept, Rhianne, on her insistence, in her own little blue tent, which Dominic had set up for her in the awning.

That first morning Rhianne woke at six, unzipped herself to find her father sitting on one of the precariously assembled camping chairs just outside. He was wearing his old white dress-ing gown and chequered pyjama shorts, his hands resting on his knees, and he was staring, blankly, at the table in front of him. He hadn't heard Rhianne, but when she crawled across the threshold of her tent, he stood, a smile breaking across his face. He had the kind of smile that was so large, so full of cheek, that his eyes all but disappeared. He bent over to peer through the canvas door into her cabin. 'How did you sleep in your little pod?'

'It was OK,' Rhianne said. 'What's for breakfast?'

'Oh.' Dominic tilted his head, looking down at the floor of the tent. 'But you've already had breakfast.'

Rhianne followed his gaze, mirroring, again, his expression. He was pointing at the snail-trails, silver and shiny, webbed across the grass outside the tent.

'I haven't,' Rhianne told him. But Dominic turned his finger on Rhianne, tracing a line from her ear to the corner of her mouth.

'But then what's that silver trail,' he said, 'going *right* into your—' Rhianne squealed, batted his hand away; up above them, the sound of Melissa rolling over, waking.

In the evenings, they sat outside and looked up at the clear, black sky, and Rhianne would climb onto Dominic's lap. One evening, Rhianne saw a meteorite, a big one that burnt up as it entered the atmosphere, and she turned to her father, excitedly, to check that he'd seen it. 'Of course I saw it,' said Dominic, but Rhianne was sure that his eyes had been closed, that he had missed it. She rested her cheek on her father's chest, felt it rise, shudder, as it fell.

Rhianne bombed down the waterslide, and Dominic wore shorts, slathered suncream into his pale, hairy calves, came out in freckles. Melissa would smooth his thinning hair back from his face, inspecting for sun damage. 'It's a tan,' he insisted, squirting cream into his palm. Around the campsite he wore his vest under short-sleeved, floral shirts that billowed as he walked. His stride was wide, his face creasing behind his sunglasses as he smiled, big-cheeked, his arm slung around Melissa's shoulders.

Towards the end of the trip, the three of them took their bikes and cycled flat routes around the villages and farmland. Rhianne wobbling, wearing a helmet twice the size of her head. The farms were filled with signs they couldn't read and the air was dry. They rode by a farmer with a pack of farm-dogs, bellies and noses low to the ground. One of the dogs growled as they passed, and the farmer hit the dog with a stick he was carrying. Rhianne clenched her fists around the handlebars. 'He's OK,' Melissa told her, but Rhianne remembered that she sounded unsure. She and Dominic pulled up and they argued over the map. The sun grew hotter.

They had to turn back twice, coming up against red circle signs that blocked their way. At the edge of the farm, again there were the dogs. This time, there was no farmer. The dogs had come fast around the corner behind them: small, yappy. 'Keep cycling,' Dominic said from the front. The dogs went faster. They passed Melissa and ran alongside Dominic, so for a moment they were going at the same pace, skidding along the dusty path, wheels and claws. But then, they skidded right, stopped, and the dog at the lead leapt up alongside Rhianne. She watched, momentarily unfeeling, as it sunk its teeth into her thigh. The dog hung there, suspended, for one long moment: its hind legs drawn up into its body, muscular, eyes bulging. Pain shot through Rhianne's thigh, and she looked down at the wild-eyed creature latching itself to her, for a moment stunned, before understanding that the horrific, high-pitched wailing sound she could hear was coming from her own mouth.

Then there was another roar, animal, as her father stepped off his bike and threw it to the ground. He was running, chest and throat open. Rhianne had never heard him make a sound like that before. The dog let go, landed on the ground with a scattering of claws, made itself small behind the wheels of Rhianne's bike as Dominic scooped her up off the ground. Then, there was a shout as the farmer rounded the corner and came running towards them. Rhianne's legs were shaking, her upper body held, tight, by her father. Her vision was obscured; all she could see was shoulder, the parched earth. Faintly, there was the smell of manure, and of lavender. Her thigh, hot with pain, pulsed. When they got home, she would need injections, a course of them, at the surgery, in case the dog was rabid. Melissa would go with her, hold her hand in the consultation room while a needle as long as her arm-bone was inserted into her stomach, and she would hate the injections more than the bite itself. But here, for now, she was safe, held in her father's arms.

She couldn't understand what the farmer was saying. She could hear Melissa talking to him in broken French. The farmer had put the dog back on a leash and she could hear it whimpering. Dominic asked Melissa what was being said; she could feel his voice vibrating against her as he spoke. Melissa translated. 'Pas de sang,' the farmer was saying, which Melissa later told them meant 'there's no blood'. The farmer was talking more urgently. 'Pas grave,' he was saying. 'Pas grave.' Rhianne saw, then, that he had a rifle slung at his side. Dominic turned towards Melissa, expectant. 'He's saying,' she said eventually, 'that he'll shoot the dog. If we want.' Dominic nodded, looked directly at the farmer, spoke in English. 'It's your dog,' he said. Melissa did not translate.

Rhianne agreed to ride, tried not to look down at the bruise that was blossoming over the top of her thigh. But even then she did not mind the pain, because her father had held her tightly. She would be bitten all over again, to be lifted off her feet like that. To be weightless, to be buried in warmth. Dominic stayed at the back, alongside Rhianne, his knees knocking against the purple handlebars of her bicycle. Her helmet wobbled on her head. There were figs squashed on the dusty pathway. Rhianne remembered, still, the sound of the shot being fired as they rounded the corner. The look on her father's face.

17

Callum let the phone ring and did not answer. He had not been intending to leave. Just to drive, to clear his head, and even as he pressed his clothes, charger and the few toiletries he had brought into his backpack, he felt sure that he would return. He threw his bag into the passenger seat. He played it, over and again. That moment: her, pulling her hair up into a band and with it taking all the warmth from her face, that narrowing look that shot straight through him. The marks on her neck; her words.

He turned the key, and he drove. He needed to be moving, to not be stuck in that little shack, waiting for her to return. As he drove, the further he went, the harder it became for him to envisage turning back. He imagined having to explain why it was that he'd packed, if he hadn't been intending just to leave her there. He pulled into a lay-by, and he sat, steadied himself.

He did not understand it: how she had turned on him. Just last night, he had sunk fingers into her flesh, felt vulnerability and strength, had felt so certain that she was his. But this morning, she had snatched that safety and handed to him instead a feeling that did not belong to him, which she had put there for reasons he could not understand. She had planted inside him a cold, hard seed of shame, which, for Callum, was unconscionable. He could not allow it growth.

He took out his phone. There were three missed calls. He wrote a message, sent it.

Had to clear my head. Can you get a lift?

Immediately, the phone started to ring. He shut off the call. He had witnessed her anger and he had left. He gave her pain no currency because he did not think of it, did not permit himself to think of it, but thought only of betrayal. The gulf between the person he thought she had been and the person she had shown herself to be that morning in the kitchen. The cut of her face, the precision of her language, passed a current through his body. On the A38 he wound the windows low, the volume high, absorbed himself in sensation, presence. Emptied his mind. He kept driving.

He didn't go back to the hotel. Not straight away. He dropped off the M5 and took the bypass. But instead of passing through Amberley, up towards the common, he turned off at Sheepscombe. It was around lunchtime, a Saturday, and the Range Rover was parked up outside Brendan and Jack's house. He had been planning, before everything had happened, to bring Rhianne here, and he'd been excited about that, to have her follow him through the tiled kitchen, out into the courtyard. They'd have a cool glass of something; Jack would tell them stories about his clients while Brendan cooked. He would hold the door for her, she would look out to the length of the garden and the sunshine that caught there, and she would be happy. He cut the engine, allowed himself to exhale. Here, he could feel calm.

Brendan would understand. Brendan had always taken care of Callum. Brendan had been there that day last year: the day he'd found out about Grace. Grace, and her bar-boy, the one she'd been sleeping with while Callum thought she was working the late shift. Callum had burst through the back way into the bar, dragged him out by the neck, thrown fists into him until there was blood, until Brendan had heaved him up off the ground. It was Brendan who cleaned him up, drove him to A&E for his wrist, which was swollen, lights passing Callum's face in the passenger seat of the car. Brendan told the nurse that it wasn't Callum who'd swung first, bought Callum a packet of Minstrels. The wrist was sprained and not broken, and Callum had stayed the night at Brendan's house. Two days later, when Callum went back to the hotel, both the barman and Grace were gone.

Callum got out of his car, knocked on the door. He steadied himself. Rhianne, he had to remind himself, was not Grace. Brendan answered in a crisp black T-shirt, watch gleaming, and, as soon as he saw Callum, stepped forwards, pulled him into a one-armed embrace, a heavy hand on his back. Brendan had this way, when he hugged, of pulling a person in towards his body and out again, as if checking them for damage, before he drew them back in. He did so now, and he could tell, straight away, that something was wrong.

'Coffee,' Brendan said, 'we're having coffee, before anything else can happen today.'

He followed Brendan down the hallway. Callum liked Brendan's house: slate tiles, a heated floor. One day Callum would have a kitchen like this one, with marble surfaces and a cast-iron stove, doors that opened out onto a large garden. He could hear Jack's voice coming down from the upstairs office. Isabella, Brendan's goddaughter, was here for the weekend; he could hear her, too, playing out in the garden. Peace; normality. Callum sat up at the island. Brendan, his back turned, switched on the coffee machine. Professional, of course, bronze-trimmed, because Brendan had only the best things, kept only the best people around him. 'I thought you were away,' he said.

'I was. We were.' Brendan knew about Rhianne. Callum had come for dinner only a few days after that first afternoon they'd spent together, and he had told them about her. Explained, with a nonchalant kind of pride, that he'd met someone, someone in front of house, that he'd been spending his time with her. 'I like her,' Brendan said. 'Smart. She'll be good for you.' Callum had been tempted to impart this knowledge of Brendan's approval. It would make her feel good; he had wanted to be the person to make her feel good. He would have told her, maybe this weekend he would have told her, if it hadn't been for what had happened. He felt it, deeply lodged, that seed of shame.

'We were away,' said Callum now. 'But I came back early.'

He was sitting up at the breakfast counter, his head in his hands.

'My boy,' Brendan said, 'what happened?'

'We argued.' Callum smoothed with his thumb the deep crease that had arrived along his brow. Already, now that he was trying to find words for it, his reaction – him, leaving – felt outsized. 'It was stupid.'

'These things often are,' Brendan said. Callum watched as Brendan ground the coffee, tamped it, fitted it into the machine. Espresso trickled, thick and dark, through the bronze spout into its cup. Then, he thought of Rhianne, standing across from him, touching her neck. Involuntarily, he put his hand to his own throat, injustice, there, rising.

'I was feeling sensitive,' he said, 'because we were talking about relationships. You know, our histories.'

Sharply, Brendan looked at him. 'Grace?'

Callum's thoughts were obscured, momentarily, by the rasp of steam blasting into hot milk. 'Grace,' he said slowly. 'That stuff. And obviously, I'm trying to be open about it. Like you said.' Brendan pushed the cup towards Callum. A hand on his shoulder. 'But I don't know. I was looking for reassurance. Maybe I didn't say it directly enough, but it's hard, you know. And then, she just got, I don't know. Defensive.'

Brendan frowned. 'Defensive how?'

The marks on her neck. Her words.

'She was just, I don't know, twisting everything. Making out like I was . . .'

'You were what?'

'I don't know. One second everything was good, and then—' He banged the heel of his hand against his chest. 'She said she was scared of me.' The words were too much for him, and the feeling. He dropped his head into his hands. The seed in his chest cracked, opened.

'Callum,' Brendan said. He pulled Callum up by the shoulders. 'Callum. That's not you. I know you. We know you.' Callum's breath was shallow, uneven, and the more he tried to steady it, the worse it became. 'You haven't done anything wrong.'

Callum spoke, whispered. 'I think I'm a bad person. I think he—' he stopped. 'I think I'm like him.' Too hard, now, to lift his chest. He stayed, cowed.

'I know you, Callum. How long have I known you?'

'Six years,' he mumbled.

'Six years. And you think you would be here, in my house, if you were that person?'

Slowly, his chest unclenched. He wiped his eyes. 'I don't know.'

'No,' Brendan said. 'The answer is no. You wouldn't be in my house. You wouldn't be in my hotel, you wouldn't be anywhere near my family.'

Callum took a sip of his coffee. He could see Isabella outside, turning circles.

'That's not what she thinks.'

'She will,' Brendan said, 'she just can't see you properly. Not yet. And she won't have meant it like you think she meant it. Emotions get heightened. That's why it's good that you've taken some space.'

'I guess.'

'Give it time,' Brendan said. 'You'll see. You dropped her home?'

'Yeah,' he said. The lie came easily. He took another sip of his coffee. He checked his phone. There were no more messages from Rhianne. 'I think space is definitely good. She has stuff to work out, you know.'

'Oh, don't we all?'

Callum nodded. He was feeling calmer. 'Because of things that have happened before,' Callum said. 'I don't know. But after that happens to you once, I guess you see it everywhere. And then someone new comes along, and, well. It's hard.'

Now, Brendan was understanding. 'It is hard. For you as well as her.'

The coffee tasted good. It was good, too, to be heard. Understood.

'Her tutor,' Callum supplemented. 'In her final year.'

Brendan shook his head. 'Well. To fuck up someone's life like that.'

'Her final year.'

'Never forget,' Brendan said, straightening. 'Men are dogs.'

He turned back to the coffee machine, blasted the steamer. Callum pulled his phone from his pocket, sent a message. *Let me know when you get home safe.* He drained the rest of his cup, studied the residue. Rhianne would be fine. They would speak later, when she was back, when things had cooled.

'Men are dogs.' Callum turned; Jack was there in the doorway, cleaning the lenses of his glasses. 'You heard it here first, Callum.'

'I'm afraid it's true,' Brendan said. 'Except for us, obviously.'

'Funny how that happens,' Jack said. He was looking at Callum, half-smiling. Callum shifted. But then, behind Jack's legs, a rustle and a movement. 'Who's that then?' Callum said, standing. A shy, trusting presence, radiating from there in the hallway: a presence that spoke straight to the child in him. He crept towards the door, his full height rounded and ridiculous. 'Who's that then? *Who* is that? Don't tell me it's my favourite girl.'

Out in the corridor, a giggle, an explosion of squealing.

Callum stepped around Jack, bent down, swept Isabella up into his arms. The giggles spilled over into uncontrollable laughter, gurgles, as Callum whirled the little girl into the kitchen, turned her upside-down in his arms. Strong arms, arms that protected, diffused warmth, affection. Callum lifted Isabella upright. She had sweet brown ringlets, and he pushed them back from her face, gathering them back up into the little butterfly clip she was wearing. Isabella closed her eyes, turned her face up towards him, trusting.

18

It was just the two of them in the house that evening. Melissa, following the dog back across the common, had a feeling of unease that had something to do with the way Rhianne appeared to have shrunk. She'd noticed it as soon as she'd pulled up and seen Rhianne waiting for her. It was a long drive, over two hours, and Rhianne had been sitting on the wall in the weak afternoon sun, her suitcase on the ground between her legs, the large, white-fronted beach hotel opposite. 'It's mouldy,' she said, when Melissa asked why she hadn't wanted to wait in the cabin. 'The sea comes right up to the back window so it's damp.'

They drove back along the A30. Winding roads alongside the Martian landscape that edged Dartmoor. They passed purple thistles; low, scrubbed land. It was lucky it was a Saturday and the surgery was open reduced hours. Rhianne slept. As they slowed for the exit, pulled down the slip road just past Bristol, she lolled forwards in her seat and Melissa, halting, put a hand to her shoulder, pressed her gently back. Rhianne blinked open her eyes. She looked weary. The hair with that unwashed look. Melissa could tell she'd been in the sea because it was crisp and salty, tied up high on her head.

'Did you swim, at least?'

'Yeah,' Rhianne said. 'We went yesterday. And then again, this morning.'

'Good.' Melissa flipped the indicator. 'Do you want to talk about it?'

'No,' Rhianne said. It was hard to believe that this was the same person that had come to the surgery just days before to tell Melissa about her interview. Clean-clean trainers, white denim jacket, holding out a fresh-bought pastry. 'I don't,' said Rhianne. They were just at the edge of town, now, heading back through Ebley. At the lights Melissa looked again at her, sideways. Her eyes heavy and, Melissa had noticed, her jacket gathered up around her neck.

'Cold?' Melissa said.

'Tired,' Rhianne said. 'I just feel really tired.'

Melissa could sense Rhianne looking at the rock on her left hand. Dominic had as ever gone oversized: a silver-set sapphire heavy enough to look precarious there on her finger. There were other colours, in among the blue, if she looked at it long enough: light shot through deep water. Melissa drew her hand back into her lap, spread and flexed her fingers, turning the stone in towards her palm.

'Well,' Melissa said, 'if you're not cold.'

She cracked the window, waiting for the lights to turn.

'Where's Dad?' Rhianne said.

'At the mill.'

Rhianne sank back into the seat and they pulled away, up towards Minchinhampton. At the house, Rhianne had stood in the doorway to the kitchen for a moment or two, before she carried her suitcase upstairs. Melissa waited. Rhianne locked herself in the bathroom. Melissa, patient, took Ludo for a walk. Returning, the light softening, her thoughts began to crystallise. She followed Ludo into the kitchen. Rhianne was sitting on the chair in the corner, hunched over her laptop, her headphones in. She had showered and changed, her hair was wet and clean, and she was wearing a cropped fleece, fully zipped, with her thick tracksuit bottoms. Slowly, Melissa poured herself a glass of water. The light lengthened across the floor. Rhianne had not moved and now she palmed back the screen of her laptop.

'Interview preparation?'

She looked over at Melissa, took out a headphone.

'Interview preparation,' Melissa repeated, 'for your interview?'

Rhianne nodded, replaced the headphone. Melissa refilled her water. She didn't know what had got into her, to be so cowardly. She pulled up the chair closest to Rhianne, who was messily typing. Rhianne looked up. 'Sooner I'm out of here, the better.'

Melissa was stung. 'Well, say how you really feel.'

'Not you,' Rhianne said. 'I just. I feel like I keep messing everything up.'

'You're not messing anything up.' Melissa leaned across the gap between their chairs, took Rhianne's hand. 'It's a false start, that's all. What happened?'

Rhianne put her thumb on Melissa's ring finger, pressed it against the big, blue rock. 'Don't know.' She heaved a breath, tried to settle. Outside, the sky was turning velvety. 'Can't explain.'

Melissa was becoming nervous. She studied Rhianne, the way the fleece was zipped up high around her throat. An instinct, old and tightly coiled, stirred deep within her. One that was rooted in fear, suspicion. 'Rhianne,' said Melissa, sharpening, 'did he hurt you?'

Rhianne shook her head. 'No,' she said. 'If anything, it was the other way around.'

Relief. Callum, hurt. This was fine. Melissa did not care about Callum.

'Hurt him how?'

'Just, I don't know. He was just messing around. Playing games.' Rhianne frowned. She looked very tired. 'It was stupid. He was pretending to interview me, because, you know.' She gestured to the laptop. 'And he brought up Alexander, and I got upset.'

'Well.' Melissa couldn't help it. She snorted. 'Alexander,' she said. 'Alexander is a talentless piece-of-trash failure of a human who preys on the vulnerabilities of young people in order to feed his diminishing ego. Of course you got upset. Callum's an idiot for bringing him up like that. Game or no game.'

'Yeah,' Rhianne said. Her eyes shone. 'He's an idiot.'

'Did he apologise?'

'Not exactly.'

'He went home instead. I see,' said Melissa. 'That was selfish of him. And stupid. What if I hadn't been there to pick you up?'

'Yeah.' Rhianne withdrew her hand from Melissa's grip, started to fiddle with her pop-socket, picking at the glue that attached it to the back of her phone. 'He's an idiot,' she said again.

'He could at least have given you a lift.'

'Yeah.' Rhianne shrank into the seat. 'We thought it would be better to come back separately.' The phone in her hand vibrated. Rhianne swiped at the screen, turned it face down.

'Is that him?'

Rhianne shook her head. 'Jess,' she said.

Melissa was weary. 'I do understand,' she said. 'It's hard to trust people. Men, in particular. I really do understand, especially after everything you went through. But not all of them are necessarily bad. Though a lot of them are, unfortunately, idiots.'

'Yeah.'

'You'll see,' Melissa pressed. 'You've worked so hard for this interview. You'll get this job, you'll be moving on to bigger, better things. And,' Melissa straightened, 'when you walk back into that place, your head held high, he'll know he's messed up. If he doesn't already.'

'The hotel,' Rhianne said. She was practically horizontal, now, and there was that strip of flesh, again, across her belly. Melissa resisted the urge to pull down the top; to cover her. Protection, or maybe something else. Self-respect. Rhianne put the zip of her fleece in her mouth, chewed. 'You think I should go back there?'

Melissa was indignant. 'Of course you should go back.' She pulled the zipper away from Rhianne's face. 'Show him that nothing fazes you. It won't be for long. And anyway, you need to save up, if you want to make a deposit. London,' she said. 'That's when life really begins.'

'How do you know it'll be OK?'

'Call it mother's intuition.'

The word, a shell. Delicate; empty. And perhaps she imagined it, perhaps not. Cruelly, almost indiscernibly, the corners of Rhianne's mouth twitched.

'It's my intuition,' said Melissa, flushing. 'I just think it's important. Not to give up on things that don't work the first time around.'

Rhianne blinked. Put her headphones back into her ears. 'I've got to finish this,' she said. She stood, and, with her phone and her laptop tucked precariously under her arm, she closed the door to the washing machine. Rhianne set the cycle, left Melissa there in the kitchen.

Melissa sat. The air was cool. Her legs were aching. Beside her, Ludo's whole body breathed; his ribcage rising, falling. Melissa stared across at the machine. The display blinked. There were fifty-three minutes on the timer. The machine began to spin.

19

Rhianne arrived from Paddington late in the afternoon and they spent what was left of the evening light in the small, overgrown square of garden behind Jess's house in Peckham, wearing their jackets lightly as the sky dipped. The garden backed on to a row of terraced houses, from which sounds and voices echoed out on the street, reverberated. 'But this is huge,' Jess said. 'I can't believe you didn't call me.'

'It is and it isn't,' Rhianne said. She was numb, distracted. 'They've been together for almost twenty years.'

'I guess that's long enough. Will you do a speech?'

'To my father,' said Rhianne, 'who is terrified of his own feelings.'

Jess laughed. 'OK. We can work on it.'

'You have to help.'

Rhianne, compulsive, glanced at her phone. The screen was blank.

Jess was watching her carefully. 'You hungry?'

'I'm not.' In fact she hadn't eaten properly since the weekend.

'Liar.' Jess stood. 'I know you,' she said. 'I know when you're lying.'

They ordered pizza and ate on the sofa. Rhianne liked the house: the living room with a long walk-through with no windows and a seventies sideboard where Jess's housemate kept his record player and collection. The bathroom and the kitchen both had peeling lino floors. There was a lamp that one of the other housemates had made, hand-wired with three pieces of wood screwed together, a single, uncovered bulb standing awkwardly on its copper bracket. The wiring fizzed and the bulb flickered. Rhianne paused to look up at the framed Frank Bowling print. She had bought it for Jess years ago, when she'd first started her degree. The original painting, which she'd seen at the Tate, was huge, taking up an entire wall: shades of orange in dilute acrylic, poured, large and vibrant on the canvas, over the obscured, layered outlines of faces, countries, continents, the paint bleeding over, across. Jess watched her, watching the painting.

'I can't wait for you to be here,' she said.

'Me neither,' Rhianne said. She crossed her fingers. 'Tomorrow needs to go well.'

She thought of Callum. His narrow double bed. Curtains closed across his small, damp window. There had been nothing from him since the weekend. A single message, that afternoon, to check that she'd got home. Her calls, messages, unanswered. She had sent one last message. *Please. Talk to me.* Then she had deleted his number. She had hurt him; it was over. Once or twice, she had thought she heard an engine idling outside, signalling his presence, but when she went out to look the driveway was empty. The churning in her chest slowed, solidified, settled into a hard, cold weight. He wasn't coming.

'You'll be great,' said Jess.

Rhianne looked back to the print – red, orange, yellow – bright on the living-room wall. The light bulb fizzing. 'Yeah,' she said.

Jess was eager. 'Marcus leaves at the end of the year. So, whatever it takes. You're coming.' She tucked her feet up under her, steadying her plate in her lap. 'But what about that guy?'

Carefully, Rhianne tore a crust, ate. 'What guy?'

'The guy, you know?' Jess said. 'I thought there was someone at the hotel. The chef.'

Rhianne shook her head. 'I thought it was something, but nah.'

The next morning was warm, and she had forgotten the heat of the city, how her make-up slid from her sweat-slicked face, how her underarms prickled. She remembered the sea, salt water on her body, freedom. As the overground pulled up, she thought she saw Alexander in the shoulders and shapes of men moving in front of her on the platform. It was Alexander's fault that this had happened. What he had ignited in her, she now could not repress. She got off at Shoreditch High Street. In the glass-fronted offices on Curtain Road, she sat opposite a woman in tortoiseshell glasses who lifted the pages of her portfolio. 'My final project,' said Rhianne numbly. 'I was creatively blocked.' She was repeating what Dominic had told her to say, when the woman asked her why she had failed her final paper. The interviewer looked at her over the tops of her glasses.

'And why fine art,' she said, 'the most useless of degrees?'

Articles, references, essays, late nights backspacing, typing. Words swam. Alexander, leaning back in his chair, his smile a provocation. Rhianne shrugged.

'I like it,' she said. 'It makes me feel good.'

They shook hands at the end of the interview. The woman smelt of jasmine. A stirring of aspiration, lost. She was glad that she'd done her nails the previous day: thick shellac, cornflower blue, worn with the rings that clinked on her fingers. There was the inescapable thought that in this time, while her phone was set to airplane mode in the bottom of her bag, Callum could have been trying to contact her. She stood on the pavement, swiped open her phone, waited for the screen to fill, but there was nothing: no messages, no calls.

Her father, later, picked her up from the station. He drove

fast, shifting up through the gears. Rhianne was quiet. She did not know how to explain how sticky this feeling was, there in her gut. They were turning up the hill, back towards the house. Melissa always slowed at the switchback, edging around the deepest bends with a caution that made Rhianne feel, somehow, less safe than she did when she was in the car with her father, who blasted his horn at the blind corners, crossing the road-markings on the hairpins with conviction. 'So long as you did your best,' Dominic said, pulling up. Those words of Melissa's, still echoing. *It's important. Not to give up.* She opened the door, got out of the car.

At the foot of her bed there was a stack of boxes she had brought home with her from London, only partially unpacked. Rhianne began to tip their contents onto the bowed floor of her bedroom. A short leather skirt that had belonged to Josephine, black-heeled ankle boots. A sheer, leopard-print top that clung skin-tight to her shoulders, her chest. She had worn that top on one of those days Alexander had been teaching, called her behind after the workshop. She fed the sleeve of the top into her mouth. She bit down on it and yanked it, biting so hard that her jaw ached, until the seam began to tear, and a loud, satisfying rip sounded through her room.

Rhianne threw the top at the bin in the corner of her bedroom. It missed, and one arm hung limply over the side. She surveyed the detritus before her. Got up to her knees. Slowly, deliberately, she began to collect, press, fold. She returned clothes and shoes to the cupboards and drawers where they had once belonged. Soft knitted sweaters, those jeans, that leather skirt, folded and neatly stacked. Make-up, bright boxes of it. Those thick gold rings – also her mother's – and a gold-plated necklace, a gift from Jess before she'd left for university. Crockery, cutlery, she arranged in a single box to be taken downstairs to the kitchen. There, within the four walls of her room, sitting upon the slanted floor, she reassembled the remnants of her former life, began, slowly, to return it to herself. She pulled out her three favourite photographs of Josephine, put them back in their old places.

When she had finished clearing, Rhianne dragged from under her bed the big folders in which the work from her degree, and earlier, from school, was kept. Drawings from that phase when she was reading manga. Another period, earlier, when she was studying, where she had become fixated on Francis Bacon – tortured images, malformed – and the Basquiat, bold colours shot through, outlines in thick black. Framed but never hung, were the paintings for her degree show. The acrylic, almost rubbery in texture, so thick it was peeling, the layers of artistry, draft and redraft, beneath which the outline of a woman was now obscured. Rhianne pressed her fingertips to the paint. The smell of it took her back, straight away, to that studio in King's Cross. The bar, lying low over the canal, mood-lighting. A slice of orange suspended in a tumbler of sticky liquid. She covered it, pushed it back under her bed.

She opened her folder again and took out a fresh piece of paper. There, on the floor, she began to draw. She heard cars pull up outside, doors open. Her father calling up the stairs; the smell of frying onion. She did not move. The backs of her knees grew stiff, her shoulders ached. Outside the sun weakened, but there on the floor Rhianne was unaware of the movements of the sky, of the drama of the light, absorbed, instead in her work. A woman, naked, lying on her side. Her waist bowing, her hips wide, an arm propping her up, but not fully, so that the lower half of her body appeared to be melting, disintegrating into the soft surface upon which she was resting. Her legs were not defined; below the knees and the thigh they trailed away into faint pencil lines. Only her jaw was set, and her eyes, round with what looked like fear, the whites shot through with little lines, which, if the drawing was in colour, would have been red. She hadn't planned it, but anyway, it had arrived there on the page. The source of that fear, there on her throat. A hand, not her own, because it was larger, roped with tendons.

She drew the tendons and redrew them. She put the image down, got to her feet, and looked at it there on the floor. The light in the corridor had gone out and she had earlier been aware of footsteps passing, pausing outside the door. It was almost dark now outside, and if she leaned out of the window, she would be able to see all the way across the common to the hotel. Instead, she stood, turned the light on, looked down at the drawing. She stepped back, looked at it from across the room. For a moment, there was clarity. Something larger than her, more pernicious. Not her anger, but his. Not her harm, but his. She hesitated, picked her phone up off the bed. She unlocked it, the screen started to light up, filling with notifications. Missed calls, three, all from the same unsaved number. Her breath caught, released only when the phone started to ring. 'Rhianne.' The voice on the other end. Not Callum, but Brendan. 'How are you?'

Her throat thickened with disappointment. 'I've just been in London. A job interview.'

'I know. Callum told me. How was it?'

So, he had spoken about her. 'It was fine. Good, I think.'

'I'm sure it was. If it was anything like your interview with me, then it was good.'

Rhianne was confused. She didn't know why Brendan was trying to be nice to her. His voice dropped. 'Callum doesn't know I'm calling you,' he said, 'but I wanted to make sure you knew that there's always a place for you here.'

'OK,' Rhianne said.

'Not that he wouldn't want me to call you. But this isn't him. This is me.'

Rhianne waited for more.

'I know you have big plans,' Brendan continued. 'But we all

care for you. And what I don't want is for you to feel in any way unwelcome.'

'I know that,' said Rhianne. A lie turned truth as she spoke it. 'I'm waiting to hear about this job. I'll let you know. When I've heard.'

The line went dead. Rhianne pushed the drawing back into an old sketchbook, closed it. She felt calmer. That night, for the first time since South Sands, she slept. In the morning, when she woke, there was an email on her phone from the woman who had interviewed her, offering her the job with a January start.

20

For the few months he had worked at The White Hart, Kieran had been largely invisible. He was good at his job: young, capable, unusually thorough when he wiped down the stainless-steel surfaces of which his corner of the kitchen constituted. He'd always been this way; always been clean. He put his T-shirts in the laundry after only one wear, and he washed his face every morning and night with a cleanser high in salicylic acid, which he had been prescribed after a Himalayan sweep of acne had broken out across his cheekbones during his exams last summer. He scrubbed his face, he scrubbed the dishwasher, because somewhere lodged in Kieran's psyche was a belief that if surfaces gleamed, if drains were cleared, limescale scoured, then there were certain terrible things – death, disease, difficult emotions – that might be prevented.

It had been a busy Sunday service. That morning at home, Kieran had put his thumb through a satsuma whose underside had turned white with mould. He was low on sleep and his mother had had the curtains to her room closed when he left. And now Brendan was here, his sleeves rolled up, standing alongside Kieran at the dishwasher.

'Like this,' he told Kieran. It was the first time Kieran had heard him sound irritated. 'You really have to get down inside and scoop.' Brendan scooped, came up with a handful of half-rotted fat from the filter. 'Otherwise it'll clog,' he said, 'that's why nothing's coming out clean.' Brendan emptied his hands into the food-waste, and Kieran understood that a point was being made: that this was dirty work, that it should be beneath nobody here, not even Brendan, but also that this was work that anybody could do. He sensed very suddenly the precarity of his position. Brendan washed his hands twice over. Callum appeared there next to him, reloading the tray of dishes that had come out dirty.

'That's not him,' said Callum quietly.

Brendan dried his hands carefully, made for the door. 'What's not him?'

Callum unhooked the hose from inside the dishwasher, blasted the filter.

'Leaving the filter dirty.' Callum pulled down the hood, pressed the lever so that water rushed through the machine. 'That's not Kieran.'

Kieran looked to Callum, and then Brendan, momentarily panicked by the confrontation.

'All right,' Brendan said. 'Good. How many shifts are you working?'

'Once a week,' Kieran said.

'Can you do more?' Brendan, holding the door open, threw the questions to Callum. 'Can he do more?'

'If he keeps turning up to school, then yeah, he can do more.'

'Yes.' Kieran was nodding. 'I can do more.' The door swung shut.

He had sensed it, lately: the opening of a pressure valve. The kitchen, before now, had been unfamiliar territory, through which he trod carefully, conscious, always, of the length of his limbs, the sharp edges, the heat. A couple of weeks later, just after the Bank Holiday, Callum handed him a pair of chef's trousers in the laundry to wear instead of his jeans. Dean, who worked mains with Callum, bumped his shoulder in the pass. He was working evenings, cycling up after school, and he'd be taking both days of the weekend, picking up shifts from Maria, who was tired, missing work. He'd better be careful, Dean told him, not to fuck with the dishwasher, because the only thing Maria loved more than her cousin was that dishwasher, he said, loves it so much she'll come up to the hotel at night and rub up against it, like this, with both hands, like that, Kez. Kieran watched him, Dean, a grown man, gyrate against the dishwasher's stainless hood. Callum, behind the hotplate, twitched, brushed his forehead with his elbow: he wouldn't laugh, he wouldn't laugh at a joke like that, and Kieran, following his lead, nervously wiped the draining board.

Kieran tugged the yellow cutlery bucket towards him, dirty water slopping at its edges. He stacked the cutlery into a basket and emptied the water into the sink, refilled it with fresh water, soap, swirling with his hand so that the suds got nice and bubbly like he would in the bath at home, then caught a glance of the delicate, agile movements of his wrist, and withdrew it, wiped his hand on the backs of his chef's trousers. Annabel came down from the staff house in tracksuit bottoms. The pressure valve refastened. She was wearing gold earrings today, and the tracksuit bottoms looked thick, soft, on her hips.

'Ke-ke,' Callum muttered, 'what you looking at?'

Kieran closed his mouth, took the tray Callum handed to him. It was full of crabmeat, and Callum was busy with his hands, his head down, working on a tray next to him.

'You need to pick it,' he said. 'Find some gloves and pick out any shell. They're supposed to take it out but they don't, and it's sharp. We need to get all of it.'

Kieran stood next to Callum, picking through the soft, juicy meat with gloved fingers, pulling out the tiny white shards of shell that had been left lodged in there. 'Good,' Callum said, every time Kieran found a piece, washed it from his fingertips. Kieran felt serious, important. He stood shoulder to shoulder with Callum.

'Where's Rhianne?' Kieran said.

'What's it to you?'

He was used to this by now, Callum's naturally combative tone, but Callum was smiling, big dimples around his mouth. He'd heard the rumours, of course. Everybody knew and pretended not to know they'd been on holiday together. Kieran shrugged. 'I like Rhianne.'

Callum's smile twitched. 'Who doesn't?'

But it was true. He did like Rhianne. Rhianne had been away the next day, too, and he hoped she was just ill and hadn't decided not to come back. The following Saturday, Kieran was locking his bike up out the back when her car pulled up, SZA blaring. It was only a week, but she looked different. Her hair soft around her face, her skin dewy with moisturiser. She was wearing bright blue eyeliner, her skunk stripes freshly dyed a brighter, whiter blonde. She cut the engine and when she got out of the driver's seat Kieran noticed that she deliberately did not look up at the staff house. She dropped her keys down the front of her top. 'Hello, Kieran,' she said. 'Did you miss me?'

He followed her down the path through the back entrance of the hotel. In the office Rhianne flipped through the rota, signed her name, shaking her sleeve from her wristwatch, and then Kieran's. Brendan was there in the office. 'You're here,' he said. He smiled, leaned back in his chair, and Kieran saw it: the flash of something between them. 'We've missed you, Rhianne. Kieran was worried you weren't coming back.'

'No I wasn't,' said Kieran: a teenage reflex. He opened his mouth and closed it again.

'I told you,' Rhianne said. 'Didn't I tell you I'd come back?'

She swung open the doors, cut through to the kitchen. There seemed, as far as Kieran could tell, to be nothing wrong. In fact, somehow, she seemed more comfortable than before. She had learned, somewhere, how to lean in over shelves, across the taut boundaries of elbows and edges that surrounded people in a hot, enclosed space such as this, how to place a friendly hand on a person's shoulders, to break her face into a smile that was warm and purposeful. Rhianne stood by the bread baskets and reapplied her lip salve, and Kieran felt relieved.

The back door opened: Callum in his pink crocs, at the top of the steps. Kieran put an apron over his head and wiped neurotically at an already-clean patch of the draining board. Rhianne, though, was unbothered. She filled a metal jug with hot water, soap, dunked a handful of cutlery into the water. 'You can help me,' she told him. Polishing, as Kieran had understood from the unspoken set of rules that separated Kitchen from Front of House, Front of House from Housekeeping, was not a job that fell within his realm of responsibilities. But Rhianne did not seem to care about such divisions of labour. She held out a cloth for him and he took it, relieved to have been given something to do with his hot, sweaty palms.

He looked at her in the reflection of the still: the bright Cleopatra lines framing her eyes were bent around a dent in the metal, and her nails tapped against each other as she polished. She was working quickly, moving her hand from the blade to the handle of those heavy steak knives, shifting the cloth so that her fingers never touched the surface. Kieran copied, slower, more clumsily. Coming loud from the top of the steps, up in sweets, was the sound of Callum's laugh. Rhianne, next to Kieran, kept her eyes down, only looking up when Annabel came in from the restaurant. 'What's up with her?' Rhianne said.

'She's fine,' Kieran said, more forcefully than he meant to. He hadn't noticed that something was wrong with Annabel, who, if anything, seemed to have more energy than usual. Next to him, Rhianne snatched a whole handful of teaspoons, polished fast, gunned them one after the other into the tray. She glanced up again, at Annabel, who was now leaning across the hotplate. Rhianne hauled the tray onto her hip, holding it out for Kieran to finish the last of his knives. She shouldered her way through the swing-door back out into the restaurant, just as Callum came down the back steps. He stood next to Kieran at the sink, pumped the soap dispenser into his palm.

'How many covers?'

'Twenty,' Kieran said.

'Good.' Callum scrubbed his hands. He was thorough. 'That's good for September. Kids go back to school, summer's over. You don't expect so many covers at this time of year. You expect it to drop off.'

Kieran didn't quite understand why Callum thought he needed to know about this: about the seasonal fluctuations of the hospitality industry. But it made him feel as though he was important. 'Hopefully they will continue to keep coming back,' he said, and it was a sentence that made him sound a little bit like a robot, he didn't know why he'd had to say such a mouthful of verbs. Callum looked at him, laughed. 'What's wrong with you?'

Callum dried his hands, whipped Kieran with his tea towel, and Kieran batted him away. But this was the thing about the kitchen. Kieran had learned that with every towel-whip, insult, the glances that punctuated every dropped plate or fucked-up order, there was a cementing of Kieran's status here. And the more comfortable he felt, the easier his work became. He was getting smoother with it, palming open the tap to soak Chef's favourite pan, heaving stacks of crockery up off the drainer, cutlery cascading into the basket regularly enough that the polishing neither piled up nor ran out. His arms ached with the strain of it, and it was an ache that signalled purpose, tenacity. Dean squeezed Kieran's bicep. 'It's coming,' he said. Kieran tugged a fresh tray into the dishwasher, pulled down the hood.

21

A work trip, Dominic had said, and this was almost entirely true. Meetings and seminars with contractors, suppliers, lecture theatres with purple lighting and talks on liquid granite and self-heating concrete. Coffee, biscuits wrapped in pairs. Dominic, lately, had been discovering that his body was no longer built for London, not even now, at the very tail end of the summer. He could not stand the stickiness of the heat in his armpits, the density of the air, the conviction, every time he descended an escalator onto the Northern Line, that he would die down here, by either suffocation or obliteration. Squashed or blasted.

There was a time, years ago, when he had loved it here. A time when he used to drive that van with missing plates down Effra Road, when he didn't ask about where the copper had come from for this job or the next, when he was taught how to roof by an uncle who also knew how to play the spoons and didn't know how old he was but would tell Dominic, either way, that he was sure he was going to hell when he died. The uncle, he'd kept tobacco in a tin box in his jacket and he'd been the one to pick Dominic up from hospital, the night he'd been punched in the eye. On the bus home he'd told Dominic, and Dominic had not forgotten, that once he had a family, he'd be better off out of the city. That was before he'd met Josephine at the bar at The Queen's Head. That summer had been hot. She'd put a can of cold Heineken to her forehead and the beer had exploded all over her face; Dominic cried laughing. They took the 345 and he promised that next time it would be a car and not a bus, and she'd told him he'd better keep his promise.

Dominic rolled over. Two nights he'd been here, more sleepless than ever. He was staying in a hotel in Docklands and in the evenings he'd catch a lungful of the polluted air that came up off the surface of the river water, luminescing. He waited until the third day – how times had changed, that three days was all he could stomach in the city – before he made the journey across town. He took the tube with his suitcase. Northern Line, Bank, King's Cross, coming up for air. He remembered Granary Square, more developed now than it was then, water fountains shooting chlorine jets across the cobbles, children screaming.

It was Rhianne who had taken him to the restaurant opposite. They'd sat and had brunch, her hair shorter back then, speaking twice as fast as Dominic about all the projects she was working on, about her supervisor, Alexander, he's incredible, she told him, you'd love him, she said, the way his mind works, it's like – here she held out her hands, wide, like she was holding an enormous brain. She'd lost weight and he'd ordered more courses than they could possibly eat, then had to ask for the leftovers to be boxed up. Rhianne had been embarrassed about that, and she'd been embarrassed, too, when Dominic had tried to pay with a big wodge of cash he'd had tucked into his jacket pocket. Dominic went to piss, sitting down because he was in his fifties and he had nothing to prove, and panicked when he came out of the cubicle to wash his hands because there was a woman there, reapplying her lipstick.

'They're unisex,' Dominic said, when he sat back down. Rhianne didn't respond; Dominic saw that she was distracted, that she was looking up at a group of young women, fully made-up and all in baggy, brightly coloured clothes, standing by the door. 'Friends of yours?' Dominic said.

'In my year,' said Rhianne. She pulled her plate closer to her, closed her cutlery.

That had been midway through her third year. That had been a clue. There, right in front of him: she was more invested in the thoughts of a forty-year-old divorcee than the social life of her classmates. A clue he somehow hadn't seen, or, more likely, had seen and chosen to ignore.

Dominic dragged his suitcase across the square. He was wearing his business shirt, his jacket pinned under his arm, and he leaned forwards, the weight of his body overriding the resistance presented by those slippery cobbles. He put the suitcase under the table the waiter led him to and sat up on the stool. He realised, sitting here on this very high, small stool, that he should have taken a booth, the sort of place a man would sit if he was trying to assert himself, particularly a tall man such as Dominic. Instead, the balls of his feet were resting against a little bar and his hands were planted on the table, on the large, A3 menu.

Alexander was seven minutes late. They had been emailing for several weeks now, Dominic using one of the false addresses Melissa used when she wanted to write bad Tripadvisor reviews. Consulting work, Dominic had told Alexander, a project in Croydon, and the man with the brain too big to hold in two hands and clearly an ego twice the size hadn't thought to ask what he, who sat in an office all day with colouring crayons, could possibly have to contribute before agreeing to meet. 'Dominic,' Dominic said. He stood halfway to shake Alexander's hand, sat back down again.

Alexander was wearing a suede jacket and shoes, and he had a thick, healthy-looking beard that appeared not only to have been shampooed but also conditioned, oiled. His skincare routine, Dominic decided, involved steps. Alexander folded his jacket and put it on the empty stool next to him. He was wearing silver rings on his middle finger and thumbs, and thick-framed square glasses, which he removed, wiped, and replaced before he sat. 'Not Dom?' Alexander said.

'No,' Dominic said. 'Not Dom. Dominic. Dominic Colvin.'

'Colvin,' Alexander touched the beard. Dominic could smell something woody on him, in his cologne. 'We haven't met before.'

'I'm Rhianne's father. Rhianne Colvin.'

Alexander pressed his hands together, held his fingertips to his lips. 'Rhianne,' he repeated. At that moment, the waiter, sweeping past their table, paused, uncapping a red felt-tip pen, asked them if they'd been to the restaurant before. Dominic, not taking his eyes off Alexander, nodded. 'I haven't,' said Alexander. He smiled up at the waiter.

'OK.' The waiter leaned over them. 'So, your table number is seven,' on the menu, he drew a large number seven that could also have been a one and put a circle around it. 'And I'd recommend getting three to five plates per person,' he said. 'We don't have the chicken,' he drew a large, felt-tip line through the chicken, 'and we only have one of the pork.' He put a small dot next to the pork. 'Do you have any questions?'

Both men shook their heads.

'OK.' The waiter stood. 'Just give me a wave when you're ready to order.'

'I think we might be ready.' Alexander eased the menu out from beneath Dominic's hands, turned it towards him. 'Unless you want to eat?'

'No,' Dominic said, 'I'll just have a coffee,' he said. 'Black.'

'A peppermint tea,' said Alexander.

In fact, Dominic would also have liked a peppermint tea: his stomach was unsettled, and he had not forgotten the unisex toilets, but to him peppermint tea felt to be a sign of weakness. The waiter wrote their order in felt-tip on the menu, before rolling it into a narrow tube. Alexander watched him retreat. 'That was very performative, wasn't it?' Then, when Dominic did not respond, 'How is Rhianne?'

'The fuck is it to you?'

'So,' Alexander said. He leaned back, peering under the table for somewhere to hook his feet. 'There is no consulting project.' He was wearing a mohair cardigan, bright purple, cut in a low V on his chest. Somehow the femininity of his clothing – and his drinks order – was more troubling to Dominic than if he had been wearing combat trousers and boots. Involuntarily, Dominic imagined the body beneath that clothing. Banded with muscle and fat, creviced, male, grotesque. This man, in Dominic's view, had no business dressing in mohair.

'Rhianne did say you were intelligent.'

'What else did she tell you?'

'Enough.'

Alexander nodded. 'I respect it. You showing up here. I like to think I'd do the same. How long was the train journey?'

'You don't have children.'

'No.' Alexander adjusted his collar. 'We couldn't.'

'Shame.'

'I don't know,' Alexander said. 'I don't know that I'd be a good father.' His tea, in a glass pot, and Dominic's coffee, arrived at the table. Alexander turned the handle, touched the side. Dominic watched. He had expected more rage to arise, sitting here. He'd considered an outdoor meeting, even, to allow space for all that righteous anger to come up out of him, and had contemplated, late at night, sitting at the kitchen table picking wax from its surface, the possibility that he would go to prison for what he wanted to do to this man, and decided, if it came to that, he would be entirely willing. But now, sitting opposite Alexander and his peppermint tea, Dominic felt suddenly very calm.

'My daughter,' Dominic said, 'has suffered. Because of you and your garbage ego, and your need to receive attention from a child. And I don't want my daughter to have suffered.'

Alexander was solemn. He nodded. 'Is she OK? Rhianne?'

'Yes, she's OK. She's more than OK. Thriving.'

Alexander nodded again. He wasn't able to look up at Dominic. It was turning out to be far easier than he had expected, Dominic thought, to hand this man's shame back to him.

'I'm glad she's OK,' Alexander said. He nodded again, long-necked, limp-headed. 'In fact, I'm glad you're here. I've thought about it a lot.' Dominic waited. He had not touched his coffee. 'Rhianne might not have told you this, but she really helped me. I was going through something, and . . .' Alexander looked up at the ceiling, this time, a widening of the eyes, displacing the glassiness that had arrived there. 'She's a very special person.'

'I know she's a special person.'

'She understood. She saw me. She saw all of me. Clearly. And it was such a long time since somebody had seen me that way.'

What Alexander had identified in Rhianne was the radiant light of her. That had been Josephine's light, too, and Dominic had loved her for that, but the way he had loved her: he had loved her as whole, as equal. As a woman. The anger, which had ebbed, rose up in him again, at this display of weakness, as if weakness was an excuse, somehow, for causing pain. Alexander was still talking.

'But that was it,' he said. 'Nothing more. And if she got the idea that—'

'She was hardly more than a teenager, shit-face,' Dominic said, 'and if she was nice to you, it was because you were very briefly impressive to her. Relatively speaking.'

'I know, I know. If she wanted me, it wasn't about me. It was about the power.'

Dominic barked. 'Wanted you? You're not Johnny fucking

Depp.' He drained his coffee. 'Bad example.' So much for calm, collected. 'George Clooney, honestly, who-fucking-ever.'

'As you say,' Alexander said, 'it's relative.' He took another sip of his tea.

'She didn't want you,' said Dominic.

'If you say so.'

'Look at yourself.'

'Look, you tell me what you want from me. You want me to talk to Rhianne? To apologise? For the confusion?'

Dominic rubbed his eyes. He had thought, long and hard, those nights at the kitchen table, until nearly all the wax was gone. 'Preferably,' he said, 'I'd like you to walk in traffic. But I'll settle for a resignation. Leave. Hand in your notice. And if I don't hear at the start of next term that you're gone, that your teaching career is over, then, well, I'm too old to be throwing punches.' He paused. 'But there will be lawyers.'

Alexander nodded. 'You think I shouldn't be in a position of power. You think it's not safe for young and vulnerable people to be in my care.'

'I want you gone. Done. Finished.'

'Well,' Alexander said, 'I'm afraid you're too late. They fired me.'

'Fired?'

'A few weeks ago. That's why I was so quick to respond to your email. Normally I'm very slow. Getting started with the new academic year. But, I thought, could be useful. A consulting job. Might help pay the bills. Nice-sounding man, Dom.' Alexander shrugged. 'I'll be gone by the end of the term.'

'Fired,' Dominic said. He nodded. 'What did you do?'

'Cuts,' Alexander said. 'Too many students not making the grade.'

'No need for lawyers, then,' Dominic said. He continued to watch Alexander. A specimen, Dominic thought. An experiment – failed – in modern masculinity. One of those men who thought that if he disguised himself with expensive clothes and beard oil nobody would notice him treating women like garbage. 'And your wife left you?' This, brightly.

'Yep.'

'Seems like you don't need my intervention,' Dominic said, 'seems like you fucked up your life enough already.'

'It would seem so.'

'I'm not sorry I came,' Dominic said, more to himself than to anybody.

'Neither am I,' Alexander said. He spun the teapot on the table, topped up his cup. 'And I'm glad that Rhianne's OK. Believe me. Not a day goes by I don't regret getting in that taxi with her.'

'Taxi,' Dominic repeated. A bar, she had told him. One drink. Rhianne, getting up, leaving. He hadn't heard about a taxi. Nor, in that moment, did he want to hear about any kind of taxi, but Alexander was still speaking.

'I do want her to be OK,' Alexander said. 'She always seemed as though she didn't have anybody.'

Dominic stood, and standing, he knocked his knee, then his cup, so that it clattered on the saucer, a noise loud enough to catch the attention of the waiter. He leaned forwards, both his hands on the table. 'I see you,' he said. 'Don't for a second think I don't see you.' Then, straightening, Dominic yanked his suitcase out from under the table, his palms and his chest suddenly hot. He turned, walked back out into the sun, his breath short and heavy. The light reflected off the glistening cobbles of Granary Square.

22

For that whole first week, it had been just her name, or the call of service. Formalities, nothing but necessary contact. He had, though, looked at her. Caught her eye, and held it with a still, blank stare. Communicating what, she did not know. She broke his gaze, walked up to where the plates were stacked, started to polish, and she felt him, still watching her. She was leaving, and she already knew that it was hurting him. This was good. He had caused her suffering, punished her without reason or explanation. She was no longer sad, she was angry. And now it was his turn to hurt. Every night, she walked to her car, saw that his light was on, and there, in the next room along, Annabel's. Rhianne did not stop. Every night, she got in her car, she called Jess. 'What's the latest?' she said.

'The latest?' Jess, on speaker. Rhianne accelerated towards the house.

'With the London dating scene. I need to be prepared.'

'Everyone eats ass now,' she said.

'Everyone what?'

'I'm telling you. I didn't know until I started dating again. You take a little time out and then you come back and, boom. Everyone's into ass. It's good you asked.'

'Boom?'

'Well, not really boom. More—'

'Yeah, yeah. I get it.' Rhianne, interrupting. 'You mean, like, literally everyone?'

'Look,' Jess said, 'you don't want to, no one's forcing you. To be honest, I don't really understand why it's got so popular. I think it's a fad.'

'OK. You send me the long read.'

'I haven't written it yet.'

'The Normalisation of Ass-Eating.'

'An essay, by Jessica Evans.' Jess paused. 'I'd say it's more dining, though.'

'Oh? Fine dining?'

'Ass-banqueting.'

Rhianne pulled over in case she crashed.

'Send it to me by the end of next week.' She was wheezing. 'We can discuss it in depth. End of Friday.'

'End of play Friday,' said Jess. 'EOP. OK. That's a hard deadline, or?'

'EOP. Hard.'

Friday was Josephine's anniversary. They used to go every year, Dominic, Melissa and Rhianne, up to Uley Bury. They would stand in the place where they'd scattered her ashes. They'd wait, all of them aware that they could be standing for an indefinite period and still nothing would happen – nobody's grief would be resolved, no meaning would be found – but nobody wanting to be the first to move. Eventually, Dominic would put his arm around his daughter. 'Ready?' he would say.

After a time, Melissa had stopped coming. Work was in the way, or there was something. The last time they had gone, it was just Rhianne and her father. Dominic took them back via the tip, and Rhianne sat in the car while he broke up their old sofa with a wrench.

'I can come,' he told her, 'it'll just have to be on the way home from work. So, late.'

'It's OK,' Rhianne said. 'I want to go on my own.'

Thursday night, she lay on her bed for a long time. She waited until she heard Melissa and Dominic go up to bed, the doors close, the lights out in the hallway. On the floor, her phone vibrated, but she stayed where she was. Jess had offered to come home, but Rhianne had declined. It was important for her to be strong. For her not to need anybody. She was beginning to identify a vertiginous kind of freedom: in anticipating nothing; receiving nothing. For a moment, she let it swallow her. Outside her door, the light flicked back on. It was late. Dominic, too, was sleepless. She could hear the shuffle of his footsteps, pausing, tentative, where the floorboards bowed. She stayed still, waiting for him to pass before she got up, picked her phone back up off the floor. On its screen, a message from an unsaved number. *Thinking of you.*

A thrill, at the sight of his number on her screen. Here, at last. Too late.

She didn't reply, and she didn't resave the number. The following day, she drove up to Uley Bury. She phoned Jess from the top and she crackled in and out of signal, Jess's face breaking up, but smiling. Rhianne had written a letter to her mother, like she had every year since she died, and she burnt it, sent it to the wind. 'I always have this feeling,' said Rhianne, 'like she's getting younger. Like the more I grow and experience, the less she knows. Like she's stuck in time, still standing by the landline in our old kitchen.' Rhianne knew this second-hand: Josephine loved to talk, ran up a three-figure phone bill when they first moved to Cashes Green, the cord wrapped around the doorframe if it was a long call or a private one so she could stand out in the hallway.

'I guess that's OK,' Rhianne said, 'if she's still there. She liked it there.' And then, confessional, 'The thing is, I don't remember it.'

'The phone?'

'I know the stories,' Rhianne said, 'but I don't remember.'

It was difficult for Jess to understand.

'But how are you supposed to remember?' she said. 'That's not your fault.'

On the way home she played All Saints, and a howl tore up her chest. And then, from nowhere, she thought of white flesh against plastic, guts poured out under cold, running water. The glistening sea and smoked coals on a late summer morning. She thought, too, about the feeling of his knuckles, pressing into the sole of her foot. In her room, she opened the message, read it over and again. Threw the phone across the floor.

At work the next day she pulled the knives from their block one by one. He was there, standing by the chopping board, and she ignored him. She was looking for the large flat-bladed one he had shown her, the chef's knife he had told her to use, all the way back then. Callum was watching.

'Are you looking for my knife?'

Rhianne let the bread knife fall back into its slot. 'Yeah.'

'You're not planning on sticking it in anybody?'

'No, why?'

Callum shrugged. 'No reason,' he said. 'Just that you seem like you might be a bit pissed off at one or two people.'

'Really?' Rhianne said. 'Why might that be?'

Callum washed the knife, dried it.

'I don't know, but I'm sure if there's a reason then it's a good one.'

Rhianne was irritated. He was holding the knife out to her, handle first.

'I didn't reply to your message because I've got nothing to say.'

'I understand.'

'Really?' The kitchen, for those few moments, had been still and quiet, but then the top door banged open. Kieran, carrying a stack of Tupperware, tripping down the steps to the dishwasher.

'We haven't spoken,' said Callum quietly. 'And that's on me. But we should.'

Rhianne snatched the knife from him.

Then, a phone call. It was three in the morning. She realised afterwards he had been calling repeatedly. She asked him what he wanted. When he spoke, his voice was scratchy, low. 'To hear you,' he said.

'You wanted to talk,' she said, 'and you chose three in the morning?'

Long spaces between them. The sound of the phone rustling against the pillow. The familiarity of his voice sent shocks through her body.

'Are you sleeping?'

'Not now I'm not. Are you?'

'No,' he said. 'I can't sleep. I thought maybe you couldn't either.'

She waited for him to say more. The silences grew longer. In the background she could hear music, wave music, the kind he used to play when he worked the late shifts, when he couldn't sleep. Rhianne closed her eyes, put the phone on speaker beside her. 'Why?' she said.

'Got a lot of thinking to do,' he said.

'Thinking? About what?'

'You.'

Rhianne stayed silent. There would have to be more.

'Except you don't seem to even want to be friends with me these days.'

Rhianne bit back. 'Seems like you've got plenty of friends.'

'Like who?'

'Kieran, Dean,' Rhianne said. She hesitated. 'Annabel.'

A pause. She knew that she had given herself away, but she couldn't help it.

'Annabel,' Callum said, after a moment. 'She's leaving next week. Going back to her boyfriend in Amsterdam.'

'That's a shame,' said Rhianne. 'No more Taylor Swift.'

'No more Taylor Swift,' Callum said.

Rhianne said nothing. She stayed on the line.

On into autumn the skies had been clear enough that through the open top-floor windows of the Colvin house the frequent metallic *puck* sound of golfers teeing off, the occasional cat-back exhaust and thudding bass, could still be heard on the cool October air. The leaves turned and the nights drew closer. Melissa's asters, hesperanthas, came up delicate and icy pink, as if they somehow knew that the frost wouldn't be coming until the New Year. The cows stood on the tarmac; traffic slowed, and the clear skies held all through to the end of the month, when at last the clouds opened and the parched earth exhaled.

Rhianne closed her window, climbed back into bed, towards her phone and the heat it was emitting there on her pillow. 'It's raining,' she said. At work, civility, but here, in the early hours, they hollowed out an enclave, during which they could exist untouched by what had happened between them. Once or twice, they edged into more difficult territory. He missed her. He asked her if they were going to be friends again, Rhianne told him no, most likely not. There was a brief power, hers to hold, there in the dark.

'You see me every day,' she said, when Callum said again that he wanted to see her.

'No. To see you. The two of us. Not at the hotel.'

Silence. 'You want that?'

'Why wouldn't I want to see you?'

'Historically speaking, you've preferred avoidance.'

'Don't say that.'

'I'll say it because it's true.'

She heard him, turning, his bedsheets rustling, his voice closer to the phone now.

'You're funny,' he said. Laughing. Voice soft. 'I forgot how funny you are.'

'That's weird.' Her own confidence was outrageous to her. 'How did you forget?'

'Must have slipped my mind.'

'Careless of you.'

'It was,' he said. 'I know it was careless.'

23

He asked again, and both of them knew that he would keep on asking. She agreed to meet, a Thursday. She waited outside the hotel with the engine on, and the heater, watching the condensation clear from the screen, watching the radio clock turn from twenty-nine past to thirty. She'd been off today, and Jess had been sending her photos of Marcus's room, asking how much of the furniture she wanted to keep. Rhianne replied to ask how her long read was coming. *Delayed,* Jess's answer. *Still in the research phase.* Rhianne sent two peaches in response. Just after half eight, Callum arrived at the bottom of the steps, throwing his jacket over his head, dashing across the gravel. He banged on the passenger side of her car, she wound down the window for him. 'Hey.' He leaned into the car. His torso filled the window frame. Dimples. The bridge of his nose wet with rain.

'I know I'm late,' he said, 'just three more minutes; I need to change.'

'Three minutes.' She looked at her phone. 'More time than that, I'm driving off.'

Callum let out a girlish scream, got out his phone. 'Siri,' he said, 'set a timer for three minutes.' He flung the phone through the window, onto the passenger seat next to her. 'Watch me,' he said. Studiously, she ignored the phone, unlocked on the passenger seat beside her, closed her eyes. Then a bang, once again, on the passenger side. He was back, his puffer jacket flecked with colour, a soft blue hood pulled up around his sweet face. 'Time?'

Slowly, she reached for the phone. 'How do you unlock this?'

'Oh my God.' Callum opened the door, slid in the car beside her. He smelt good, something with sandalwood. Snatched the phone. 'Two minutes fifty-seven,' he said. 'Minus the four hours it took you trying to unlock my phone.'

She looked at him. 'Hi, Callum.'

'Rhianne,' Callum said. He reached out. Pinched her cheek with his finger and thumb. They drove. Callum wanted to get away from the hotel, as much distance as possible, he said, as they turned up out of the drive.

'Away from the drama?' Rhianne said.

'Just away.' Callum sank back in his seat. He fiddled with the temperature dial.

They came down off the common, heading back up the other side of the valley through darkened lanes. This hill was steep, and the engine of the little car struggled. 'Have you been putting on weight,' Rhianne shifted down to second, 'I normally fly up here.'

Callum slapped his belly. 'Probably. Eating my feelings.'

'Already?' Rhianne kept her eyes on the road. 'Annabel's only been gone a few days.'

'Not Annabel,' said Callum. 'Definitely not Annabel.'

They found a sticky-tabled corner booth in the Railway and ordered two lime sodas. Rhianne sipped her drink. Lime syrup, not enough ice. He had been the one who wanted to meet, but now it seemed as though he was waiting for her to speak. He looked small to her.

'So. January?'

'Yeah,' Rhianne put down her glass. 'January.'

Callum nodded. The corners of his mouth twitched. 'A month.'

'Six weeks.'

Rhianne gave nothing more away, sat back in her seat, waited.

'Look,' he said, 'I wanted to see you.'

'I'm still waiting for you to tell me why.'

'You know why. You know I was upset with you.'

Rhianne nodded. She was ready for this, had been ready for weeks, and all of it had grown so tangled. A relief, now, to have it all laid out for her. She had anticipated the blows. Callum shifted his drink away from him. His face, his smell, the sound of his voice, all of it so familiar to her. He leaned back; Rhianne tilted forwards. 'But not any more. That passed. Almost as soon as I left it passed.'

'As soon as you left.'

'Yeah, like, not even halfway home.'

'You mean,' Rhianne sharpened, 'when you left me in the middle of fucking nowhere without telling me where you were going? And you waited almost three months to say this to me?'

'Two and a half,' Callum said. He was smiling, and this made her angry. 'You're an intelligent woman. You figured out a way home.'

'Yeah. Cool.' Rhianne reached for her jacket, pulling it over her shoulders, stood.

'Where are you going?'

'Got somewhere to be,' she said, 'you're an intelligent man.'

'Hey,' Callum said, 'hey.' He stood, and suddenly he was there, his arms around her, and he enveloped her. 'I'm sorry, I'm sorry. I'm being a prick.'

She spoke into his chest. 'You are.'

'I've protected you,' Rhianne said. 'Told my family, told Jess we agreed to go back separately. So that nobody would think you were an asshole.'

'I don't care what they think,' Callum said. 'I care what you think.'

'I still think you're a prick,' Rhianne said. But she stayed where she was.

And he squeezed her, tighter, and his touch was the end of all the pain, all the guilt she had carried. Him, holding her. There was a world in which she peeled his arms from around her shoulders, stepped back, looked for her keys. He breathed in tight, then he let her go. She sat, put her head in her hands.

'I felt so guilty about what I said. And you didn't give me a chance to apologise.'

'We could have spoken.'

'I thought, I don't know.' Rhianne's head was foggy with the facts, the chronology. The realisation that all this time it had been him waiting for her to reach out, close that distance between them. 'I thought you didn't want to.'

'What?' Callum said. He was smiling, wicked. 'You were scared of me, or something?'

Rhianne shook her head. 'Fuck off,' she said. 'Don't. It's not funny.'

'I'm joking, I'm joking.' He reached across, touched her face. Put a thumb to the tears, now falling. 'I knew as soon as I left it was ridiculous. I know you know me. I know you don't think that way of me.' His touch, electric. 'I've moved on. You should too.'

'Moved on?'

'Moved on from, you know. What was said.' He caught her expression, and she knew that her fear was readable. From nowhere, the image of Annabel. Pink-cheeked, leaning towards him. 'You thought I meant moved on from you?'

'I guess.'

Callum shook his head. 'No,' he said. 'No fucking way.'

Rhianne said nothing, bowed her head. At some point, he had started holding her hand, and she could feel it, how he was pulling them back from the brink of something. She was still thinking of Annabel. Fears, unfounded and tightly held. She loosened her grip.

'What is this,' Callum said, 'some kind of self-flagellation? I didn't know you were Catholic. But it would explain a lot.'

'Well, I'm sorry for what happened.'

'Don't be,' he said. 'You've got nothing to be sorry for.' He leaned forward, reached across the table, dipped his fingers in her lime soda. 'I absolve thee,' he said, dabbing the drink on her forehead, 'of thine sins . . .' her chin, 'the sins of the father . . .' left cheek, 'the son . . .' right cheek, 'and the holy ghost . . .' nose.

Rhianne closed her eyes, frowned. 'Did the holy ghost sin?'

'Yeah,' he said. 'Really fucking naughty, the holy ghost.'

'I think you might have got that wrong.'

'Look,' he put his fingers back in the glass, flicked it at her, 'do you want my absolution or not? Because this stuff doesn't come cheap.'

Rhianne snatched his hands away from her face. 'I don't want it,' she said. 'Keep it.'

They drove the back way, down the hill the car had struggled to climb, through the lanes in the dark. They drove along the driveway to The White Hart. The shutters of the hotel were closed, their edges bordered with the warm interior light of the restaurant and bar. Rhianne swung right, pulled up outside the staff house. She wrenched the handbrake on, left the engine running. Earlier this evening, she had made commitments to herself: that she would hear him out, but that she would not soften. Now, though, beneath the noise of the fan heater, in the warmth she could feel radiating from his body beside her, the memories his flesh contained, these commitments seemed to dissipate. Callum looked at her. In the dark, his expression was soft. He put his fingertips to the side of her face.

'What about you?' she said.

'What about me?'

'What about your absolution?'

'That's between me and my priest.'

'You don't have a priest.'

'That's what I keep trying to tell him.'

She put her hand to his, held it, there, on the side of her face. Looked at him steadily.

'You haven't said you're sorry.'

Outside the hotel, the security light came on. Callum blinked.

'I'm sorry,' Callum said. He inhaled deeply. 'I'm sorry that I will always look younger and more handsome than you, even though I'm at least six months older.'

Rhianne snatched his hand back from her face. 'Get out of my car,' she said. She shoved him, once, and then again, harder. Callum, laughing, fell out of the half-open door.

'All right,' he said, 'I'm going, I'm going.'

She drove fast along the lanes in the dark.

24

Tonight, they were going to The White Hart for a tasting. Melissa put on her best top with its big flower pattern, and it felt ridiculous cutting in under her armpits, her breasts heavy and low and that old mulberry lipstick making her lips look somehow small and puckered and not full like she had wanted. She was driving because, she told Dominic, she had no plans to drink. 'Wine,' she insisted, 'is wine.' Mostly she was here to keep an eye on the portion sizes, make sure they were big enough. She backed up into a row of vintage cars and yanked the handbrake, checked her reflection.

Melissa told herself to relax. She'd had fears, none of which had been realised. Rhianne was happy, working hard, head high, and it had paid off: she'd got her London job. Melissa was proud. She hadn't allowed herself to be cowed by idiot boys. There had been none of that noise, no engines, idling. And Dominic, well. He seemed to be happier, too, these last few weeks. 'I told you,' he said, as they crossed the car park towards the hotel. 'I told you everything would be good again.'

The White Hart had been renovated since the last time Melissa had come, and quietly, she was impressed. To her mind it had been one of those grubby places with sticky tables and dirty carpets, but it was cleaner than she remembered, more compact. The lights were low, warm, velvet cushions on big, comfortable-looking sofas and logs stacked high in the grate, that rich, woodsmoke smell that Rhianne brought home in her hair at the end of every shift. Brendan put a hand on Melissa's mid-back and walked them through, past the bar – Oscar Peterson, bass soft, amber bottles stacked – and to the kitchen, just as the white swing-door kicked open, Rhianne emerging, pulling her hair up into a ponytail.

'I hope you're hungry,' she said, 'because there's a lot of food.'

A window table, even though there was nothing to look at except the inside of the closed shutters. The restaurant was full and nobody else had worn florals. There was a pregnant woman with a manicure wearing monochrome overalls and white trainers; men in thin, high-collared jackets. Melissa had missed the part where rich people had started to dress like communists.

Rhianne wasn't eating with them because, she said, she'd eaten everything already. 'More times than I'm willing to tell you.' She smiled; said she would keep an eye on the chefs for them.

A week earlier, at the end of a twelve-hour shift, she'd recited her favourite dishes and Melissa had been struck, not for the first time, by how together she was. Melissa watched the way she unpicked the tie on her tracksuit bottoms, hitching them higher on her waist, and she felt that old fear, that old protective impulse, rise, and then recede in service of something else, something a little less habitual. Trust, maybe. Or faith.

'If you like the prawns,' Melissa had said, 'then we'll have the prawns.'

Rhianne tightened the tie on her tracksuit, thrown. 'But you love a bit of mozzarella.'

'You like the prawns,' Melissa said again.

Even Dominic had been thrown – he knew Melissa didn't like the little whiskers they had, thought they were creepy and extra-terrestrial-looking – but now they had arrived, and Melissa was tucking her napkin into the front of her flowery top and she was twisting the head off one of those big, juicy prawns, resisting the temptation to tell everybody about what manner of E.coli was contained there in the brown stringy bit she was pulling out of its spine.

She had done her best to disguise her discomfort. Managed not to interrupt Dominic talking about Roberta's son's new job, took Dominic's hand under the table when he put his fingers through hers, gave her opinion on the salmon, the creaminess of the sauce, the balance of salt and sweetness and lemon combined with the wine sips Dominic insisted upon. She'd been worried about the food, that there wouldn't be enough, but it kept on coming, small plates and big plates brought to the table by Rhianne and another waitress. Dominic had wanted everything to be right. And then they were cleared, and Melissa was full, but this was not something she was ever likely to admit, and more was coming: a cheesecake, New York style.

'With compliments from the chef,' said Rhianne.

Melissa took a fork to her dessert.

'The chef?' she said. 'What's he complimenting us for?' She'd said it more loudly than she meant to, and Melissa had the feeling that the other people in the restaurant were waiting for her to say stupid things. Rhianne was coy, shrugging.

'Don't know,' she said. 'He just sends them.'

'We'll take them.' Melissa mashed a piece of cheesecake beneath the fork. 'Some of us these days have to take the compliments where we can get them.'

'I'll tell him,' said Rhianne.

The kitchen door swung open again. A blast of noise and light, voices. Melissa turned back around, feeling suddenly conscious of how thin everybody in this restaurant was. She didn't believe any of them had ever eaten five courses. She was feeling uncomfortable, irritated.

'What is she, DPD? Can't he come out and send them if he wants to send them?'

Dominic started to eat. 'Have you decided what you're wearing?'

'Not sure, maybe a suit. Depends on the legs.'

'Oh,' said Dominic.

'The veins,' Melissa said. 'Hopefully they don't take any of the important ones.' She didn't know why she was being like this, why she felt the need to ruin nice things, and Dominic, across, was giving that look he gave her, the one that betrayed his disappointment and affection all at once. But she had done it. At last, Melissa had showed Taschimowitz the veins, planted her Velcro-fastened shoe up on the chair and rolled up the hem of her scrubs. 'I know it'll be expensive,' she said, 'and it'll need to be both legs. This one's the good one.' Taschimowitz stood up, walked around his desk, and put on his glasses, as if he needed them to focus on something so large and monstrous as a middle-aged woman's inner calf. She pulled the hem higher.

Taschimowitz had taken the glasses off. 'Hasn't this been terribly painful?'

'Nothing I can't get used to,' she said. She didn't know where it came from, someplace subterranean, but it rose up inside her, horrible and unignorable: a quiver, in her voice, as though she was about to cry. She withdrew the leg. 'Can she do it? Your person?'

'She'll do it.' He would put her on the list, right at the top.

'I might even have supermodel legs in time for our holiday,' said Melissa, now, to Dominic. She hesitated, and then corrected: a concession. 'The honeymoon.'

'Lake Como.' He brightened, and she was glad for this. 'Full of wankers, I heard.'

But she didn't go with Dominic into the kitchen at the end of the meal; she put her bag over her shoulder, went instead to the Ladies. She was queasy and full, and all the cream they'd served with the salmon had done something to her stomach. She took her time in the toilet, flushed three times, and, feeling lighter, she washed her hands and reapplied her lipstick. She stood back to look at her reflection, took it off again.

Outside in the car, she watched Dominic, lopsided and

drunken, patting his pockets as he came out of the hotel. He was giddy about the food, about the place, he was excited about the party, and he wanted to ask his friend with his covers band to play, and Melissa was glad he knew to call it a party and not a wedding. She shifted up a gear, cutting back towards the house.

'So,' said Melissa, when they got upstairs, 'did you see him? He won't spit in the food, you don't think?'

Dominic shuffled from the bathroom to the bed.

'No,' he said, 'of course he won't spit in the food.'

'He might be bitter,' she said, when he climbed up in beside her. She propped herself up on her elbow. 'Or stupid. Or something.'

Dominic turned onto his side, towards her.

'You were the one who thought she should go back there.'

'I was,' Melissa said. 'I am. I don't believe in women being chased away from places.'

He smoothed his fingertips across her brow.

'He's a normal idiot boy,' he said. 'And she's stronger than you give her credit for. And,' he said, 'she's moving, anyway. Big smoke. Big shmoke.'

Dominic was quiet, curled in on himself.

Melissa leaned over, turned off the light.

'Lights out, guv,' said Dominic into Melissa's armpit.

But she didn't sleep. Lactose, really, as much as instinct, and always with the heating up too high at this time of year. The salmon had been too creamy. Dominic, next to her, had fallen into a heavy, apnoea-choked sleep. At least he was sleeping better these days. Good for him. Melissa swept up her pillows and stepped out into the corridor. There was the flash of headlights through the window. Outside, the sound of Rhianne's car pulling up, the engine cutting. Melissa listened for the sound of the door, keys dropping into the bowl. She was late; later than she should have been. Melissa lingered at the top of the stairs. Then, she hugged the cushions closer to her, shuffled off down the hall.

25

All through December the lights in the restaurant had been turned low, the fire stacked higher. Fairy lights glittered in the hall, and outside the common was frosted, crisp. The hotel closed for the holidays, and Callum, as he always did, spent Christmas with Brendan and Jack. There was whiskey and too much dessert, and on Boxing Day, after lunch, Brendan and Callum occupied one sofa each, vinyl softly spinning in the corner of Brendan's living room. Jack, upright by the bay window, shifted his book closer to the reading light.

'*23 Things They Don't Tell You About Capitalism*,' Callum said, tilting his head to read the title. 'Just a light Christmas read, is it?'

'My revolutionary,' Brendan said, adoringly. He was almost horizontal, collapsing in his chair, a plate of cheese resting on his stomach. 'Careful, Callum. We want him onside come the uprising.'

Jack looked over his glasses. 'It's too late for you, Callum, I'm afraid.'

'Oh, Jack, don't.' Brendan shifted, rebalancing his cheese-plate. 'You know how sensitive he gets.'

'It's cool,' said Callum, distracted. In his pocket, his phone had started to vibrate. He pulled himself upright, extracted it. 'The revolution comes,' he said, frowning at the screen, 'you do what you have to do.' He stood, stepped out into the hallway.

Rhianne, on the other end of the line, was tearful. She wanted to know where he was.

'I'm still at Brendan's,' said Callum. 'What's going on?'

'I really need to see you.'

'Where are you?' He glanced back into the living room. Jack, in the corner, was oddly still. Callum straightened. 'It's OK, don't worry. Are you at home? I'm coming to pick you up.'

'No, no, don't,' Rhianne spoke quickly. She took a breath. 'Don't go there. I'm already here, at the hotel. Can you please come?'

Callum packed up his bag and left Brendan and Jack there at the house. Rhianne, he told them, needed him. He'd been static for too long, and stepping out into the cold, he was energised by the drama, the urgency of her phone call. As he pulled up outside the staff house, Rhianne got out of the front seat of her car. Her face was pale except for the tip of her nose, which was pink. He put his arms around her, and he held her.

'What's happened?' he said. 'Talk to me.'

Rhianne shook her head. 'I can't,' she said.

'Hey.' He pulled back, studying her face. She looked younger, her eyes wild and unfocused. Her breath was unsteady. 'It's OK. Just try to breathe. Breathe in.'

Rhianne took a large, shuddering inhale, stopped.

'And out,' he said, 'Jesus. I meant in both directions.'

Rhianne exhaled, burst into laughter, which immediately turned into tears. Callum pulled her back in, his arms wrapped around her. She crumbled, collapsing into him. 'And in again,' he said.

Her voice was muffled. 'You don't have to say it every time,' she said.

'You sure about that.' She nodded into his chest. It felt good, to hold her. To lessen this pain she seemed to be carrying. He had missed this: her body, her warmth.

'I hate Christmas,' she said, petulant.

'I know.' Callum wrapped his arms around her tighter.

'I thought you'd be here. That's why I came.' Blearily, she peeled herself away from him, gathering herself, determined. 'Did I make you leave early? What did Brendan say?'

Callum shook his head. 'It's OK,' he said. 'It doesn't matter. Let's go inside.'

He took her by the hand, led her across the living room and up the stairs. She followed, unhesitating. In his bedroom, he pulled the cap from the bottle of whiskey on his desk and poured a glass for her. She sat down on the edge of his bed, took a sip. Callum sat beside her.

'So, are you going to tell me what happened?'

Rhianne looked down at her glass. She was calmer now. 'It's him,' she said.

He couldn't help it. 'Santa Claus?'

She shook her head violently. 'No,' she said. 'No. Callum, it's Alexander. You know. *Him.*' Of course, he knew exactly. 'He's at the place. Where I have the new job.' The job, the one she had taken for January. 'Freelance stuff,' she said. 'He does consulting now.' She took her phone from her pocket, and she handed it to him. *Merry Christmas . . .*: its subject. And, in its body, a continuation, *and congratulations. I hear you will be starting at Oren come January. The founder is a dear friend. I look forward to our paths crossing.* Signed, with a single initial. *A.*

'That's Alexander,' Callum said.

'They were at university together,' Rhianne said. 'Him and the founder. I looked them up.' She rubbed her eyes. 'The woman who interviewed me. They're obviously friends.'

Callum was derisive. 'He has friends?'

'They always have friends,' Rhianne said. 'That's how this works.' He felt her tense up beside him. 'I can't be around him again.'

'I know,' he told her. 'I know. You don't have to be.' He was quiet for a moment. 'So you got that email? When?'

153

'This afternoon.'

Callum nodded. He squeezed her tighter. 'We'll figure it out. Don't worry.'

Rhianne was quiet in the resonance of that turn. *We*. Then she nodded. 'Yeah,' she said. 'We will.' She shivered.

'You cold?'

She shook her head. 'Not really.'

'Liar.'

'I'm not lying,' she said. He'd cleared the room since she'd last been here, hung up the Yayoi Kusama print he'd gone into Bristol and had framed on his day off, thinking about what she'd told him about picking out the colour when he was choosing a frame, to go to a good shop that would do it custom-sized, mount the print properly so that it didn't wrinkle away from the glass. Rhianne looked at the print. She turned, looked up at the wall behind his bed, looked back around. 'You got the lamp,' she said.

'On expert advice,' said Callum.

Rhianne shrugged. 'Whose advice was that?'

'Just someone I know with impeccable taste,' said Callum. He stood. 'Here.'

He took his bathrobe from the back of the door, put it round her shoulders. Rhianne climbed to her feet so he could fasten it around her waist, except she hadn't put her arms through the holes, so now her arms were tied up inside of it. She spun from left to right: the robe's sleeves flapped around her.

'Do I look like I've been recently hospitalised?'

Callum took the sleeves and tied them, too. He started to laugh. Rhianne was standing close to him, pouting, checking her reflection as though they were fashioning some couture garment. 'Just . . .' He flicked the hood up, began tying the strings of the hood around her chin, so that her face was now a small, squashed circle, framed by the fastenings. 'Beautiful, darling,' he said. He wiped the make-up, which had smudged, from underneath her eyes. Rhianne thought she looked like a woodland creature entering its winter hibernation. A squirrel, cheeks full of acorns.

'Yeah,' Callum said. 'You look much less fuckable.'

Rhianne tilted her head. 'And why would I want to look less fuckable?'

Callum stood very still. Electricity, quite suddenly, between them.

Then, she laughed. 'All right,' she said. 'So, me and you are going to get along fine? Just so long as I wear an extra layer of fleece and have no available arms?'

'Pretty much.'

'OK,' she said.

'OK,' he said. He untied the sleeves. 'So, what are you going to do?'

'Stay here, I guess.' She lifted the hood back off her face, lay down on Callum's bed. 'Until I find somewhere better to be.'

'You want to stay tonight?' He couldn't keep the hope from his voice.

Rhianne nodded. 'Yeah,' she said. 'I do. I don't want to go home.'

He sat down next to her, tugging playfully at the rope of the dressing gown.

'Did you talk to them about it? Show them the email?'

'Yeah,' she said.

Callum let go. He had known there was something else. 'And?'

Rhianne shrugged, rolled onto her side. 'My dad was upset. Angry. And Melissa, well.'

Callum sharpened. 'Angry?'

'With him,' Rhianne said, 'obviously.'

'What did Melissa say?'

'Dunno,' Rhianne said. She was small, curled in on herself. 'They were both just upset.'

*

That night, simply, he held her. He smoothed her hair away from her face, took her phone from her hand, put it on charge, over the other side of the room where she wouldn't look at it. He inspected her hands, saw that she had picked all the polish from her nails. He pressed her palms between his, pulled her closer. He had forgotten the feeling of having her in his arms. How every touch drew a response, how expressive her face. Her mouth. How it was, sinking himself inside her, arriving at all his edges. 'Stay,' he told her after.

'I am staying,' she said.

'No,' he said, 'I mean, stay. Don't leave. Stay here with me.'

They had been awake for hours, and now she was making half-promises in the dark, resting her cheek on his chest, her fingertips moving across the skin of his arm, across the taut gleam of an old burn.

'I hate it here on my own,' he said.

She rested her hand on his ribcage and he breathed more deeply so that it widened beneath her, grew fuller, and he felt her fingers spread across his ribs.

'You missed me?' she said.

'I missed you,' he said. 'This whole time, I've been missing you.'

She was still, quiet. His breath became more regular. They slept, and in the morning, he went across to the hotel. The ground was icy and the kitchen empty and quiet. He put the radio on loud, took a box of pastries from the freezer and put them under the grill. He got two steaks, too, put them out to defrost. If she stayed, he would cook them for her later, and he'd take a bottle from behind the bar up to her, too. He filled a cafetière with the good coffee, folded the pastries into a napkin and brought them back to the room.

'OK,' she said, propping herself up on her elbow. 'I'll stay.'

He kept his voice level. 'Yeah?'

'Melissa won't like it.'

'Why won't she like it?'

Rhianne watched as he laid the pastries out on the bedside table.

'To be honest, she doesn't like you.' The confession, blurted. Rhianne flushed.

'Well,' Callum shrugged, looked away, 'in that case it's good that she's not invited.'

'But I like you. I always liked you.'

He climbed into bed beside her, and she turned to make space for him, her body still holding the warmth of the night. She, wearing only his T-shirt, him already dressed, his clothes rough against her bare skin. She needed him. He had known that she needed him. He pushed the T-shirt up over her thigh, waist. Her mouth, his, and her, clinging, arms around his neck. Wanting to not let go.

26

The days after Christmas slid one into the next. This year, Jack had persuaded Brendan to keep The White Hart closed for a little longer than usual. The curtains in Callum's bedroom were pulled shut, the hotel empty. On one of the mornings, Rhianne went barefoot down the stairs of the staff house and ran the shower until the bathroom filled with steam. She stood in a blast of hot water, watching her skin turn pink, and she sat on the lid of the toilet, waiting for the mirror to clear. Then, she wiped condensation from the screen of her phone, and she drafted an email explaining that for personal reasons, regretfully, she would no longer be accepting the job she had been offered. It was New Year's Eve. She was supposed to be moving to London in a fortnight.

Rhianne read back the email and sent it. Upstairs, she dried herself, wrapped her hair in a towel, and dressed in the clothes Callum had put out for her on his bed. All week she had been wearing his T-shirts, sweats, the smell of his laundry detergent, the clothes thick and soft. She went down again to find him there on the sofa, flipping through the channels. She stood in front of him, blocking his view.

'I've done it,' she said.

Callum shifted, looking past her to the screen. 'Done what?'

'I'm staying,' Rhianne said. 'I told them, I'm not starting.'

Now he looked at her. 'OK. And you spoke to Jess, too?'

'I already told you I spoke to Jess,' Rhianne said. The

conversation had been tense: Jess had wanted her to come to London anyway, had been upset when Rhianne stood her ground. 'She's going to try and fill the room.'

The screen flickered. 'So it's just your parents you're keeping me secret from.'

Rhianne threw down her phone, climbed up on the sofa on top of him, Callum trying, but too slow, to wriggle out from under her. 'Why are you like this?' She pinned down his arms, grinning. 'You're an idiot. Obviously they don't think I'm just here on my own.' Her hair unravelled from the towel, fell across his face. 'Nothing has ever been less of a secret.'

'You're soaking,' Callum said. He snatched at her hands but she launched herself forwards, slamming him to the sofa. Callum tensed. 'Go and dry your hair, you fucking lunatic.'

She squeezed his face between both her palms, kissed him.

'All right,' she said. Now she was serious. 'I'll go and dry it. Then we can go to the house. We'll get my stuff.'

Callum, slowly, watching her, shifted upright. He pointed the remote at the television, turned it off. 'OK,' he said. 'Go dry your hair.'

Rhianne hadn't gone back to the house since Boxing Day, and there had been just a handful of messages. She'd shared with Callum only pieces of what had happened: the arrival of the email, just after lunch, how she had handed her phone across the table to her father, who, reading it, swore, and stood up so quickly that he tipped a whole, freshly made coffee onto the back of his hand. How Melissa had dragged him to the sink and turned the cold tap onto full blast while Rhianne sat, numbly watching the way Melissa rubbed his arm, coaxing him back under the water, hushing him when he tried to pull away and turn towards Rhianne. That had been it. Rhianne's anger, the injustice, all of it had coalesced around the sight of her father, cowed over the kitchen sink, and this woman who was not her mother, soothing him. Rhianne got to her feet, kicking back the chair.

'Why don't you just let him do it?' Rhianne said. 'He's not your child.'

She hadn't told Callum that part. How Dominic had whipped around, anger and hurt in his expression. The shame she had felt, knowing these were words that could not be unsaid. Rhianne shunted her chair out of the way, stepped straight out of the kitchen and into the hallway, ignoring her father, who called after her. She'd gone straight upstairs, picked up her bag, her keys. On her way back down, she paused outside the kitchen. Her father was holding Melissa, her back to the door, her face buried in his chest. Rhianne hesitated. And here was another part she had not told Callum. How Dominic had looked up and seen her, about to step forwards. Silently, he shook his head, held on tighter to Melissa.

'Some people are just sensitive,' Callum said now, up in Rhianne's room. They'd come straight upstairs when they arrived, and they were speaking quietly, both of them aware of the stillness that emanated from down in the kitchen. Callum grinned. 'Or maybe it's that sharp tongue of yours.'

Rhianne shoved a box into his chest.

'What do you know about my sharp tongue?'

'I know enough,' Callum said.

They stood, facing each other. Downstairs, there was the sound of the kitchen door opening. Callum took the box from Rhianne's arms, put it on the floor. 'And still,' he continued, 'somehow, it's New Year's Eve and I'm here packing boxes for you.'

'This is it,' Rhianne said, 'the last one.'

While he took the box out to the car, Rhianne sat across from Melissa and her father at the kitchen table, stuck her thumb in a knot in the wood. Outside, there was the sound of his engine starting up.

'You know I didn't mean—'

'Oh, I don't care about that,' Melissa said. She pushed her coffee away from her. 'I just think this is all very hasty.'

'Not everybody feels the need to wait nearly twenty years before committing to a relationship,' said Rhianne. She said it gently, teasing. Not an apology, but trying, at least, to goad a smile. Melissa was brisk, composed. But Rhianne could not help noticing the way her father's hand rested on top of Melissa's, the way he squeezed it, protective, every time Rhianne spoke. He was looking down at the table.

'Are you really sure this is right?' Melissa said. 'I didn't even think you and he were speaking. I drove halfway across the country to collect you because it all ended in such a mess.'

Rhianne looked from Melissa to her father and back again.

'It ended,' she said, 'and then it started. And I'm an adult.'

'I know you are,' Melissa said, 'we just—'

'He's made me feel better,' Rhianne said. Tears started to spring. Her father still was not looking at her, still holding Melissa's hand, pressing his thumb tightly over hers, and Rhianne could not stand it. How he could not look at her. 'He's the only person who's actually made me feel better.'

On New Year's Day it began to pour with rain, a whole month's rainfall in forty-eight hours, and the common was immediately saturated, puddles sluicing across the high, straight road that ran through it. Rhianne, on her way for groceries, drove her car into floodwater and Callum towed it back to the staff house, where they left it to dry, in case the engine choked. It was Dominic, years ago, who had fixed the hotel's foundations, and the main building stayed solid, dry. But in the downstairs bathroom of the staff house, Rhianne, looking up from the toilet seat in the early hours of the morning, saw how quickly the patch of damp on the ceiling had enlarged.

For Dominic, there were callouts, favours. There were emergency works on the flood defences, there were sandbags to be moved to the entrance of the electricity sub-station out past Whitminster, and Dominic was fuelled, as he worked, by a renewed sense of purpose that hinged on the possibility of destruction and the promise of repair. In the evening, he drove back out to the mill where the waters surged higher. He revisited old calculations – rainfall, waterflow, the gradient of the riverbank, density of the soil there – and decided that it was time to move his filing cabinets, his paperwork and the boxes he kept stacked in the back office up to the first floor. He heaved sandbags onto his shoulder and he felt assuaged by the fact of his bulk, the service of his body, here, now, of use.

His anger, since Rhianne had left in such a blaze, had blunted and turned inwards into a dull depression that sent him to the kitchen in the early hours, standing in front of the refrigerator, sawing great hunks of bread from the loaf, eating cereal with his hands, his waist thickening, his mind, too. Dominic closed the fridge, went to the bathroom, pissed. This pain that had lodged inside him, it needed excavating. Those words of Alexander's, which had worked their way deeper, through his ribs and right between his lungs so that they stuck like a fishbone in the cavity of his chest. *She wanted me.* Delicately, Alexander replacing the teacup on its saucer. *She always seemed as though she didn't have anybody.*

Dominic washed his hands, looked at his reflection in the mirror above the sink. The pupil of his right eye, burst from a knuckle-blow to the socket. He remembered how, standing, that day in King's Cross, his knees had knocked into the table. He thought of Alexander, desired. Rhianne, desiring. He thought of Rhianne in the back seat of a taxi, turning fast through darkened streets, and Alexander, firing one short email that had derailed, all over again, his daughter's life. It had been too hard for Dominic to face her. He had been cowardly, and he had never thought of himself as a coward. Now, his anger rose, but this was preferable to what lay beneath it: fear, and the fact of failure. He climbed quietly back under the covers, buried his cheek in the space between Melissa's shoulder blades, pressed his face against the soft fat of her back.

27

Upstairs in the staff house, as the skies cleared, Rhianne pushed Callum's shirts to the far end of the rail and filled her section with all those clothes she had not worn since she'd come back from London. She unpacked her make-up into the bathroom, stacked her pens and her sketchbooks into the space beneath Callum's bed. She opened up the windows and cleaned the dust from the ledges, hoovered the cushions of that big beige sofa, and she asked Brendan for a dehumidifier to set up in the bathroom so that they could clear the mould. The Hart had reopened, and the ground that surrounded the hotel began to drain, great pools of water slowly sinking into the earth.

'It's normal,' said Callum, when Rhianne checked the bookings, asked him why it was so quiet. 'That's just January in hospitality. And it's been pissing it down.'

He was right. The shifts were long, and because there were so few guests, time dragged. Her car remained marooned in the driveway. Callum had kept the keys because, he told her, he knew someone who would fix it. She didn't know where he had put them. On the day she was supposed to move to London, she cleared out the cupboard behind the kitchen, starched and refolded the napkins. She did a stocktake of all the glassware, restacked the linen in the laundry, wiped and polished the breakfast trays. She took the master key from the office and went up to the bedrooms, packed the kettles up into a cardboard box and brought them to the kitchen.

'I'm descaling them,' she told Callum, though he had not asked.

He looked up from his chopping board, stared at her blankly. It was the two of them and Dean in the kitchen, and Dean kept his head down, scraping bone stock into a large, plastic tub. At work, even though there were so few guests, Callum had been busy, recipe testing and menu planning, and Rhianne had the feeling, now, that she had interrupted something important. She flushed.

'They've got loads of limescale in them. I don't think anybody's done it in years.'

'OK,' Callum said. He looked back down at his board, continued chopping. Dean, next to him, was carefully fitting the lid onto his plastic tub. He picked it up, moved past Rhianne.

'Excuse me,' he said, carrying the tub up out the back. 'Hot stock coming through.'

The back door swung shut, Rhianne stung by humiliation that felt both ugly and disproportionate. She kept her eyes down, pouring vinegar into each of the kettles, and then water, filling the silence with the sound of the tap. She was facing the window. Callum came to her, wrapped his arms around her waist, digging his chin into her shoulder.

'What's up with you?' he said. 'Why are you so grumpy?'

'I'm not grumpy,' she said.

'Liar.' Callum pushed his chin deeper into her shoulder.

Irritated, Rhianne pulled herself from his embrace, turned around to look at him. 'When are you getting my car fixed?'

'Next time I'm off.'

'Why don't I take it?' she said. 'Since you don't have time.'

He looked at her, steady. 'I told you, I'll take it.' Then he smiled. 'Otherwise you might go and not come back.'

*

She couldn't sleep that night. Callum had taken to plugging her phone in over on the far side of the room, next to his on the desk. She'd stopped taking it to work with her, leaving it in the laundry during her shifts in case he saw her using it during service and gave her one of his looks. Swiping through her settings he'd paused, frowning at the screen. 'Scrolling,' he told her, 'you know it's not good for your depression.'

She had spoken to Melissa, to Jess, in only stilted exchanges. From her father, there had been a short series of messages during the rainfall: he'd asked about the hotel's flooring, whether anything had leaked. She'd sent him some photos of the mould patch in the bathroom, and he'd told her to draw a circle around it so that she could check if it got larger. Now, lying beneath the weight of Callum's arm, sleepless and full of thought, it felt to her as though her phone was burning a hole in the wood.

She slid out from under him. Creeping over to the corner of the room, she unplugged the phone, pocketed it. Then, she knelt, quietly pulling her sketchbook and pens out from where they were kept under the bed. The door made a sticking sound as she pulled it open, turning the latch and stepping out into the corridor.

She had been intending to go downstairs, to sit in the living room, scroll and maybe send some late-night messages. But she didn't want Callum to come looking for her there. Instead, she pushed on the door to what had been Annabel's room. It was unlocked, the bed stripped and the walls bare. She switched on the light. In the corner, like in Callum's room, there was one of the old hotel mini-fridges, and a kettle. Beneath the window, a desk, across which the bulb's bright light fell, holding dust suspended, spinning.

Rhianne stepped inside, gently closed the door. She took her phone out of her pocket: it was nearly four in the morning. Of course, nobody had messaged. Now she was alone, the urge to make contact with the outside world had dissipated. She sat down against the wall, opening her sketchbook on the floor in front of her, wrapping her sweatshirt around her shoulders. It was quiet in here, and peaceful, and it was months since she had looked at her work. She flipped through the book, its contents familiar, tracing her hands across the lines.

At the back, she paused. There, tucked in as a bookmark, was the photograph of Josephine. Rhianne pressed it against the page. She had memorised this photograph. The way her hair fell over the shoulder, so that the line of her jaw was thrown into relief. The arch of one of her eyebrows, the soft, dusty light, that made Josephine appear almost luminous. The point of her chin, which was Rhianne's, too: her inheritance.

There was a smudge in the bottom corner, where a finger had covered the lens, added an unintended depth. She had not opened the book in a long time, knowing what memories were contained there, not wanting to use them up. But now, more than ever, she needed them. Outside, it was still dark. Rhianne turned back through the book. She had left the painting from her final year – the one that she had torn – at her parents' house. But everything else, all the sketches, paintings, designs, were here. They were not as she had remembered: they were better. She held the sketchbook further from her, trying to see it clearly, and she saw how her mother's face was filled with warmth, light; despite the fact that these drawings were in graphite, it was held there in her eyes. Rhianne turned the page, and she started to draw.

It was Callum she was thinking of. Callum as he had been in the summer, and again over Christmas. Callum, not as he had been since she had moved to the hotel – watchful, uneasy – but the Callum she knew best, wanted most. She moved across the page, softer strokes, then firm, working the architecture of his jaw, those deep, sweet indents that bracketed his mouth. But something was happening. She paused, held up the book. The drawing, she saw now, was flat, his face asymmetrical, one eye small and misshapen, unseeing, none of his warmth, his light captured here. The backs of her eyeballs itched, and Rhianne felt, rather than recognition of her own artistry, that the sleeves of her sweatshirt were thick and damp and unclean, that her shins were dry, that she needed not just a new set of clothes and perhaps a shower, but also a new skin.

Rhianne closed the book, rested her head against the wall and looked up at the lampshade, in which, she could see now, dead insects had collected, burnt by the bulb. Her lungs were taut and leathery and the room, suddenly, was too still, too quiet. She had been here for more than an hour. She put the book back on the desk, went downstairs, pulling on the big Timberland boots by the door, Callum's jacket. She went out, round the back of the staff house and to the top of the gardens, numb to the cold air, and sat down on the mound of earth that edged the valley.

Her lungs, at last, grew larger. Rhianne took her phone from her pocket and called Jess twice. It was before six; she wouldn't be awake, and Rhianne, later, would be working and would miss her returning the call. But she had tried, at least. She gathered the jacket around her and watched as the cables of the Severn Bridge began to swing. The jacket was thick, and it smelt of him. Sandalwood; detergent. She put her hand into the pocket. She pressed the pad of her thumb to the ridged blade of the car key – her key, the key he had kept – pressing, turning, until it grew warm.

28

Callum had been right. As the days grew fractionally lighter, longer, the hotel became busier again. Rhianne, in the mornings before work, let herself into the next-door room, and opened her sketchbook. She drew, and the hours slipped by, and the room felt large and light. She kept hold of her car keys, said nothing of them to Callum. Then, on an afternoon in February, she got in the car and drove down into the town. All day Callum had been busy, distracted. As she accelerated down the switchback, Rhianne was thrilled by her sudden freedom.

At the garage Rhianne sat looking up at Miss February on the wall calendar while the mechanic wheeled himself under her car, checking for any lasting damage. There was the smell of grease, rubber. He wiped his hands, told her there was nothing wrong with the engine, and Rhianne rolled her eyes. 'I knew he was worried about nothing,' she said, handing over the cash. The mechanic took it, buffed the scratches from her bumper for free. Afterwards, she felt better, knowing she had her car, knowing that the hotel was filling up. Callum, she hoped, would be happier, less irritable.

She parked outside the staff house. In the kitchen, she tore a piece of bread in half. 'I took it,' she told Callum, chewing. 'There's nothing wrong with it.'

Callum looked up. 'Took what?'

'The car.'

He wiped at a smudge on the worktop, flicked his dishcloth over his shoulder.

'All right,' he said.

She took her lunch up to the staff house. That night, he kissed her on the top of her thigh, the fleshy part, and behind the kiss, a bite. Slow, getting stronger, until she thought that he would pierce her flesh. The door, from his bed, felt very far away. Afterwards, she lay in bed alongside him, wired. He had his eyes closed, but she knew he was awake.

'You're upset about something,' she said.

'Why would I be upset?' He pulled her close, squeezed her. So she had imagined his anger.

'I don't know,' Rhianne said. 'Why else would you want to bite me like that?'

'Bite you?' He kissed her on her nose, cheeks, mouth, kept on kissing her. 'I want to bite you because you taste good, that's why.'

She pushed him away. 'Well, just be careful,' she said. 'Jack and Brendan are coming tomorrow. We both need to be in one piece.'

He shuffled closer, clamping her arms to her. 'One piece,' he said. 'I promise.'

He'd fallen asleep before her, and it had been hard to drift off with his arms so tightly around her. The next day she felt sleep-deprived, sallow; everything dragged. In the bathroom, she traced her fingers over those two ridged crescents on her thigh. At the start of her evening shift, she reapplied her eyeliner, her lip-gloss, dark and thick. Her nails were chipped, and she'd had to put on a second coat of concealer. She swept up a silver tray, walked back down the hallway to the bar. She paused, gathering herself. She could hear Brendan's voice on the other side of the door.

'It's the oak. From the Algarve. It's stronger. A little bit spicier.'

'You two. All I can ever taste is alcohol.'

Jack rarely came to the hotel, but tonight they were celebrating.

'A big investment,' Callum had said, 'the place down in Bristol. Nobody's supposed to know, so. You don't know.'

Rhianne stepped around the door. The three of them: Brendan, with his arm slung around the back of the sofa. Callum, swilling an amber glass. Jack, whose glasses twinkled when he saw her. 'I thought you were away,' he said to Rhianne. Turning, now, to Callum, 'Rhianne's here? Why isn't she having dinner with us?'

'You want to swap?' Callum said. 'You can do the dishes as well, if you want.'

'Next time,' Brendan said, waving his hand. 'Next time, we'll have Rhianne to ourselves and we'll put Callum to work.'

Rhianne was standing in the doorway, the tray pinned under her arm. She was looking at Callum. The crisp cuff of his shirt, one she had not seen before, lifting to reveal a watch that caught the light. He'd woken early that morning; she hadn't seen him all day. She could feel the marks of his teeth on her thighs. And, perhaps she was imagining it, but when she caught his expression, it was a flat look, unseeing.

Brendan squeezed Jack's arm. 'We had to pull out all the stops,' he said, 'throw all our best staff at you. Make sure you leave us a good Tripadvisor review.' He stood, clearing the empties. He was energised, excitable. 'You know Rhianne is a very talented painter.'

'I did know,' said Jack, 'and somehow they've got you waiting tables?'

'I like it,' Rhianne said. 'But it's temporary. I haven't figured it all out yet.'

'This is what happens,' said Brendan. He smiled at Jack. 'You would know. Don't fall in love. Especially not with a reprobate chef.'

Jack, though, was watching Rhianne. 'And what do you want to do, after?'

'I want to be an artist,' Rhianne said. The words came: bold, unexpected.

'An artist,' said Jack warmly. 'There you go.'

She spoke loudly. 'Maybe I'll go back and study more. I don't know.'

She could not help it: she glanced at Callum. He took a slow, careful sip.

'But,' Brendan stood, 'we're going to try our best to keep her. At least until she's too famous for us.' He squeezed Rhianne's elbow. 'Bristol,' he said. 'Big creative scene. And good universities.'

'So I heard,' Rhianne said.

The three of them followed Rhianne to the restaurant. Wine selection, bread. She caught snatches of conversation, but she was attuned mostly to body language: to Callum's left hand, the movement of his shoulders. Kieran was helping with starters tonight. He filled the soup bowls to their brim, garnished them quickly, expertly. The bowls had been sitting under the hotplate, and Rhianne was only halfway out of the kitchen when the porcelain began to burn through the napkin to her hand. She walked as quickly as she could without spilling, the bowls stacked in one arm. There was a kind of clarity to the burn, a satisfaction in the knowledge that she could endure it.

She put down the bisques, and she thought of Callum's room, darkened, the curtains pulled. The pain in her thigh. She played back the night. He was not upset. He'd told her he wasn't upset. They'd laughed, he'd kissed her. He'd told her she tasted good. But now she was consumed by the feeling that, if he did not look at her soon, she might flicker out of existence. Brendan was talking about knocking down some of the old outhouses, making space for new guest rooms. Rhianne moved around the table, pouring water. Briefly, she felt Callum's eyes fall on her, and her breath caught, waiting for him to say something, but instead he leaned back in his chair, pulling out his phone for Jack.

'This is the one,' he said, 'we can walk up to it later.'

Jack leaned forwards.

'Where the copper bathtub is,' Rhianne said. Inserting herself, because she had not been invited, forcibly into the conversation. She pointed in the direction of the hut. Callum did not look up. 'On the other side.'

At some point, she had begun to move as if through water. She took the red wine from the bar, opened it. As she poured, she imagined upending the bottle across the tablecloth, tearing off her apron, walking out, never coming back, and Callum, as if he could read her thoughts, leaned forwards and caught her by the wrist as she stepped around the table. He was smiling.

'Brendan,' he said, 'tell Rhianne how much that bottle cost.'

'I told you,' Brendan said. He dabbed his forehead with his napkin. 'Reprobate chef.'

'What?' Callum was still holding her wrist. He tugged on it, smile widening. 'Brendan, what is it? Five, six hundred?'

'Nine,' Brendan said. He at least looked embarrassed.

'And what is that? In pounds, per drop?'

'Oh, don't.' Brendan hit Callum gently on the back of his arm, and he let her go. 'Ignore him,' he said to Rhianne. He pushed his glass towards her. 'Don't let him make you nervous.'

She was pouring, and now everybody was looking at that single drop of wine that had beaded there on the rim of the bottle.

'It's probably about five pounds,' Callum said, answering his own question. 'Per drop.'

'I'm not nervous,' Rhianne said.

'And how much is that? Of your hourly wage?' Callum said, reaching for her wrist again as she moved closer, but Rhianne – irritated, humiliated – snatched her hand up out of his grip. 'Or,' he said, 'how much of the cost of getting your car fixed?'

There it was: the car.

'Drove it into a swamp,' Callum said. 'Car her daddy bought her.'

'Oh, Rhianne,' Jack said. He put down his glass. 'Tell him to fuck off.' Rhianne saw now that his face was flushed, something like genuine anger in his expression. He took a swig of his wine. 'Or, tell him to pour it himself.'

'It was a puddle, actually,' Rhianne said. 'And the mechanic said there's nothing even wrong with it.' She had finished pouring for everybody but Callum. She smiled. 'You know what?' she said. She put the bottle down on the table just next to his right hand. Callum looked at the bottle, up at her. 'Don't spill it,' Rhianne said.

Slowly, he poured his glass. Rhianne did not wait for him to drink. She could feel Jack watching her, and somehow, this made it worse. She pushed through the swing-door, back into the kitchen. Her breath kicked. She steadied herself next to the still.

He was back late that night. The men had gone in a taxi to the new place down in Bristol, and Rhianne had sat on the edge of the bed waiting for the sound of gravel beneath tyres, for headlights to move across the ceiling. The humiliation, the injustice, had ebbed as quickly as it had risen. She wanted his touch. She wanted him to touch her because his touch, its clarity, would erase the uncertainty that now engulfed her. Just before, she had hated him, but now she wanted him. She wanted urgency, desire. There was something terribly wrong with her: she wanted his desire even if it arrived in the form of pain. They'd finished their meal and she had loitered, there behind the door of the restaurant.

'Late,' he said, when she asked what time he'd be back. 'I don't know. It's work.'

'Do you have to go?'

'You're not exactly stuck here,' Callum said. His eyes were glittering. 'You can leave, can't you? If you want to leave.'

She finished her shift, and she went back to her room, undressed. She removed her make-up, sat, looking at its residue, its boldness, there on the cloth. It had all been too bright. She dressed in his T-shirt. There, beneath the hem, was the mark on the inside of her thigh. Those bruises that had turned from red marks to purple, mottled. She played back the scene in her mind. The way she'd slammed the bottle down. Her warning. The thought occurred to her that tonight he would not come back. She did not know if it was pain she would feel, or relief.

She lay back on the bed, pressed her fingers to the marks. The hairs on her skin stood up. Her body felt raw, alert, all of her attention now oriented around that sensation, the memory of pain, and something beneath it, softening, opening, into pleasure. She moved her fingers between her legs, and straight away she felt calmer. It was the feeling of sinking into a warm bath, waves moving up through her body. The movements of her mind slowed, and the mattress broadened beneath her as she sank back into it. 'I was touching myself,' she told him, when, later – much later – he returned. He unbuttoned his shirt, threw it into the laundry. His chain sat on his chest. 'Thinking about you.'

'Oh yeah?' He climbed up, sank his fingers into her hips. 'Thinking about what?'

'Last night.'

He held her, tighter. Her fears sank into the floor. He was here. 'You liked it.'

She nodded.

'You made yourself come?'

'No,' she said. Her breath caught. She knew, of course she knew, that there was something very bad happening here: something noxious, disguised as intimacy. But she did not know how to stop it. 'I waited for you.' Callum nodded, his cheek into hers, his breath growing heavier, and she waited for it. His hand rested, as it often did, on her lower belly, before moving down between her legs. 'You're wet,' he said, and she nodded. Gently, the hand moved. She waited for him to give her what she needed; to finish what he had started. And then, she felt it. The movement of his hand slowing; him slipping.

175

'Jack likes you,' he said.

'He's nice.' Rhianne was very still.

'It's good,' Callum said. 'They want you there, in Bristol. I can tell.'

She was caught between the fear of silence, stillness, and the fear of making promises she didn't know that she would keep. 'How can you tell?'

Callum did not reply. Instead, there was another question. 'Do you like him?'

'I like him,' said Rhianne. 'Why wouldn't I like him?'

The hand stopped moving.

'You like him,' Callum said. 'You like everybody, except for me.'

29

Kieran's fingers were greasy from the Happy Meal he had demolished at the sticky white table in McDonald's. Callum had paid; he always paid, snatching Kieran's wallet up out of his hand whenever he tried to get out his savings card. The fries had been delicious, crisp, molten inside, and Kieran had finished his portion, began eating what was left of Callum's while Callum, sitting back, watched. 'You need to eat,' said Callum.

Kieran waited for the follow-up, the joke, whatever comment Callum was about to make about his appearance or his appetite, but nothing came. Callum could be like this, away from the hotel. Earnest, oddly sweet. Kieran sat back, feeling as though a thick rubber ring had set around his lower belly. He put his hands there, hoping that the coagulation of fat was something he had imagined, was disappointed by the fullness beneath his hands, a rubbery band below his belly button he could grab in both palms.

'I think I'm getting fat,' he said.

'You're growing,' Callum said. He pushed the rest of his chips closer. 'Eat.'

'I'm gonna start working out,' Kieran said.

'Oh yeah? Weights?'

'I think so,' Kieran said. 'Or maybe jogging.'

Callum took his keys up off the table. 'You do you,' he said.

Kieran followed him out into the rain-washed car park, got into the passenger side of Callum's car. It was dark, and as they drove up towards the hotel, headlights blurred in the mist. Kieran's stomach churned. He'd thought about it before, once or twice, throwing up what he'd eaten, but he could never quite bring himself to do it because he hated the taste of bile and whenever he got close to the toilet seat the smell of urine around the rim made him recoil. Next time he ate too much, he'd go to the gym instead. Maybe he'd go with Callum, or one of the boys in the kitchen. He'd already got stronger, this last year, from all the lifting of trays and crockery. He fiddled with the stereo. Drake, the Weeknd.

'I like this one,' he said.

'*Certified Lover Boy*,' said Callum, glancing sideways at Kieran. Kieran shrugged. 'Could be.'

'Say no more.' Callum shifted down into third.

Kieran sank back. His bike had a puncture that needed repairing, but it was OK because he liked being driven around by Callum. Callum's car had a currency which blinded him to certain aspects of its condition: the almost-empty packet of chocolate digestives on the passenger seat; the stereo that sat halfway ejected from its console, wires exposed, and the faint burnt-clutch smell as Callum turned up off the roundabout.

'Macros, is it?'

Kieran watched Callum stuff the biscuit packet, which had rolled out on the turn, into the door pocket. A sensitive soul, attuned to the needs and movements of others, Kieran was unconscious of his ability to pick up the speech patterns, even accents, of the people he was surrounded by, the 'is it', the gentle sarcasm, was a verbal tic he'd collected from his long days in the kitchen. Vegan food, Callum had told him, filling his bowl with broccoli, with tahini and quinoa, was the best way to balance the macronutrients in a diet. He'd bring in extra for Kieran, he said, if he was serious about getting into his fitness.

'Macros,' Callum said. 'What do you know about macros?'

They were up on the common, now. On the far side from the hotel, just above the ice-cream factory, Callum swung in. 'All right then,' he said. He unbuckled his seat belt, turned to face Kieran. 'Big man. Let's see what you've got.'

For a short, insane moment, Kieran thought that he was being propositioned. He opened his mouth, closed it again. Callum took the keys out of the ignition, threw them into his chest.

'Let's go,' Callum said, 'before I realise what a terrible fucking idea this is.'

Kieran got out of the car. He thought about saying something about police, or insurance, but he had an instinct that he might end up getting left here in the middle of nowhere if he did, so, instead, he got into the driver's seat, and he fired the engine. It sputtered, cut out. 'You've got a shit car,' he muttered.

'Your mum's car is worse,' Callum said back.

'Yeah, well, my mum's too depressed to drive.'

'I would be, too, if I was your mum,' said Callum. As always, he'd bitten, thrown back. Nothing could be serious, when he was with Callum, and the relief of this freedom was intoxicating to him. Kieran turned the ignition again.

'Clutch,' muttered Callum, 'clutch, clutch.'

Slowly, Kieran started to lift the clutch. He felt it bite, he felt the car shudder, wheels soft on mud. Callum whooped.

'Gas,' he said. 'Slowly, slowly.'

Slowly, Kieran pressed the gas. The car rolled. He looked over his shoulder, checking for traffic, and Callum turned with him, his arm on the back of Kieran's seat.

'You're good,' he said. Kieran pulled out. 'More gas, let's go.' And the vehicle sped, juddering, just a little, but it responded to his touch, quicker now, the engine pitching, across that high road he'd cycled so many hundreds of times. 'Clutch again,' said Callum, and with his right hand, Callum shifted up through second, third. 'And again,' he said. 'All right, easy. I need to keep hold of my licence.' It was the same quiet, steady voice he used when he was working with Kieran in the kitchen, and Kieran, obedient, responded.

Kieran checked the mirrors, eased, cruising. The car was small but now, to him, it felt wide and powerful, and there was that feeling he always seemed to have in Callum's company: it was the feeling of having crossed a threshold. It was the feeling that, perhaps, up until this point, he had been lied to about the nature of transgression, disobedience. Here he was, on the other side of that threshold, and nothing bad was going to happen. The opposite, in fact: here was freedom, possibility, Callum's arm on the back of his seat. Callum leaned across, flipped the indicator. 'Second,' he said, 'whenever you want to turn.'

Kieran, when they pulled up at the staff house, was buzzing. He handed back the keys.

'Next time,' Callum said, checking the erratic angle of the bumper up next to the window, 'parking.'

Kieran went inside and pissed, a princely stream. In the living room, he leaned his elbows on the coffee table, sprinkling a pinch of loose tobacco into the L-plate he was constructing. Callum didn't touch the stuff, but he let Kieran smoke outside. Later, they would play GTA, and Kieran would pretend he liked it when really he just liked the slow, bass-y soundtrack, the odd, off-beat movements of the characters on screen, and the feeling of the sofa cushions moving underneath him every time Callum twitched, sprung forwards in his seat, jolting the remote. He was still wired from the drive; he needed the edges to be blunted. He smoothed off the Rizla, twisted the end.

'Where's Rhianne?' Kieran said.

Callum hissed the cap from a beer.

'Why do you always want to know where Rhianne is?'

Kieran shrugged. 'I just wondered how she is.'

'Oh yeah?' But Callum was smiling. 'I get it. Trust me.' He took a swig. 'She's at her parents' for the weekend. Left me.'

Kieran took his spliff outside. He leaned against the wall. The lights in the hotel's upstairs suite still lit, the night sky velvety and broad. He inhaled, deeply, dropped his head back against the brickwork. He took a deep drag, and then another. Behind him, he was aware of the sound of a door closing. Usually, the weed made him feel calm. Slackened his jaw, unfocused his gaze. Tonight, though, it seemed to have had the opposite effect, as though somebody had forced a huge air bubble down the back of his throat where all the oxygen he now tried to inhale was being held. Shadows lengthened; shapes, human more or less, took form.

He went back into the staff house with his head still spinning; great, vertiginous swoops through his skull. He sat down on the sofa next to Callum, who slung his arm around Kieran, handed him another beer. Kieran took it, sipped, trying to steady himself. The lights were too bright in here, and he could smell the alcohol on Callum's breath. 'I smoked a lot,' Kieran said, foggy.

'That's OK,' Callum said. And he seemed to brighten. 'You can stay here.'

Kieran tried his best to focus on the bottle in front of him.

'I don't have my toothbrush.'

'You forget your teddy bear, too?'

'No,' said Kieran, frowning. 'I mean, yeah. I don't have one.'

Callum drained his beer, threw the bottle into the waste basket. He seemed to have had a sudden burst of energy. 'Just as well,' he said. 'I probably shouldn't drive.' Kieran swallowed, swaying. Callum laughed. 'What's up with you, man? Come on. Bedtime. You can leave that.'

Slowly, Kieran made his way upright. The nausea caught him, swept through his stomach. He steadied himself, but Callum appeared not to have noticed, held open the living-room door.

Kieran followed Callum up the stairs, holding on to the wall while Callum opened the door to the middle bedroom. Probably, it was the weed, but he was suddenly aware of how empty the staff house was; how still. He stepped into the bedroom. It was bare, except for a stack of paper over on the desk by the window and a thick pencil case.

'Is this Annabel's room?'

'It was,' Callum said. 'It's empty now.'

Kieran glanced over at the bed, which was coverless.

'She didn't leave her bedding,' Callum said. He was watching Kieran. 'In case that's what you were hoping.' And then, before he closed the door, he paused. 'Bed's pretty comfortable, though.'

'How would you know?'

Callum's expression was innocent. 'New mattress and everything.'

Kieran waited until the door was firmly shut, until the pipes of the building had stopped running. He didn't know if it was the weed or if it was just Callum being Callum. Annabel had given Kieran her number before she left, and now Callum was talking about the mattress in her bedroom. He opened his phone, scrolled through his WhatsApp. The message he had sent Annabel had delivered; she'd never replied. Kieran was uneasy.

Shadows moved outside the window. He could hear Callum next door, opening cupboards, closing them. Kieran sat down at the desk, shuffled the papers aside. Underneath was a sketchbook. He opened it. He knew it was Rhianne's; he had seen her with it, carrying it under her arm out to the gardens. The effect of the marijuana was slowly wearing off, his vision clearing, and his throat. Next door, Callum had stopped moving, there was silence. The drawings were good. There was a woman Rhianne had drawn over and over. Her expression was bold, like Rhianne's, her face alive with light, movement. These drawings – he could see from the dates – were older, all of them from last year or earlier.

But there was newer work, too. Sketches of the common, the gardens below the hotel, bursts of colour and broad skies. A dog with a wet-looking nose. Bodies, too: hands, hips, thighs, in smudged charcoal. Kieran, making sure that his hands were clean, touched them, one by one. He thought again about the look Callum had thrown at Annabel's now-empty bed. Nausea passed through him, this time nothing to do with what he'd smoked. He turned, carefully, to the back of the sketchbook, to the image that had caught his attention. Charcoal, a woman's body. There was the curve of her waist, the indent of her thigh, shaded. And there, a hand on her throat. Powerful, sinews, tendons, standing out from the skin. Kieran looked at the picture, and he looked at the date. September. He closed the book, quietly sat.

30

They'd met in Peckham, the magnolias closed-cupped against the sky. Blue, but drained already of the day's warmth. 'There's a place,' Jess said. 'Under the arches.' The seating was mostly outdoors, sheltered beneath the cover of a trellis through which thick vines grew, and an iron staircase led up onto a partially covered platform, draped in red and purple fairy lights. Large heaters blasted out dry, synthetic heat.

'I thought it would be good here,' said Jess, 'because we don't have to book.'

Rhianne nodded, vague. She was looking behind Jess, at the big table. A woman sitting right in the middle of the far side, dressed in a black sequinned top, balloons tied to the back of her chair, the man, next to her, leaning close. Jess's voice cut through the noise.

'In case I had to cancel,' she said. 'Honestly, I didn't think you'd come.'

Rhianne took off her jacket. 'Why?'

'Don't know,' Jess said, 'seems like you're too busy these days.'

Rhianne bit the inside of her cheek. Jess did not know, because Rhianne had not told her, that she'd lied before coming here. Home, she'd told Callum. Just for a night. She'd looked in her rear-view mirror for his reflection, disappearing, as she rounded the corner. Exhaled.

'Is this about the room?'

'It's not about the room,' Jess said, 'it was easy to fill the room.'

It wasn't about the room. It was about the missed calls, the unanswered messages. The phone calls, which, when Rhianne actually picked up, were stilted, heavily edited.

'I'm sorry,' she said.

'You didn't even tell me you were together again. I had to find out from Melissa.'

On this, she couldn't argue.

'I'm sorry,' she said again, because she didn't know what else to say, and she was glad, then, when the waiter arrived, bringing their drinks, big plates of mezze, stacks of vine leaves, olives, hummus and pitta. Rhianne pulled the nearest plate towards her and tore a chunk of fresh bread. She handed half to Jess, who took it without looking at her, dunked it in oil. Rhianne watched as she stuffed the bread into her mouth, oil splattering on her blouse.

'Careful.' Rhianne picked up her napkin, held it across the table.

'Yeah. Thanks.' Jess sniffed, dipped the napkin in her water. She rubbed at the stain.

'But you understood, right? About the job? Why I couldn't just—' Rhianne stopped. 'I couldn't come and just dredge all of that up again.'

'I know that,' Jess said, 'I understood that.'

'But—'

'But it also felt like you just didn't want to. Come, I mean.'

'That's not true.' Rhianne was vehement. She knew, Jess knew, that it was only partway true. The napkin had disintegrated where Jess had rubbed it against her shirt, and she brushed the little pieces into her palm. They both knew that choices had been made. 'I did. It just felt too hard. That fucking form.'

Jess nodded. 'I know. The form.'

'You helped me with the form.'

Another chunk of bread, which she dunked, this time, more

carefully. 'Obviously,' Jess said. 'I helped you because I want you to be happy. And I'm glad that you're happy. I get it. You met someone. He makes you happy.'

Rhianne took a swig of her beer. Not happiness, not that. But neither, really, its opposite. More some kind of numb in-between state. She was watching over Jess's shoulder. Behind Jess, Birthday Girl was smiling, the man next to her brushing her hair back from her face. Occasionally, she would put a hand on his shoulder. To push him away, or to draw him close, Rhianne couldn't tell. The place was pretty, with its vines and those lights, the smells of grilled meat and incense, but somehow, everything was flat, drained. It was this odd, back-of-awareness feeling she'd been having so much lately, that her senses had been razed. She tried for honesty, or something closer to it.

'He's helped me through some really difficult stuff.'

'Yeah,' Jess said. She sounded unsure. 'That's good.'

'And I've helped him, too. He needs me.' This part, she was sure was true. She couldn't help but hold a hint of pride in her voice, because this – him needing her – this was something that felt good to her. Because, otherwise, she did not know what it was all for. Her location, off. Her car, parked up at the back of the long-stay, in case he went through town and saw it there. 'I know he needs me.'

Jess gave her an odd look. 'Well, yeah. You're great.' She carried on eating. 'Maybe it will be different when I meet him,' she said. 'Obviously, it's a wedding, so everything's heightened. But I think it'll be good.'

'The wedding.' Rhianne nodded. She kept forgetting about the wedding. 'He'll be helping, actually. With the food. But yeah. You will meet him.'

'And, you know, when you do actually move here, he can come and stay.'

Rhianne took a slow sip of beer, looked up again, at the lights.

She couldn't explain it. She didn't know how she knew, but she would never bring Callum here.

Jess was still speaking. 'I mean, what about job applications? How's that going?'

Rhianne put down the bottle. 'They want me to go with them to Bristol.'

Jess frowned. 'They?'

'Callum, Brendan. The owner. They're opening a place, and Callum is running it.' That pride, again, in her voice. 'They want me to help. I haven't decided yet, but. There's a creative scene there. And it would be something new.'

She tried not to look too much at Jess as she spoke. She looked, instead, at Birthday Girl, who was standing now, at the end of the table. Her cake had arrived, and as she straightened, clapped, Rhianne saw that there was a large sunflower tattoo on her thigh, a glittering metal bar stuck through her belly button. She leaned towards the cake, her face illuminated by the bright circle of candles, the restaurant filled with the sound of singing, the woman's name, *something something*, lost beneath the noise, hands all over her, touching her, holding her. Rhianne looked back at Jess. 'Maybe I would actually be good at it.'

'Bristol,' Jess said.

'I might like it,' she said. 'Being somewhere new.'

The blinds in the room Jess had set up for her were thick, blackout, and Rhianne had fallen deeply asleep, had not woken until it was after ten. She stirred naturally, her body full of rest, her pyjamas clean against her skin. Missed calls. She left the phone on the bed, came barefoot down the stairs. She stood in the doorway to the living room. Jess sat on the sofa. Above her, the Bowling print, colours bleeding. Orange, red. 'It's so bright,' Rhianne said.

Jess closed her laptop, pulled her feet up under her. 'I love it,' she said quietly.

She seemed, at least, less upset than she had been in the restaurant. Guiltily, Rhianne perched on the edge of the sofa.

'I miss you,' she said.

Jess was cool, steady, watching her. 'I know,' she said. 'I miss you too.'

'I have this feeling, lately. That I can't do anything right.'

'Like what?'

'Everything.' She felt suddenly cornered, childish. 'It's like, I just lost my confidence. And it's like,' she steadied herself, 'I'm always upsetting people. Melissa, my dad.' She paused. 'Callum.'

'But you know that's his fault.'

Rhianne sat very still.

'Alexander. He built you up,' said Jess, 'and then he destroyed your confidence. That's why his students kept failing. That's why he got fired.'

Rhianne slid down onto the sofa next to Jess.

'He built me up,' she said, the words spilling out of her, 'because he wanted to fuck me. Not because I was any good.'

'No.' Jess was firm. 'He built you up because he could see that you were talented and hardworking and he wanted that to belong to him.'

Rhianne shook her head. 'I wasn't good.'

'What? Bullshit. You're so good.'

'I'm not,' Rhianne said. She'd never said it out loud. 'I was never good.'

Jess put down her coffee, pulled Rhianne in towards her.

'Who's been telling you you're no good? I'll kill them.'

Rhianne buried her face in Jess's lap. 'Nobody.'

Jess pushed her hair back from her face.

'It must be someone. Tell me. I'm coming for them.'

'Me,' Rhianne said. Her voice was muffled. 'It's me who's been telling me.'

Jess was disappointed. 'Well, I'm not going to kill you.'

Slowly Rhianne turned, so that she was looking up at the print on the wall. In it, behind the burst of orange, she could just make out the outlines of buildings, faces. Upturned, hope filled. She spoke quietly. 'I've been trying. Drawing again, I mean.' She thought of the room. The false starts, torn-up pages. But also, one or two that she had liked. One or two that might actually have been something. 'Callum says I don't believe in myself enough.'

Jess rested her palm on Rhianne's forehead.

'I think he might be right about that.'

Numbly, Rhianne nodded. The painting blurred. Now, she was thinking of Callum. The map of his body. His happiness. Betrayal. She missed him. Jess shifted out from under her, knelt down in front of the cupboard under the record player, rifling through a stack of old papers. Rhianne moved herself upright.

'I know you think it's too late.' Jess handed to her two pieces of paper, folded.

'What is this?' Rhianne opened the paper. She recognised it. The university's lettering, there at the top. The boxes, all of them filled. 'Why did you print it out?'

'I thought we should have a copy,' Jess said.

Rhianne stared at the page. The story of the last year and a half of her life contained in five short lines. She read it once, twice, mouthing the words. Images flashed in front of her. She folded the paper back over. Jess was watching her.

'I don't think it's too late. In case you wanted to try again.'

'It was the bottom of Caledonian Road,' she said, 'not Holloway.'

'OK,' said Jess. She took back the paper, pulled out a pen. Drew a line. 'The bottom of Caledonian Road.'

Rhianne chewed her lip, watching. 'I have looked at it,' she said. 'Once or twice. The MA, again.'

'Yeah?'

'Just to remind myself.'

Jess nodded. She folded the paper. 'So then,' she said, 'you should keep this.'

She took the overground to Liverpool Street, across the city to Paddington. In the station, she stood, holding her overnight bag in both arms. The domed, glass roof arched away, out of sight. She picked her way down the train until she found a carriage, empty except for a few laptops, suits, big coats. She sat down at the window seat. Although she had slept, she was still tired, the kind of tired that emerged only once acknowledged. They rushed through tunnels into the dark. She rested her face against the cold glass, falling towards sleep, until there was a jolt: the sudden sounds of a train coming towards them, rocking them back on adjacent tracks. On her phone were messages from Callum, asking how her night had been, how her parents were. *Good*, she told him. A thrill there, beneath the lie. A piece of herself, held back. *It was good. We got an early night.*

For a moment, she allowed herself to consider how it would be – to end it. To leave. Painful, yes, but the engine thrumming beneath her. That open road, a sky expanding. Nowhere to be. But then, also, nowhere to be.

She put her phone away. Jess had said goodbye, told her she'd see her soon, at the wedding. Rhianne opened her bag. She hadn't brought much. A small notebook, a pencil case. She unzipped the case, turned to the next fresh page. With the brightest colours, she started to draw. She was only half-present in her mind, her hand moving as though it belonged to somebody else, and she drew a sun, its rays bleeding out into the sky that surrounded it. She didn't know where they were, or what time it was. The train plunged into a tunnel. Outside, darkness. She held up the page. Felt its heat, its radiance.

31

Melissa, in the overheated changing rooms of Cabot Circus Zara, stood in front of the mirror and faced, head-on, the disparity between the image she had seen on the advertisement behind the counter – the ten-foot-high woman with green eyes and the jacket's deep, cream neckline revealing bare olive skin – and what she now saw reflected back at her. Here, precisely, was the reason Melissa had been nervous about all of this. She was a person who knew rationally that it was absurd to expect people to be young, in good health and thin at the moment they walked down the aisle. It should have been easy to reject such clichés, given that they were both whole people, him married before and a father, both of them already old and a little fat. And yet, here she was, measuring herself against expectations that were not only unreasonable but also irrelevant.

She had not thought she would look like the big model woman, but nor had she anticipated the reflection she now encountered. Beneath the bare, strip lighting, the flesh of her thighs strained against the fabric, the inner seams aching. The trousers, which were supposedly a wide-leg fit, were tight not only around her thighs, but also, somehow, her knees and the bulk of her calves. Melissa had not thought it would be possible to have knees that were too broad, but now, looking at her reflection, she could see that there was a problem with her bones. No, the trousers were too tight, or the legs were too large, except at the ankles where the material fanned dramatically out around her feet, and the waist, where it sagged.

The jacket was all wrong, too, its shoulders padded, pinching at the waist and flaring out so that she looked like some kind of television magician. Melissa had stripped the clothes from her body, and was angrily re-dressing when the shop assistant asked, from out in the waiting area, how the fit was.

'Terrible,' said Melissa through the changing-room door. 'I have to leave.'

'I think maybe,' the assistant said, 'with that cut you want to be a bit taller.'

'Too short,' Melissa said. 'I'm too short for a suit.' She paused, holding on to the suit, which the assistant reached for. 'I'll take it.'

She had one more shop to visit before leaving, Superdrug, two doors down from Zara, Rhianne's favourite shop when she was younger. Rhianne didn't know that Melissa knew all about how she and Jess used to come in and peel the barcode labels from mascara wands, put them up their sleeves. 'It's not for me,' Melissa said to the assistant, handing her a box of neon eyeshadow, blues and greens and purples. It was expensive, but she knew it was good because she'd already looked it up online, checked the brand and the price, the reviews underneath to make sure it was one that Rhianne would like. 'For my daughter.'

In the car, she fiddled with the radio. Pulled up off the motorway, onto the lanes. She missed Rhianne. It had been almost three months since they had properly spoken. At first, Melissa had been waiting for her to call. That was the way it had always been, when Rhianne had gone to university, moved to London, the first time she'd gone on holiday without them. It would always be Melissa she came to for guidance, reassurance. Of course, there had been that argument, those sharp words of Rhianne's. And Melissa had been wounded, prideful. Petty, she knew, to be upset that it was

Dominic that Rhianne had gone to about the floodwater and the mould. After all, Melissa knew very little about floodwater. But it would not have been so hard, for Rhianne to find an excuse to call. Melissa had been able only to conclude that she had not called because she hadn't wanted to, and it was only lately that Melissa had really begun to consider that there was some other reason that Rhianne had grown so remote.

She pulled up outside the staff house, wrenched the handbrake. She checked her phone. A message from Dominic. She had not told him that she was planning to come here, and she knew he wouldn't like it. Meddling where she wasn't meant to be meddling. She got out of the car, crossed the gravel, holding the plastic sales bag and the box inside it in both hands. She hadn't been in the staff house before, and it had a fusty smell to it, the rattan carpet ragged and dirty as she went on into the living room. The television was on, screen flickering and volume low, and the coffee table was dirty and covered in tobacco. In the window there was a single orchid, dead-looking but not quite dead, and the pot-wash was napping on the sofa. She recognised him: in Rhianne's absence, finding her way to the hotel's socials, she'd zoomed in close on all the staff pictures. She coughed, and he stirred, sitting up, shocked and alert.

She announced herself. 'I'm not a guest. I'm here to see some-one. Rhianne.'

A guilty, shuffling looking about him, and acne. 'Rhianne,' he said, 'she's working.'

'I don't mind that you're sleeping, by the way,' Melissa said. 'You don't need to look so guilty. I just came to deliver some-thing.' She hugged the Superdrug bag closer to her chest. She didn't know how to say that she didn't want to leave her gift with Kieran. She hadn't imagined that the staff house would be like this: so bland, oxygen-less. She didn't know how to say that she wanted to hand the make-up over herself.

'I think she's on a straight,' Kieran said. 'But you can leave it.'

Melissa looked towards the door at the far end of the room. Kieran, observing the pointedness of her glance, stood. She followed him through the fire door and up the darkened stairway. The door at the top of the stairs swung shut, and Melissa's stomach knotted. Kieran walked past the first door on the left, paused in front of the second. He turned, hesitated. Then, he opened the door.

Melissa stepped inside, stopped. Her breath caught. The curtains were drawn back, and it was sunny. The cupboards were open and empty, and there were no covers on the bed, but there was a bedsheet, large and paint-splattered, spread across the floor. On it were palettes, brushes, pencils. And, on the walls, paintings; drawings: iterations of the same but different image – bright, bold – torn from sketchpads and notebooks. The paintings started in the top left corner of the room and ran all the way across. Carefully placed, neatly lined, so that the colour filled almost the whole of that far wall and came all the way around to the door, growing in brightness, density, so that the entire room felt, to Melissa, to be vibrating.

Rhianne had been drawing the sun. Some of the top-left iterations were faint, yellow, pencil-drawn. They were simple, childlike. Less technical than the paintings and drawings Melissa had seen in her sketchbook, which were complex, layered with texture. But brighter, somehow better. Melisa sat, stared. This was not skill, or technical ability, none of which mattered to Melissa. This was vibrancy, volume, persistence, each of these suns seeming to grow brighter, so that the more Melissa stared, the more she felt the heat of those colours – reds, yellows, oranges, and more oranges – small fires, before her.

'You can leave it here,' Kieran said. She had forgotten that he was there, but he was watching her with a nervous, twitchy look. 'She'll find it.'

'What do you think of this?' Melissa said, turning. 'You like them?'

194

Kieran nodded. 'I like them.' He was looking up at the wall. 'She'll run out of space, if she keeps going.'

Melissa's gaze slid to the far wall, towards the next room. 'What does he think?'

Kieran chose carefully. 'I think,' he said, 'he doesn't know it's here.'

Melissa looked back up at the wall, down at the pencils, brushes. Palettes laid out on the floor. They were old, and she could see that the paint-wells were crusted, some of them very nearly used up. 'And paint,' she said. 'She'll run out of paint.'

In the kitchen, Dominic paced. He ate half a loaf of bread and went up into his office to make the call, closed the door. Melissa waited downstairs, patient. She pushed her fingers into Ludo's fur. 'Tired,' Dominic said, when at last he emerged. 'Busy and tired.' He sat; the armchair heaved beneath him. 'Depressed, actually,' he said. Clouds gathered across his face. 'Gets that from her daddy. My great gift.' Melissa leaned forwards.

'Depressed,' she said. Of course she was depressed. 'What else did she say?'

'She didn't,' Dominic said. He held her gaze, firm. 'It was Callum I spoke to.'

'Callum?'

'Her phone was off. So I called Callum.'

'Off?'

'I know you don't like him. But he cares about her.'

'Right.' Melissa stood up, swiped the car keys from the side.

'Where are you going?'

'Back,' Melissa said. 'I'm going back to speak to Rhianne. To find out why she's stopped calling and why she's found it necessary to fashion herself a padded cell.'

'Sounds like she's made herself a studio,' Dominic said. 'If she's painting again.' Now it was Dominic whose eyes were shining, 'It's good, Melissa. She hasn't painted in so long. I know she's been struggling.' His voice pleading. 'But all of this. Believe me, it's so much harder when you're alone.'

'There are worse things than being alone.'

'He loves her. I could see it, Melissa. I know he loves her.'

'You don't know anything,' said Melissa; 'you don't know anything about men.'

Dominic sat back down. 'I am *men*,' he said. 'Of course I know about men.'

'That's exactly why you don't know.' Melissa was putting the keys into her pocket, stuffing Ludo's lead into her pocket, because suddenly, she didn't want to leave him here.

Dominic folded his arms. 'I know she didn't tell us everything,' he said. He hesitated, then spoke. 'About Alexander. The mohair-wearing prick-professor.'

Melissa was thrown. 'Alexander?' she said.

'I wasn't going to tell you. But. There was something that happened. In the taxi.'

'What taxi?'

'The taxi,' Dominic said, 'there was a taxi she didn't tell us about.'

Melissa fell silent.

'She told Callum. He knows about it. That's why she's been so withdrawn. She's been going over it all, and he's helping her. And he must be doing something right, if she's doing her art again. Please.' And it was only because he looked so tired, so worn out, so weak, that Melissa hesitated. That she swallowed all her instincts, put down the keys. 'She was so unhappy here, when she came back. I couldn't bear it. Let me fix what I can fix. Let her stay.'

'Fix what?' Melissa said. 'Fix how?'

Dominic lowered his head. He looked so small, there in that big chair.

'I know it's too late. I just need to make it right.'

32

The decision about the flowers had come to her the day before the wedding. Early, Melissa had opened the kitchen doors, crossed the garden and stood there, surveying the bed at the very back, just below the hedge that separated the garden from the rest of the common. The light was best up here, and the rain they'd had earlier that year had been good for growth. It had been perfectly planned, the brassicas large and green, the spring roses in full bud so if she cut them now, they'd bloom tomorrow. This was precisely how she'd wanted it. But she'd thought about it all night, listening to the sound of Dominic's deepening breath. She'd thought about it, sitting up alone in the kitchen, listening to the washing machine turn. She thought about it now, crossing the garden in the morning light. She thought about it because the other thing, that was too difficult to think about.

He'd been away, and now he was back. Work, he'd said, down in Bristol. But he'd come back last night, and he was looking funny, walking funny. Swelling on his knuckles – some fucker, he said, dropped a big fuck-off plank – and that old pain in his right shoulder, the one that shot down his back and caused him to walk with his weight to one side, a shuffle down his right leg. Nerve pain, Dominic said, pinching the meaty pad of muscle that lay on top of his shoulder. She'd missed him. And last night, she'd moved towards him in the dark. Found, momentarily, what she had been looking for. The grip of him. That old urgency. Heat, all of it indicative of desire. She had kissed him, put her hands on his; felt the heat of his bruised and swollen knuckles. But then, when she reached for him, he was soft. She held him, persisted. Endured, even, the humiliation for them both of her climbing down under the covers, of putting him in her mouth, the panic of unresponsiveness that settled in among a shuffling of sheets. The sound, repugnant, of spit. Dominic put both his hands on her shoulders, heaved her up.

'Don't,' he'd said.

'What's wrong?'

'Nothing's wrong,' Dominic had told her, squeezing. 'I told you. It's better.'

'Dominic,' she said into the dark.

But there was the sound, only, of his breath deepening. She asked him again what was wrong, and again he didn't answer. He had fallen asleep, curled up on his side like a little boy, leaving Melissa there in the dark. She lay and looked up at the pattern of light across the ceiling. The usual thoughts, as irritating as they were predictable: infidelity, secrecy. It couldn't be that. But there was definitely something.

She knew there was something because she knew so well his voice, his body, and she could hear, feel, sense, that something in him was altered. Melissa rolled over, reached for her phone. Closing her less-good eye, she logged out of her own email, and into Dominic's. She knew what she was looking for. Train tickets, and they didn't take long to find. A bright little survey, asking Dominic to rate his trip. Not to Bristol, like he'd said, but to London. There it was. The pointless lie of a man who wants to be caught. He'd said that he would fix it.

Now she was fully awake. Melissa got out of bed, went downstairs to the kitchen. There, she turned on the light, opened the washing machine, into which Dominic had emptied his suitcase earlier that afternoon. It was closed, but not yet set, and one by one she extracted its contents. The clothes, they smelt of him. Detergent, sweat, cologne. He'd been wearing a suit when he returned, but the rest of these clothes, they were working clothes. Soft cloth, torn jeans, oversized T-shirts. She inspected them, one by one, feeling that she was mad but feeling certain, too, that this was something she needed to do. A T-shirt, white or off-white, the logo of a roofing company across the chest. And there, on the hem, across the belly, an ugly spatter of dried blood.

Melissa looked up, now, at the bedroom window. The curtains still closed. She had sat in the kitchen until dawn. She had set the washing machine, listened to its sound. The house quiet. Rhianne was coming today: had agreed to come, after Melissa had messaged, called, then messaged again. Melissa had so wanted to be well rested for her arrival, but instead she was brittle, fatigued. She had known that if she went back up to her and Dominic's bedroom, it would be dark, and there would be the smell of sleep, of breathing. Now, there was movement at the window, the curtains drawn, the glint of Dominic's wristwatch. For Melissa, that certain clarity that a night without sleep could inspire. She went in to find him in the kitchen.

'I've decided,' she said, 'we won't bother with the flowers.'

Dominic was standing by the kettle, waiting for it to boil.

'What do you mean? What flowers?'

'For tomorrow,' Melissa said. She ran the tap, soaped up her hands. 'I don't think we need the flowers.'

The kettle clicked. 'The flowers,' Dominic said. 'For the wedding?'

'I like them up there,' Melissa said. 'Up in the garden. They'll be in bloom right through to the summer.' The reasoning was clear. She had gone up there with her shears to consider how it would be to cut them at their stems, and, she decided, it would be a waste. So much effort, and such fortune with the weather, to cut them now, leave the garden bare. 'It just seems like such a waste,' she said now. Melissa dried her hands. 'Just for the sake of a party.'

Dominic wasn't saying anything; he was standing with his back to the worktop, both his hands gripping its rim. The worktop they'd built themselves, which Dominic had tiled – and the floor, too, shuffling in kneepads across the kitchen for twelve hours straight – all those years ago. Then, his strength, his persistence, had built things for them.

'I guess we won't bother with food, then, either,' he said. 'Given that it'll all just get shat out at the end.'

She had been ready for this: the irony of his tone, its bitterness.

'We need to feed people.'

'I know we need to feed people.'

'So we'll need food; don't be ridiculous.'

'So, no flowers, you think. Not necessary. Bit of a waste, really, just for the day.'

Melissa was holding tight to the shears because right now, she did not want to reach out and touch Dominic. In that moment, she felt repulsed. She saw his eyes were shining. He was upset, of all the things to be upset about, about the flowers.

'Right,' Dominic said. He collected his keys up off the side. 'Well. I need to go, anyway. Do the tables. And the little pyramid thingies.'

'I know,' Melissa said, as Dominic turned to go. 'You've done something to that man.'

He paused, then, and he nodded.

'What will happen to him?'

'He'll be fine,' Dominic said.

'And what about you?'

Dominic shook his head, said nothing.

'Dominic.'

'You know she liked him,' he said. 'You know she, she—' He started to speak, and then stopped. Tried again, his voice almost a whisper. 'He made her have feelings for him.'

'Feelings?' Melissa said. She could have smacked him with the flat edge of her shears, but she wouldn't, didn't. 'Feelings, Dominic? Just what is so terrible about having feelings? All of us having feelings, except, apparently for you, who has fists and a thick fucking skull for hitting with.'

Dominic only blinked, stood straighter.

'I'll be fine, too,' he said. 'Thank you for asking. I'll be better than fine. So long as you're there tomorrow, I'll be fine.'

Melissa waited until she heard the door close before she went up to the garden. She knelt before the beds she'd spent the last year tending. She'd forgotten about the little boxes. He'd ordered them, ninety in total: little cardboard boxes which would be filled with truffles that Dominic had asked Callum to organise, three for each guest. She'd thought it was a stupid idea at the time, one, typically, he'd failed to think through: a great stack of flat-packed pyramid nets with edges that needed scoring and triangles to be folded over, which had sat for the last two weeks on the kitchen table unassembled. She imagined him now, crouching there on the floor, his big fingers. It would be bad for his back, which was worse than ever these days, and suddenly Melissa's heart hurt. She hated it, the thought of Dominic in pain.

But always, he'd kept it inside him. Lodged there, turned inwards, it had been possible to pretend that it did not exist. Whatever it was that lay beyond that surface contentment, it had remained hidden. But now, she could not unsee it. Something pernicious and all too familiar. Cold and hard. All those years ago, she had sunk into him. And what a relief it had been, after all that time, to let go of fear. But here it was again. Here it had always been, because it always had to be, in potential, even if not realised. There, in the dark, existing in the little turns between his breath: violence, and its possibility.

Melissa hated it. Not because of the fact of harm – she didn't care about that man, the professor or tutor or whatever he was, she didn't care about his wellbeing, he could be flattened by a freight train for all she cared – but because it was Dominic, her Dominic, moving bluntly through the world. Bending it to his will. It was stupid and it was useless and she had thought – for all this time she had thought, and she'd been so glad about it, so smug about it – that he was above it. He had been so solid, and she had been so sure of him. She had thought, all this time, that he was better than other men.

Melissa cut roughly, uncaring. If he insisted on the flowers, then they would have the flowers. She'd cut the shrubs bare, and the garden would be empty, if that's what he wanted. She worked her way through the thick, thorned bush. She had been so looking forward to having them for the party, but now she hated the idea of the party, because if what they were really celebrating was the misery Dominic had added to an already miserable little life, then Melissa did not much want to partake. She thought of Dominic, how big he must have felt, and she was ashamed. This was not the man she knew, a man who needed to cause pain, to know that he had power.

When she was finished with the roses, she spread them out onto the tarpaulin. She checked the time, and her phone. No messages, and this made her nervous. Rhianne should have been here by now. Melissa was wearing her thick hide gloves but still she'd cut her upper arms, scratches that bled tiny red beads, and she was starting to gather up the detritus, when, at last, she heard the car. It pulled up fast, spraying gravel as it came up the lane, parking in the empty spot out front. Sitting there, with the engine idling. The slam of a car door. Melissa exhaled. But then, behind it, a second door, echoing across the valley. Melissa stood. She crossed the garden, the roses abandoned.

She saw them from the top of the steps. They did not see her. If they had looked – and they were not looking – the reflection of the glass would have prevented it. They were there in the kitchen. Him, as well as her. She'd seen neither of them since that day at the end of the year, and he was standing, now, with his back to Melissa, his arms folded, in front of Rhianne.

They were having a conversation. She couldn't hear what either of them was saying, but she saw how Rhianne reached out her hand, and she saw, too, the way Callum shrugged the hand from his shoulder, stepped back.

It wasn't so much the shrug, but how Rhianne was primed for it, straight away recoiling. Melissa stood still, just for a moment, and then, knowing what she had always known, knowing that she needed to see no more, took the steps two at a time, pulled open the door. The pop of it against the runners. Compressed air, bursting out.

Both of them turned, looked at her.

Melissa did not consider how she must have appeared. Thick, hide gloves up to her elbows, her upper arms – muscular, these days, from all the work she did out in the garden – mapped with little cuts from the thorns, and the shears, held tightly in her right hand.

Callum was the first to assemble himself, and he did so quickly, easily: his face, cracking open. 'We made it.'

'Hello, Callum,' Melissa said. 'What a long time it's been.' She looked at him, and then she looked at Rhianne, took her in. She looked different from the last time Melissa had seen her. The wide expression, open, but the light of it somehow drained. Melissa resisted the urge to step forwards, take a hold of her. Instead, steadying herself, she sat. Her hands still on the shears. She was aware, holding tight, that there was strength roped across her shoulders that was inappropriate for her age, her sex. 'Rhianne,' she said, 'I need you to help me with the flowers.'

'We've got time.' Callum checked his phone. 'I just need to be back for the prep.'

Slowly, Melissa shifted the shears, turned them towards Callum.

'I think,' she said, 'you should go.'

Callum looked back at her. He turned to Rhianne, but she wasn't looking at him.

'Dominic says he needs you,' said Melissa, her smile forced. 'Something to do with the menu.'

The departure was slow, measured. He washed his hands before he left. Took his time about it. Ran the water until it was warm enough and then soaped and lathered and rinsed and dried. Before he left and went out into the corridor, he put his hand on Rhianne's face. Tenderly, he kissed her. And then, he walked out. Melissa could see through the crack in the door that he was checking his pockets – keys, phone, wallet. The door opened, and it stayed open for a while. A minute, maybe more, before it closed.

33

She knew what to do, because she had been here before. Not to force it. Not to rush to judgement. Not too much pressure, because who knew how much of that she was already under. Melissa stood. She had been right. Rhianne had lost her colour. The bleach-blonde strips had grown out, the new roots were dried out, wiry, and there were circles hollowing beneath her eyes. Melissa resisted the urge to touch her, knowing that even tenderness, in this moment, might feel to Rhianne like violence. Instead, she picked up her shears, slotted them into the pocket of her gardening apron. 'I could use some help.'

Rhianne followed her up to the garden. Melissa directed her, clearly, not too soft, to collect the wheelbarrow. Together, they began to shovel the cuttings into it. Load by load, Melissa waited while Rhianne pushed the barrow over to the compost. Melissa could see that it was an effort for her. Only now that she was paying attention – later, she would find a way to forgive herself for this: the fact that she had not been paying enough attention – could she see that Rhianne had lost weight, that she was clumsy, her coordination off. But this was important. She ought to do things like tip a wheelbarrow, and she ought to do them now. Melissa knew that if she could not do a thing like tip a wheelbarrow, then nor would she be capable of leaving a man she thought she loved.

They scooped the flowers into two large tarpaulins. 'You'll find a box of vases,' Melissa said, 'in the shed. You collect it. I'll go and get the big buckets.'

Rhianne got to her feet, hesitated.

'Go on,' Melissa said. 'Big box of vases and a second set of shears. You'll know it when you see it.'

Melissa, as they worked, was acutely aware of Rhianne's movements. Her breath was sharp and her hands unsteady. She cut under Melissa's direction, snapdragons, tall and quivering. Greenery, to give texture, bulk, eucalyptus and myrtle, but not too much. Melissa tore dead petals from the outer edges of her pink camellias. 'Colours,' Melissa said. 'None of this green and white virginal bullshit,' she said, threading a tulip, fire-coloured, its petals crinkled like crepe paper, into her bunch. 'Lord knows I'm too old for that.'

Rhianne smiled, only halfway. Any kind of a smile: that was good.

'How is Callum?' Melissa said. She had been sure to speak while Rhianne was busy with her hands, so that she would have an excuse not to look up. Rhianne nodded.

'He's good,' Rhianne said. 'Stressed.'

'Stressed?' Melissa nodded. Precision was important. There had been a rupture between them, and each word, now, another tear, or a stitch. 'Stressed why?'

'Work.' Rhianne hardened. 'The wedding. He wants to get it right for you both.'

Melissa nodded. 'Too much red,' she said. She handed Rhianne a tulip. Rhianne took the flower, inspected the head. She was concentrating. 'He's nice to you,' Melissa said. A statement, not a question.

Rhianne pushed the flower into her vase. 'I know you don't like him.'

'It's not about who I like. It's about you and your happiness.'

206

'I am happy,' Rhianne said. She hesitated. 'Or sometimes I'm not. But that's my stuff. It's me who's causing problems.'

Melissa nodded. Stripping leaves, threading. 'That's what he tells you, is it?'

'He doesn't have to. It's obvious.'

'Not to me, it isn't.'

'We're working through it. And he's helping me.' The rising tone in her voice, the shrillness, all of which Melissa had expected, like trying to prise a bottle of liquor from the hands of an addict. She knew this. The harder you pulled, the tighter they held.

Melissa stood, dusted off her thighs, and she knew that Rhianne was surprised by the movement, the sudden abandonment. 'My legs,' Melissa said, rubbing the insides of her thighs. 'They're getting worse.'

'I can finish,' Rhianne said, and Melissa noted the tone of sulkiness in her voice.

'You know I'm always here,' Melissa said, 'if you want to talk.'

'I know that.'

'Oh, you do know?' Melissa said. 'That's why you got the eyeshadow I bought you and never thanked me for it? Don't reply to my messages except when you feel like it?'

'I meant to message,' Rhianne said. 'I just don't always get round to it.'

Melissa nodded. 'She doesn't always get round to it. Fine.'

Coolly, Rhianne shrugged. 'I've been busy,' she said. 'There's been stuff going on.'

'I'm sure there has.'

'Big stuff,' said Rhianne. 'There's a job.'

Melissa waited for more.

'A new place. In Bristol. Callum's going.'

'And you? Do you want to go?'

Rhianne looked at her then. 'I can't just end it,' she said. The words spilled out, her voice pitching higher. 'It's not that I haven't thought about it. It's just. I don't know who I am without him. Not any more.'

Melissa was quiet, clear. 'Then remember.'

Rhianne stared up at her, startled. She was holding the shears, still, in one hand, a bright bouquet in the other. Minutely – and this, for now, was enough for Melissa – she nodded. Outside, was the sound of Dominic's car pulling up, Rhianne, starting. Melissa softened, took the shears from Rhianne. 'It's just your dad.'

Rhianne stayed with them, just until dinner. They spent the afternoon finishing the boxes, which Dominic had brought home with him unfinished. He'd been distracted, he said, by a change in the table layout and some alterations to the menu. Something about the fish not being salty enough, something else about adding ham. He was finding it difficult to look at Melissa. Melissa sat at the kitchen table, finishing the rest of the flowers; Rhianne sat across from her, assembling the little boxes, placing them one at a time onto the floor, covered, now, with gold and purple pyramids, the very last of the preparation. Occasionally, the afternoon sun caught one of those golden surfaces, turning.

For a moment, watching Rhianne, Melissa thought that perhaps it had been enough. Rhianne would stay here tonight. The wedding – the party – that could be navigated, they'd disinvite him or relegate him to the kitchen or, quite frankly, and without hesitation, Melissa would have him fired that morning. 'Pizza,' Melissa said, who never ordered pizza and didn't understand it. 'I think we deserve a pizza.' But then Rhianne stood up, surveyed the detritus, the little boxes now finished.

'I can take these tonight,' she said, 'save you the trip in the morning.'

'I made up your room,' said Melissa.

It was true. Two days earlier, knowing – hoping – that Rhianne would come today, she'd wrestled a fitted sheet onto Rhianne's bed, hoovered the floor.

'That's OK,' Rhianne said, 'I've got a bed.'

There was no cruelty. There was, though, pity, and that was a gut-punch. But Melissa kept her composure, let Rhianne have her pride. Callum, Rhianne said, was already on his way. Dominic helped Rhianne pack up the boxes. They all heard the car outside. And then she was gone, and it was Melissa and Dominic alone. They ate pizza in the dining room and the night grew cool. His knuckles were still raw, he had not thought to dress them, and Melissa would not offer. She could feel him, studying her face.

'You decided we'd have the flowers,' he said.

Melissa nodded. 'I did.'

'I'm not sorry,' Dominic said. The hardness in his voice, and the difference it confirmed, she had known it was coming, but still, to hear it, it hurt. To hear the man she loved announce himself, proudly, that he had fallen short. 'And I'd do it again. To protect my family.'

Melissa was tired. She took off her glasses, rubbed her eyes. 'But you haven't.'

'Haven't what?'

'Protected your family.' She could have laughed, knowing what she knew, knowing of his ignorance. But she didn't, because there was the hardness again in his voice, which she was so unused to hearing, and which hurt her, how sure he was that she was wrong and he was right. 'That's not how you protect your family.'

'I disagree,' he said. 'I very obviously disagree.'

'All you've done is lower yourself.'

'No. I did it to protect Rhianne.'

Melissa shook her head. 'You did it to make yourself feel better.' Her eyes started to sting. 'I love you,' she said. 'But you did it to make yourself feel better. If you cared about protecting your family, you would be paying attention.'

'I am paying attention. That's all I'm doing.'

'You know Rhianne's thinking of going to Bristol. Moving. With Callum.'

'I know. And I know that she loves him. She told me. She loves him.'

Melissa shook her head. Fixing her gaze on the glass of water in front of her. She imagined herself speaking, finding the words – twisting them – to make them land. She imagined the table shunting, the door slamming. Dominic's wheels spraying dirt on the corner. And her, sitting here and waiting. Callum deserved it. Bruises, breakages, pain. He deserved it for what he was doing to Rhianne, because Melissa could see how he was eroding her. But she could also see that it was all too blunt. Dominic's tools, all of them were blunt. More than this, they were irrelevant to the task of restoration that awaited. She felt no longer anger, but pity, and the desire, deep-rooted, to protect.

'Melissa,' Dominic said, 'this again. What are you trying to say?'

She looked at him. She reached out, put a hand to his cheek. It was dark now, and she felt that she could see the whole of the night sky in his face. She shook her head.

'Nothing,' she said. 'There's nothing to say.'

34

For Dominic, it was a good day. Standing side by side in The White Hart, in that place whose foundations he himself had once re-laid, he felt that he had earned it, somehow, and he had stood taller than usual, feeling that his feet were familiar with the land far below, the land as it had been before buildings, the foundations he had mapped, reconstructed, made sturdy. There would be both mystery and context: the memory of the ground beneath them, held as soft earth in his hands.

For months he had lain awake at night, thinking about the wedding, and he had imagined Melissa standing beside him in her suit, and he had imagined that she was content: that, at last, he had done enough to make her content. For a time, he had slipped into terrible dreams, but now, he would sleep soundly. That old pain, the one that had been lodged in his chest, he had transformed it. It had worked its way to the surface, and though his knuckles were bruised and raw, the thick pad of muscle on his shoulder tight, sending shooting pains down the inside of his scapula, this pain was no longer the ache of inertia, but spoke instead of strength, sacrifice. His pain had meaning, and it had purpose.

It hadn't been hard to find the address, a quick search of the Companies House register, a scroll through his website to check the location was in date. He'd gone there intending to talk. He'd had whole speeches planned, and threats. Lawyers, he'd told himself. A case that was already half built, one that was career-ruining. But arriving at that flat in Brixton, looking up at the freshly painted portico, the wisteria growing across its front, catching the expensive gleam of that Patek Philippe wristwatch as the door opened, and the expression arranged so quickly into one of concern when he saw who was calling, he knew that there was only one way this was going to go.

'Dominic,' Alexander said, 'is it Rhianne? Has something happened?'

That was it: it was the sound of Rhianne's name in this man's mouth, more than anything. Dominic stepped over the threshold, closing the door behind him. He did not stop to consider whether there was anybody else here: pets, women, children. He took in only the large glass staircase, the corridor leading through to an open white kitchen, marble-topped, vaguely, that the walls were covered in artwork. He only wanted to erase those soft sounds, her sweet name, and, unthinking, he'd swung his fist at Alexander's mouth, and it was when he made contact – the blistering clarity of knuckles on bone – the dull thud of soft flesh colliding, which sent the man staggering back, clutching his jaw and spitting, that Dominic saw this was what he should have done from the start, what he was always meant to have done.

Alexander straightened, his eyes large and bulbous through the thick lenses of his glasses, clutching his jaw with one hand, reaching for his phone with the other.

'I'll call the police,' he said.

Dominic shook his head. 'Don't,' he said, 'trust me. That won't go well for you.'

And Alexander, seeing that there was one clear and fast way through this, barrelled forwards into Dominic, pushing him back against the opposite wall. Dominic let the first blow land, and there was a clarity here, too, a pain he was sure on some level he owed if not to this man, then at least to somebody, before he threw back. Once, twice, into Alexander's jaw, his nose, kept throwing, until Alexander came swinging for him again – strength, but a lack of precision, Dominic could tell he'd never been in a bar fight – and Dominic watched white dots explode across his retina, felt his legs weaken momentarily.

Alexander, following through the weight of his punch, stumbling forwards in the narrow hallway, and Dominic caught him under the armpits, lifted him upright. Dead straight he looked at him, holding him like a large and monstrous toddler, before folding him over, throwing a knee right into his ribs, and then another, and then another, straight to his face, and there was the sound of the soft tissue of the nose giving way beneath his kneecap, and a corresponding pain that shot right down Dominic's shoulder, causing him to release Alexander, while Dominic, opposite, stumbled back, slid down the wall and landed, seated, legs out long, on the floor.

Dominic was breathing heavily, his lungs wheezing. He thought, possibly, he might be sick. Alexander, opposite, appeared to be conscious, though bleeding heavily. Dominic nudged him with his foot, and Alexander heaved himself halfway, spitting blood.

'Enough,' Dominic said slowly. He pushed himself to his feet. 'That's enough.'

His jacket was torn, and Dominic pulled it back over his shoulder, straightened his glasses, miraculously unbroken, and staggered to his feet. Outside, on the pavement, he threw up twice. Vomit, blood.

For the next three days, he lay in a hotel room with an icepack on his knuckles and heat on his shoulders. He waited for a phone call, and when none came, he had the satisfaction of knowing that he had been right to follow his instincts. Self-preservation would always win out. On the fourth day, he took the train home, he unpacked his clothes into the washing machine, and he went up to Rhianne's room. There, he knelt on the floor, and from under the bed, he pulled out the final piece of her project, the one that she had kept hidden since she'd come home from London.

But he had known all this time it was there, because he'd tried to look at it, at least once every two weeks since she'd returned. He'd pulled it out and he'd tried to make himself look at it, except that he couldn't, because to witness her pain and to be powerless to prevent it, it was too much for him to bear. Now, though, kneeling on the floor of his daughter's bedroom, pain shooting down the whole right side of his body, his jaw still gently throbbing and a cut in his tongue where he'd bitten straight through its flesh, he found, at last, that he was ready.

He looked, he kept on looking, and he understood what it was that had been so very difficult to confront. It was the thickness of that paint, where it had been scraped away, repainted, and that spot where the canvas had been torn right through. The fragility of it, and the textures, how alive it felt, how animated with feelings, and none of them straightforward. A nice, smudgy charcoal drawing, that, he would have liked. Or a painting in watercolour. Something flat. He would have liked that. Something flat would have been just like a photograph. But in this painting, whose surface had been chiselled away, torn, re-layered with paint squeezed straight from the tube, whose edges spilled over onto its frame, this painting, for Dominic, seemed to contain such desperation. The way that it had been worked and reworked, it contained so much longing, and he understood that longing too well. It was the longing to reach, grasp, hold that which was no longer reachable. The memory of almond oil on sun-drenched skin. The memory of her disappearing inside her own pain, the memory, too big to carry, of his failure.

And Melissa, she had worn the suit and she'd worn her transition lenses. She'd stood opposite Dominic at the register office, made her vows, sat beside him at the desk and blinked as the camera flashed, drove the Saab with streamers running from its wing mirrors up to The White Hart. Last night she'd let him hold her. His ribcage, she had always said, was large enough for two whole hearts. They'd come early this morning to finish the set-up, boxes filled with vases, and the little cardboard pyramids, which Jess distributed, one on each place setting, Rhianne following with a tray full of truffles, dropping them, one by one, and then pinching the boxes closed.

The speeches had been absurd. Dominic's, twenty-seven minutes, a list of inelaborate thanks, delivered like a roll-call. 'Nice woman,' Dominic said, when he got to Melissa, placing a heavy palm on her shoulder. He looked at her. 'Some of you know her. Her hair looks very nice today.' Melissa didn't know whether to be insulted or to laugh, but the room in its entirety had erupted, and she could see that Jess had put her head on the table, that Rhianne, too, was laughing. She watched how Rhianne buried her head in Callum's shoulder, how he put his arm around her, held her with something that looked so much like love. 'Callum,' Dominic said, 'thank you, Callum; he cooks, he cooks very well.' Jess, on Rhianne's other side, was watching them, her drink untouched. She looked across at Melissa, who, catching Jess's expression, nodded. Shifted, gently, Dominic's hand from where he held her.

She waited until after the dinner was done, until the tables were stripped and pushed to the sides of the room, before she stepped out into the corridor. It was dark now; they had a few more hours. Melissa, though she did not show it, was afraid. She had felt it, since Rhianne had left yesterday, knowing that Rhianne, although she might not have the words for it, understood what Melissa could now see. And this future, mapped out: Bristol, a new beginning, which would be for Rhianne a kind of ending. Melissa sickened. She had seen Brendan, his arms around both of them, Rhianne glowing. She thought of that darkened upstairs room, imagined the curtains drawn against the sun, and next to it, the orange room; Rhianne's.

Melissa followed the path out of the back entrance of the hotel, up the steps, across the car park. She was wearing white, flat-soled trainers, and she was quiet as she crossed the gravel. She unlocked her car, and from the boot she lifted the bag that she had packed there. She let herself back into the staff house, went upstairs, opened the door. She turned on the light, and for a moment, she stood and she surveyed those covered walls. Not one wall, but all four, edging right up to the window-frame, the back of the door, so that there was almost no wall-space left, and those colours had spilled over, now, onto the large stacks of paper on the floor. Melissa did not sit. She had to get back to the party, the sound of which she could hear through the half-opened window, music and voices carrying up from the hotel. She lay the bag on the empty, stripped-down bed, where she knew it would be found.

35

After the wedding, spring came into its fullest. Melissa's tulips had gone over, eclipsed by the drama of peonies – dewy and round-headed, bursting their petals over the ground – and the very beginnings of the dahlias which, in Melissa's garden, were coming up fast, small buds: pale green and bullet-like. Brendan had neglected the garden at The White Hart that year. It was unlike him, but then he'd been distracted; the hotel busy and contracts and building surveys for their Bristol project coming through. The air had grown warm already, the early-summer sunshine burning off the morning dew.

Upstairs in the staff house, Callum switched on the fan. He checked his phone, put it back on his bedside table, lay, looking up at the ceiling. It was late afternoon, and he was uncomfortable. The synthetic duvet sprung back as he pushed it to the end of his bed, pulled his eye-mask over his face. His body was tired, heavy. Fourteen-hour shifts, six days a week, and the physicality of it, too. The spikes of adrenalin that kept him alert to the demands of every service. And now this unwelcome warmth. His body felt old: the habitual tightness in his shoulders and that twinge, always, in the lower part of his neck just behind his right ear, as though the muscles there needed to pop and release. He rolled over.

Two weeks had gone by since the wedding, and even though the day had gone well – Callum back and forth to the kitchen in his suit and all the food coming out just as he'd wanted – he had known that something was not quite right. Rhianne with her moods – lately, so flat. They were making him uneasy, restless. Of course, she had been anxious in the run-up, and her anxiety, the low mood that inevitably followed it, had put a strain on things. But at the end of the night, Dominic had pulled him in for a warm embrace, tight. 'Thank you,' he had said, 'for everything.'

Callum liked Dominic. He was funny, like Rhianne. That same sharp wit. And a steadiness to him, a warmth Callum would have liked if he'd had a father like that. Dominic and Melissa had driven off in the Saab, and later, in his small, dark room, Callum peeled Rhianne's dress from her, and she held him, her arms gripping tightly around his neck as he sank himself into her.

He asked her, after, in the dark. 'Will you be happy now? For me?'

'Is that what you want?'

It wasn't a proper reply. A question for a question.

'You know it's all I want,' he said. 'For you to be happy.'

He was resolved: he would make her happy. Tonight, for example, he'd booked dinner, just the two of them. He'd spent days looking for the right place and he'd read the menu several times over. He had thought about having her sit across from him, her skin all soft and her make-up especially done. And today, in the kitchen, for the first time in what felt like a long time, there had been that old thrill. Despite it all, heat and chemistry, the dial of their energies inching incrementally higher. The sight of those two faded peroxide strips disappearing out the door, the little losses, every time the swing-door banged after her, the reignition of desire every time it reopened. The sight of her body, the knowledge of its freedom, agency, and at the same time the pull: the safety in knowing how her movements would end, always, with her folding in, under, him.

The bedside fan whirred. Agitated, Callum turned.

He was trying, just like he always had. And still, somehow, it was not enough for her.

His phone vibrated on the bedside table. Callum sat up, pulled the eye-mask up around his forehead and read the message from Rhianne asking where they were going for dinner, squinting at the screen with one eye closed. *What's the place called again?*

She didn't know what he knew.

He waited. Ten minutes, maybe more.

Yeah, he wrote. *I don't think tonight's gonna work out.*

The hotel was busy tonight. He worked quickly, calibrated himself to the pressure of a full restaurant, shut out the noise of her discontent, the slowness of her movements. She was making mistakes. Desserts on table six went to table four, a gluten allergy missed so that he had to do starters twice over on ten. He could feel her orbiting, carrying great stacks of plates up past the pass, all of her movements loud, all of it jarring. He looked at her only once, and he saw that her eyes were wide, tearful. He looked away, turned up the heat. He did not want to see her sadness, which was cavernous, ugly. The checks gathered, emptied, the kitchen quietened. Callum cleared down. Rhianne waited for him outside the restaurant.

'What's going on? Are we not going for dinner?'

'I don't think so.'

'You haven't replied to my messages.'

'Later,' he said. He peeled her hand from his arm. 'Not here.'

He took off his whites and got back into his jeans, threw his sweatshirt over his shoulder. On the way, he paused in the office, took the order sheet down from the board. He could remember that first time she had come to him, sat by him, helped him fill in the orders, how tired she had looked, soft. He sat down, took his pen from his whites, scribbled numbers. He looked up at the CCTV screens, flickering. He could see her there in the hallway, leaning in towards the mirror, checking her reflection. She took her lipstick out of her pocket, reapplied it. Callum hardened.

He took the stairs two at a time back up to the staff house. First, to the kitchen. He took a case of beers from the cooler, carried them upstairs. Not to his room, but next door, the spare room, the one he'd let Rhianne use, whose floor was covered in a big, torn bedsheet. He turned on the overhead lights, and then, feeling that this was not an occasion for lights, turned them off again, turned on the desk lamp, the fan. He plugged in the little refrigerator in the corner, filled it with the beers, sat. The can hissed. He drank. He looked up at the drawings. He'd been in here a few times, these last weeks. Waited until she was at work, gone inside to see what Rhianne was doing in here without him. The drawings, paintings, they were bright, childlike. He'd liked that: the purity of it. Big circles, rays. Messy. Nothing here, he thought now, leaning back in his chair, that was out of his grasp, beyond him. Simply, they were colours. He began to feel calm.

An hour passed. There had been a full restaurant tonight. Callum checked his phone. There were no messages from her. The only notifications were the missed calls from earlier that afternoon, the sight of which made the tiredness spike in his bones, the fact that he had been deprived of his afternoon's rest. And then he heard the sound of feet on gravel outside, the fire door on the stairs swinging shut. There was a knock, quiet. 'It's open,' he said. Again, louder, because his voice had come out scratchy and low. 'It's already open.'

She opened the door, came inside. Her face was clean, fresh with make-up. Those bold flicks that made her dark eyes glitter, and her hair just loosed from a day of wearing it high. Only this morning, she'd lain there beside him, her face split into a smile, one that he had put there. The make-up could not conceal the angst, now, on her face. Wings beat in his chest. He steadied them.

She looked nervously around the room, at Callum.

'Are you going to tell me what's going on?'

Still, she was standing there. 'You want a drink?' he said. He nodded across to the corner of the room, where Brendan's minifridge stood. Rhianne followed his gaze. She crossed the room, knelt down in front of the fridge. She was still in her uniform. 'One of these?'

'Help yourself.'

'Do you want another one?'

Callum shook his head.

'You don't?'

Again, his voice was scratchy. 'I'm good.'

Rhianne stood. She was holding a can of beer. With two hands, awkwardly, as though she had forgotten how, she hissed the can, opened it. 'I don't know why you're upset with me.'

He looked at her. And this was painful to him, because even in her dulled state she was bright and full of light that was not for him. 'You don't?'

'I have no idea.'

In the chair, Callum turned. Tugged the folder from the desk. 'You don't know.'

Rhianne opened her mouth, closed it again.

'You weren't going to tell me.'

'I was going to,' she said.

'So now you're lying.'

'I'm not lying.' The beer was limp in her hand. 'I just wasn't ready.'

Callum nodded. He flipped open the folder. Pulled out the three printed pages he had found there. The first, headed and typed. '"The incident,"' he said, quoting. '"Alexander Hadley was my senior tutor in the third year of my undergraduate degree. I agreed to go for drinks with him because—"'

'Stop,' she said. She stepped forwards, reached for the paper. 'Please.'

Callum thrust it into her chest.

'Because what? It's tiring, Rhianne. When are you going to stop with this? Do you have any idea what it's like trying to live with someone who's constantly miserable? All I'm trying to do is make you happy.'

Hurt flashed across her face. She had not moved. 'Maybe I do know.'

'You know, and you inflict this on me anyway? Because why? You want to hurt me?'

'I don't want to hurt you.' She was speaking calmly, and this was unsettling to him. 'I want to move on from what happened. And I need the university to know about it.'

'But why do you need them to know?'

'Because.' Rhianne stepped back, sat down on the bed. She shrugged. 'Maybe one day I'll want to go back. Study.'

There it was: he had been ready for this.

'You want to go back. And you thought that wasn't something I needed to know?'

'It's just a form, Callum. It doesn't have anything to do with you.'

'It has everything to do with me. Because I'm here picking up the pieces.'

'That's what you think you're doing? Charity work?'

'No.' Callum started to pace. She wasn't understanding him. 'Not charity work. That's not what I said. But it affects me. Your mental health.'

It didn't come out how he'd wanted it. It was lashing, petulant. He saw it land. He was watching her expression. Something in her face had shifted. Something was steadier, cooler.

'My mental health,' Rhianne repeated, 'affects you.'

He was in front of the door, now. He turned, stood with his back to it.

'That's what it means. Being in a relationship. We have to do things together. Decide things together. Or did you think it was something else?'

'I didn't say I was going back.'

'You didn't say that, no. But who knows, with you? I'm always in the dark.'

Outside, the security light blinked off. Rhianne's eyes flickered towards the window.

'What were you doing in here, Callum?'

'I live here, don't I?'

Rhianne paused. 'You do live here.'

'I came to see your paintings,' Callum said. He couldn't keep the hurt from his voice, and he hated it, how childish he sounded. 'I wanted to see what you were doing. Getting up early every morning. Wanting to be away from me.'

'I don't want to be away from you.' Rhianne paused. Her voice sounded odd to him. Sicklier, sweeter. She held up the piece of paper, the form Callum had found. 'Me writing this. I had to do it. Just for me. It doesn't mean I'm going anywhere.'

He watched from the door, the way she was leaning on one arm, her head tilted. He did not know if anything was real. It was painful for him to look at her. She kept on talking.

'Bristol, the new place. Us. You know that's what I want.'

Callum leaned back against the door. He had finished his beer; the liquid was cold, now, in his chest, his belly. His wrist was loose, his fingertips gripping the can only lightly. On the floor, in the corner where Rhianne's sheet had been lifted away, there was a perfect knot in the wood. Perfectly round, crossing between two planks, a darker, shinier shade of pine. He fixed his gaze on that knot, and he blurred his eyes, so that he could see nothing else, except for that knot in its blurry, outline form, so that he could see, only peripherally, Rhianne, standing up from the bed.

'Where are you going?' His voice was flat.

'Nowhere,' she said. He felt it, her hesitation. The knot, under the force of Callum's unfocused gaze, became blurrier, lost in the mass of its surroundings. She stepped towards him, reached for his hand. He snatched it up out of her grip.

'Don't,' he said. She faltered.

He would not look at her, and she knew that he would not look at her, because she didn't touch him again. She stepped back, and she dropped down. To the floor, to her knees.

'Callum,' she said, 'you know I'm sorry.'

'Sorry for what?'

'I'm sorry,' Rhianne said. She didn't get up. She stayed on her knees. 'I'm sorry I didn't talk to you about it. I just didn't want to burden you. I know how hard it is for you, hearing me talk about that stuff. But I feel like you think this is about me trying to leave. And it isn't that at all.' He let the words wash under him, they sounded good. 'I'm drawing a line under it so that I can move on. So that we can be together and I'll be better.'

Now he looked down at her. Studied her face, drank her in.

'Why is nothing ever enough for you?'

'It is,' she said. 'You are.' She looked up at the walls, her eyes shining. 'Look at this,' she said. 'I'm doing this, aren't I? I'm here.' Slowly, he nodded. 'I wouldn't have done any of this without you,' she said. 'I don't know who I am without you.' He softened. He could not help it with her. Always, he would soften. He held out his hand; she took it. 'You've helped me so much,' she said. 'I know I can be difficult sometimes. And I'm sorry. It's just that I've been through some things.'

He nodded. 'It's OK. I understand.'

'Callum,' she said. His name. So sweet, to him, the sound of it in her mouth. 'I know you don't want to,' she said. 'But please, let's go for dinner.'

He took his phone out of his pocket. Nine o'clock. They could still just make dinner.

Still, he could sit across from her, bathed in her light.

He pulled her to her feet.

'To celebrate.' She smiled up at him. Pliant, open. 'New beginnings.'

36

Before the surgery and prior to the anaesthetic, Melissa had to fast for eighteen hours. An insult to add to the forthcoming injury. Only a week since the wedding she was already being wheeled into surgery. At breakfast, she sat across from Dominic, who sat with wide elbows spooning cereal into his mouth, spreading sugared crumbs across the table. 'Not even water,' she said. He told her, chewing, that she would be absolutely fine.

'I know that,' Melissa said.

Dominic drove her. He'd taken the day off work. Melissa had never had general anaesthetic before, and she tended, best she could, to avoid hospital, because hospital took her back to a place she didn't want to go. This was, at least, a private procedure, which meant that she was spared the chaos of a regular inpatient clinic.

'Nervous?' Dominic had said.

'A television,' Melissa said, 'is this what the four thousand pays for?'

'And a chocolate mousse,' Dominic said, picking up the laminate card on which the post-operative menu was printed. 'The chocolate mousse is quite good, actually.' He flipped over the card like they were in a reputable restaurant and not a hospital room. They had come here after the second baby. Melissa's stomach rumbled.

'A television,' she repeated, correcting herself, 'and a chocolate mousse.' But then, because she couldn't help herself. 'I would have preferred the lemon thingy,' she said.

The procedure went well, except for the stitches, which had torn on her inner thigh, bleeding into the dressing. When she'd come round in post-op, where the bed had been rolled, she'd woken up sobbing, she didn't know why. She knew that could happen sometimes, sometimes people got good dreams, sometimes bad, sometimes nothing at all. She hadn't dreamed, but maybe that was why she was so sad when she woke up to faces in blue masks, talking about how her heart rate had dropped, which had frightened her, and she hadn't realised that the sound of whimpering was coming from her own throat until the nurse leaned over her and said everything went well, Mrs Colvin, the surgeon's happy. Melissa, wide-eyed, had turned her face up to the nurse, and she had asked where Dominic was, because she felt suddenly sure that he was dead, but then the nurse arranged her bedclothes and told her that Dominic was coming later this afternoon, and Melissa stopped crying, and she heaved in a breath, and she blinked up at the light overhead.

'Who's Mrs Colvin?' she said.

There was a damp patch on the back of her leg. She thought she'd wet herself, but when she put her hand to the back of her thigh, which was bandaged up tight and dressed in those big beige stockings the doctor had warned her she'd wake up wearing, and that paper underwear that hardly covered her, it didn't come back smelling of urine but of copper, and when she held her fingers up to her face, they were red. She whimpered again. Blood, the memory of loss, so deeply buried. You're all right there, Mrs Colvin, said the nurse, and it wasn't a question, but Melissa held out her hand unspeaking, and the nurse explained that it was nothing to worry about, that there was a bit of bleeding under the dressing. They didn't keep her in overnight, sent her home in the afternoon, gave her a leaflet about how long she had to keep the stockings on and a cellophane pack of blue gauze, which the nurse told her to push down the stocking if the bleeding started up again. When Dominic came, that afternoon, she put her arms around his neck, and for the second time that day, she began to cry; this time, whole, body-wracking sobs, shuddering through her chest, her arms, where she clung to him. He peeled her from him, smiling, confused.

'But you're OK,' he said.

He pushed her hair – that wild, wiry halo – back from her eyes.

'When I woke up,' she said, 'I thought it had happened again.'

'Thought what had happened?'

'There was blood,' said Melissa. 'There. There was blood.'

Dominic pressed his hands to both sides of her face. His forehead to hers.

He drove her home, and she woke in the driveway with her face squashed and her mouth smeared against the window. Melissa had not anticipated the discomfort the anaesthetic would cause; the afternoons lying on the sofa, the sickness, the constipation. The worst part was having to keep the stockings on the whole time. She had to keep them on or else the veins would open up again. The surgeon, Dr Taschimowitz's friend, had told her right now they were closed up, dried out and dead, like a shed snakeskin just under the surface. They would dissolve, she said, the flesh around them would just eat up the dead skin, but you have to keep the stockings on, otherwise you'll be back here in a few years and next time it might not work so well. For those first two days, Melissa had stayed on the sofa downstairs, dozed in and out of sleep.

Every few hours, her phone vibrated.

The first message had come the day after the wedding. Rhianne's name and a single photograph. Colour, filling her screen. *Some new material*, the message had said, and nothing else. Melissa had replied, and there had been no response. But the next day, the same. A photograph, and a short, one-line message.

Dominic, every night, asked if she had heard from Rhianne. 'Every day,' Melissa said. Dominic twitched, nodded.

She heaved her legs up onto the settee. The stockings were thick and they were tight around the tops of her thighs, so that the flesh there spilled out. They were held up by long, Velcro straps that attached and fastened around her waist like a suspender belt, the straps digging in, too, across her buttocks and the fronts of her thighs, so that she felt like some prime cut of meat, strung and stuffed. She had seen a photograph of Josephine when she was so terribly ill; she had been skeletal. Melissa was distrustful of any paradigm that associated emaciation with beauty, or worse, with worth. She shuffled her hips down the sofa to give her legs more height, let her feet fall out to the sides so that there was room for her thighs to breathe. She lay back, attuned to the stillness of the house, its emptiness.

She couldn't shower so she washed standing next to the bathtub with a cloth and hot water and soap that marbled on her skin if she didn't wash it off properly, making the dry skin and itching worse. Dominic was back at work, but he came home every few hours to check on her. She would wake, sometimes, to feel him checking her temperature, his hand on her forehead. Sometimes, he would just be standing there in the doorway. She could sense him, the breadth of him. She called his name from there on the sofa. He came to her, then. Sat down, heavy. Melissa wrapped her arms around him. He lay down, his weight only half-falling on her, and she clung to him. She asked him if this was the honeymoon he'd wanted. Ludo rested his nose on the edge of the sofa. His ears twitched. She thought she heard an engine idling outside the house, a car pulling up, and she waited for the door, but nobody came. She kept on waiting.

On the third day, Melissa moved from the sofa to the chair.

Her appetite had returned, as she had known it would, and she started to take walks around the garden. She moved slowly, cautious of the stitching on the insides of her thighs. Melissa was not squeamish, but once or twice if she moved too abruptly there would be a sharp pain on the inside of her left leg, and an image – which made her nauseous – arrived in her mind of her skin splitting, as if it had seams. Five days after the operation, Melissa unfastened the stockings and rolled them down over her thighs. She cut the bandages underneath them, which ran all the way from her hip to her ankle, peeling them from her legs, and though the inseams of her thighs were marked with stitches, and the skin was red and dry, stained with dried blood, the veins were gone.

She'd never spent so long in the bath, soaking, peeling off what was left of the dressings. She dried her legs, patting them with the towel. She moisturised, as she had been instructed, with aqueous cream. Briefly, Melissa inspected her reflection. She did not like to spend time with it and so was largely unaware that there was beauty there. But, for a moment, she allowed herself to contemplate the point of her chin, the two crescent rounds of her cheeks. The breadth and sweep of her collarbones carrying the pride of her shape. She did not care to measure or acknowledge them. These were not markers of a person's character. They were arbitrary, accidents of genetics that went on to inform a person's standing, worth, good fortune in life. She had more important things to worry about. Her legs were not yet dry, but she pulled on her jeans, hiking them over her hips. She went downstairs, and she waited. Hoped that in her patience, her faith, she had not been mistaken.

37

'New beginnings,' she'd said. And, just as she had wanted, he held out his hand, pulled her up off her knees and in towards him. He gathered her in, pushed her hair back from her face. He kissed the top of her head. And for a moment, she let him. For a moment, she felt that this was the safest she had ever been, would ever be. He squeezed her tight. All of his anger, his hurt, dissipated. 'What am I going to do with you?'

'Don't know,' she said. She smiled. 'Take me for dinner?'

'All right.' Callum stepped forwards, away from the door. Rhianne's heart pounded. But then he opened it, they stepped out together into the corridor.

The door swung shut behind them, taking with it the light.

'I just need my jacket,' Rhianne said. 'It's at the hotel. I'll meet you back up here.'

Callum hesitated, about to follow. Rhianne smiled.

'I'll be quick,' she said. She touched his arm, squeezed it.

Then she walked, half ran, back down the steps to the hotel. There were guests in the bar, but their presence did not register. She went the back way to the laundry.

The morning after the wedding, she had slipped out from under him. Just as she had every other morning these last weeks, she had stepped out into the corridor, opened the door. The wedding was over, she'd woken under the weight of him, and she had felt alone. Except, she was not alone. In her room she saw what had been waiting for her, there on the bed. She opened the bag. Not a palette this time, but tubes: big, fat tubes of acrylic paint, their seals unbroken. The paints were thick and bold, and she knew exactly who had left them there for her. She emptied the bag onto the floor.

She could not describe it in words, what she was making in that room. It was too radiant, too bright. It filled the pages too fully and too easily, and her hand knew too well where required shade, where redness, where orange flames that licked out from the centre across the edges of the paper. Until the day after the wedding, she had felt that this – this colour – surely could not have belonged to her, not if she could not even stand the real sun that poured in through the single-glazed windows of the hotel. She could not be made of sunlight, if even the sensation of it on her skin was too much to bear. Not if the light of it made the backs of her retina hurt.

But that day, squeezing great tubes onto paper, pushing her brush into the paint, spreading it thick and bold, she felt sure that she was creating the purest expression of who she was beneath the detritus her life had gathered. She felt sure, as she painted, that she was pouring out onto paper the most essential part of herself. She stood up, looked down at what she had drawn. And, at last, she saw herself there. She sat for a moment, took her phone out of her pocket to check the time. She was late for her shift, but it didn't matter. Carefully, she positioned her camera, took a photograph of the painting, still glossy there on the floor, and sent it to Melissa. The phone buzzed straight away, but she did not read the reply. She was looking up at the wall, the duller drawings, looking for spaces she could brighten, layer, fill. She would need time to go over it all. She would need time, if she wanted to finish it.

Rhianne, though, did not have time. Not even for that small, blank space, which, this evening, she had stared at while Callum stood right there in front of the door, and she had become aware of his bulk, the breadth of his shoulders, filling the doorframe. She understood that in this room, there would not be a tomorrow. So, instead, she had knelt down on the floor in front of him. She told him the only part of the truth he was capable of hearing, just enough of it for him to hold out his hand and step away from the door.

From the laundry, she took the jacket, her phone. She went back up the steps, her legs hollow. The rhododendrons were heavy headed: summer was beginning, pollen dusting the concrete. Rhianne went back up the path and stopped at the edge of the car park, looking up at the staff house. In the orange room, the blinds were drawn back, the walls illuminated in a bright block. She could not see him there, and nor could she see if he was in his own room. The thought occurred to her that he was already downstairs, waiting.

She stepped onto the gravel, her keys in her hand. The security light clicked on. She crossed towards her car, her hands steady as she opened the door and climbed into the front seat. Weeks since she had driven. Thoughts knotted behind her vision. The engine would stutter, flood. The petrol drained from its tank. Still, she turned the key and the engine juddered. Flipped on the lights, pulled out, fast, in reverse. Her heart pounded. Above her, his bedroom light flicked on. She looked up.

This morning, she'd lain next to him, studied the architecture of his jaw, those cheekbones. His face had been soft. Now, all she saw was his silhouette, there against the light. She froze, fixated by his outline. She conjured images. A windowpane, splintering. Bone colliding with bone, a grip tightening. But it hadn't been that, not really. Or, at least, not quite, or not yet. Really, it had been that look. That long, flat look that drained her of light. The look she could feel, now, through the glass. Simply, he looked. And then, he turned away, and the security light blinked. Rhianne pushed the car into gear, and she drove.

38

Later, once Melissa's stitches had healed, they went swimming. The spot was a drive away, and it was just the two of them, Melissa and Rhianne in the Saab. Rhianne had her shoes off in the car, and she kicked them out onto the grass where they had parked. It was still fairly early, so the grass was wet, and she stood barefoot, feeding her feet slowly into the straps of her sandals.

Rhianne heaved her rucksack onto her back, followed Melissa. Both of them moved slowly, steadily, hands pressing against the smooth faces of the rocks around them to steady themselves. Rhianne watched Melissa move, how carefully she held herself, how, although she moved slowly, she was sure of her footing. The bottom of the path fed into woodlands, which opened out into a wide, smooth rock, hanging over the lip of the river. On the opposite side of the water, a hundred or so metres downriver, was a family: a white Labrador in the shallows, the mother sitting on a rock while her children clambered down into the water. Melissa got undressed first, laid out her clothes in a patch of sunlight. She was wearing her black swimming costume, her short hair tucked behind her ears. Her legs had been covered for most of the summer, and Rhianne watched her climb down into the water, then she slowly began to undress.

Rhianne had not swum since South Sands. She lowered herself into the water. It was river water: icy, and she took it. The shock to her chest as she plunged beneath the surface, gasping, regulating her breath. It was early summer, and she and Melissa had run out of conversation. This was a relief. Those long walks across the common, Melissa leaning her weight on Rhianne's elbow, they had talked themselves in circles, and Rhianne had come to learn that there was nothing she could not say. If she said that she loved him, Melissa understood. If she said that she missed him, Melissa understood. If she said she hoped that he would be crushed in the driver's seat of a burning car, Melissa, well, she understood, and Rhianne knew that this woman who was not her blood but who loved her with the ferocity of any mother would understand anything that needed to be understood.

It had been a month now. He had contacted her only once, just after she left. That night, she had handed Melissa her phone, and Melissa had answered. Melissa had waited for him to speak, but he'd hung up. He had known. Then, he must have known. She'd waited for the sound of his engine idling, the slam of a car door. She feared his return. In equal measure, she craved it. 'Dopamine,' Melissa had said, pushing her hair back from her face. 'Nobody doesn't like dopamine.' They'd heard the sound of a door slamming outside, Dominic calling from the hallway.

Rhianne lay on her back, the water holding her body, adjusting to the shock of the cold. Here, in this silver pool of light, trees tall on either side, a slice of sky above her, she was momentarily free.

Melissa got out first, half-dressed by the time Rhianne followed her out of the water. Rhianne climbed up the rocks towards her, the stone warm on her skin, and traced her wet footsteps up to where they'd left the clothes. She could hear the wood pigeons, the sound of the motorway in the distance. Melissa handed her a towel, and Rhianne wrapped herself in it. Perhaps Melissa knew that Rhianne was thinking of him, as still she did. He would be working a straight finish now, and for a moment there was that old feeling that only within the closed-off sphere he had created for them did the possibility of love exist. The logic didn't hold up to any scrutiny, because even though there, in his arms, there was the possibility of love, there was also the certainty of pain.

Rhianne knelt, cautiously, the towel still balancing on her back, and began to dry herself. Melissa stood, unwrapped her own towel from her hair, and held it up, around Rhianne, shielding her, so that she could dress. Rhianne dried herself as quickly as she could, hitching her underwear up around her legs, sticky on her cold, pimpled skin. Melissa folded up the towel and knelt down, packing up her bag. 'He's left,' she said.

'Left where?'

'The hotel,' Melissa said. She wasn't looking up. 'I heard last week. He's gone.'

Rhianne stood in the cold clearing, unmoving. Melissa stood, hitched her bag onto her back. 'Let's go,' she said. 'I want to get a caramel latte before the hut closes.'

On the way back, Rhianne fell asleep in the passenger seat, the heating on full. She took a long shower in the little bathroom next to her room, then came downstairs to the living room, where Ludo was curled up on himself, his small body breathing. So, he was gone. Rhianne lay down, rested her cheek on Ludo's warm fur. He was gone, and it was finished.

Dominic didn't know what they talked about on those long walks they took together. Callum, he assumed, the sudden end to their relationship. But she was young, and he hoped, after everything she had been through, that Callum had reminded her what it meant to be loved. He hoped it wasn't just about that; he hoped, too, that they talked about the future.

'I'm going to do it,' Rhianne said over dinner. 'Put in an

application for the MA.' She kept her eyes on her food. 'And I'll talk to them about before.'

The night she returned home, Dominic had come back to find Rhianne and Melissa out on the patio. Two women, backs turned to him, the fairy lights on and the little gnome illuminated. Dominic stood, observing them from the kitchen. Rhianne saw him first, and, turning, he saw how Melissa stayed her. For a moment they were still. Then, Rhianne, in her chair, leaned forwards, fell into Melissa's arms. Dominic stepped through the open doorway, and in the moment that Melissa saw him, she made eye contact with him over Rhianne's shoulder. Minutely, Melissa shook her head. Dominic paused, stood, for a moment, before he went back inside.

The next morning, Jess arrived. There were the sounds of the two girls speaking, low and fast, under the door of Rhianne's bedroom. In the mornings, they too went for long walks. They curled up on the sofa, limbs intertwined. He thought, once, he had felt Rhianne flinch when he touched her. But then she stood, held him close, and he was sure that he must have imagined it. It could not be him that she thought capable of harm.

'Did you tell her?' he asked Melissa, one night in the dark. 'About London?'

Melissa shook her head. 'Why would I tell her a thing like that?'

He knew that there was reticence, and he knew that there had been a rupture. But he also knew that there had been a repair. He had understood, the day he came to collect Melissa from the hospital, how fully she loved him. He understood what, for years, he had failed to understand: that those parts of herself she held back from him, she did not hold out of greed, or because she was not generous, or because she did not love him. She held them back out of fear. And fear, the fear of loss, of failure, of rejection, these were all fears that Dominic understood on a cellular level, and they were fears he did not meet with coldness, or with punishment, but, as he always had done, with persistence, relentless as it was bold.

Dominic was not sorry for what he had done. He slept soundly.

Melissa and Rhianne had just got back from swimming. Dominic walked alone across the top-floor corridor. He paused, looked up at the drawing, framed there on the wall. Originally, he had put up Josephine, Rhianne's ruined painting – textured, thick, the loss of her – but Rhianne had protested the gesture, told him she didn't like it. 'This one,' she said. She hesitated, and then handed it to him. 'If you want to put something, put this one up.' It was a line drawing. A hip, thick bands of muscle, lines in heavy pencil and charcoal. Dominic held the drawing in both hands. Her torso, her neck. Visceral, a shock. The hand, there, around her throat. He had not expected these gradations of black, grey, lead yielding to paper. The precision, and the softness. Dominic blinked. Rhianne was looking at him, waiting.

'I'll take it tomorrow,' he said, 'to the framers. Roberta's cousin in town.'

He'd stood in the shop and chosen between seven types of varnishes, got picky about the width of the mount. 'My daughter,' he said, although the framer hadn't asked him, 'she's an artist.'

Now he turned away, towards the window, where Melissa appeared, fitting a dust mask to her face and dragging, with both arms, the chainsaw she used twice a year to trim the box-hedge. She paused, pulling the rope, starting the engine, and then, steadying herself, she lifted it up above her head, wielding it there for a moment, before bringing it down upon the hedge, and the muscles of her arms, shoulders came alight in sunshine.

39

The day Melissa had come to the hotel, Callum had been working. She'd picked up the suitcases Kieran had helped him carry down from his room and into the laundry. He hadn't seen her, but the door to Brendan's office had been shut, and later, when Brendan sat down across from him, he could not quite meet Callum's gaze. 'It's experience,' he said. 'We just think that Dean has more experience setting up somewhere new.'

'Jack?' Callum said.

'Jack, me. We need you here,' Brendan said, 'looking after things.'

He'd stayed for only a handful of weeks before he told Brendan he'd found somewhere else. He'd taken his pink crocs with him, and his favourite knife, and soon descended the steps to another kitchen, keeping his eyes down. The fridge opened the other way here, and the pass was narrower, the grill hotter, but he'd get used to that. He'd get used to all of it, given time.

The kitchen door banged open, and Callum glanced across, under the pass, saw the tug of long dark hair pulled back, the sweep of eyelashes, carefully made up. The flush from the kitchen's heat travelling up the base of the throat. The gleam of gold pushed through the top of an ear. Callum flicked the dishcloth back over his shoulder. Sparked the grill.

Brendan had gone himself to check that the room was clear. It was the sort of thing Callum would normally have done, because

Callum had always made himself useful, indispensable. For a long time, Brendan had thought that Callum was a person who could not be replaced. Brendan pushed open the door to his bedroom. The curtains had been torn down and they needed fixing, and there were scratches on the little table by the window, the bed-frame. Light poured through the bare windows and onto the dirt-stained carpet. The bed was stripped, and that, too, was stained, and on it, there was a folder, thick, full of paper. He would have to confront it, someday, the too-soft love that he had for this man, who, to Brendan, would always be a boy, incapable of harm. But he could not do it now, not today. 'Noxious,' Melissa had said, sitting across from him. Jack, next to him, folded his arms. 'And difficult to see. For those of us who aren't looking properly.'

He picked up the folder. Some of the papers were sticking out and he could see that there was colour, there, orange and yellow and red, but he did not open it. He turned it over in his hands, opened it, thinking – hoping – that Callum might have left something: a message. There was nothing.

Kieran cycled away across the common, a tobacco-tin of weed in the pocket of his hoodie. Passing the turning to The White Hart, he did not pause, but kept flying, straight. The expanse of the common opening out in front of him, bombing straight down towards the long grass. He lay back beneath the wide-open sky, the grass crisp on his lower back, popped open his tobacco tin. Music tinny on his phone. A deep inhale. Kieran blew smoke, allowed the fuzziness to settle over his brain. Felt, here, he was content. In his back pocket, his phone vibrated, and he rolled over onto one side, extracted it. Brendan, asking if he could take on another shift next week. He read the message, took a long, slow drag. Watched the tip of his joint fire briefly red, then black.

40

Summer again, congested heat. A Friday, Kingsland Road. Rhianne was taking the day off; she'd booked herself a pedicure. She had messaged Melissa to inform her of the indulgence, its spontaneity. Part-confessional, but also to get ahead of the accusation that she was spending twice the pay she'd receive for an hour's work to have the rough skin grated from her feet and her toenails decorated with some intricate pattern that would likely not even be seen. Boastful, too. These days, she took care of herself. Melissa, at last, had made it to Como, but she responded immediately, with a picture of Dominic eating an ice-cream and wearing a large, inelegant sunhat.

She did not tell Melissa what had happened this morning, that she had seen him.

The finished product – polished toenails, soles briefly soft – was the least exciting part of the procedure. Sitting back with her arms resting on a sturdy cushion, feet elevated: that felt good. There was no bathtub in their flat, so the sensation of having her feet fully submerged in hot water was good, too. And the touch. The briskness of it, the roughness, the way the technician looked over to the front desk, speaking a language she did not understand as he kneaded Rhianne's soles with his knuckles, all of this made it impersonal. She did not attempt to decipher the tone, the contents of his interaction, but instead handed herself over to the alchemy of this stranger's touch, which made her feel that her body – independent of her, her history, the story of her life – simply as a body, possessed unimpeachable worth.

This fantasy of a democratised touch had lasted up until her feet were deposited back on the stool, the final layer of moisturiser not quite embedded, the technician retreating into the break room with the butt of his phone held to his ear to listen to the voice-notes that had been arriving in his pocket throughout the treatment. Rhianne had put her socks back on, her feet still oily inside her shoes. At the door, she had tapped her card on the reader, stepped out into the late-afternoon warmth.

The bar was in Shoreditch, just past the fire station, and she was early. It was half-empty, but in a couple of hours it would be busier, the floor a dance floor, sticky with Red Bull and rum. It was the last weekend in May, and the Champions League final was playing on a screen on the wall outside. Rhianne ordered a drink, drew a line in the condensation on the outside of her glass.

She had known that he was in London because Kieran had told her, but it had been almost a year and she hadn't seen him, hadn't heard from him either, and she'd allowed herself the possibility that he had been fired. Once, she'd been to the restaurant where he worked, under the arches in Haggerston, and she'd stood against the wall opposite, waiting for him to emerge. It had been winter, and it was cold, and she stood there until the restaurant was empty and the lights were out and she had expected him and she'd had it planned: how she would step out of the shadows and confront him, how she would say everything she had considered saying, how she would make him see all of the things he had done to hurt her, and she knew that even though he would know, then, that he still had power over her, at least she would have spoken. But it wasn't Callum who appeared – dressed in whites and holding two black bin bags, edging through the glass front – but another chef, a woman.

Rhianne watched as she slung the sacks into the bin. She didn't step out of the shadows.

Sometimes, she considered the possibility that he was happy.

The door to the pub opened; Rhianne looked up.

Three men in Arsenal shirts, bodies loud.

She sipped her drink.

She hadn't gone back to the restaurant, but she indulged fantasies in which she walked into the kitchen, put a meat knife through his hand, or his neck, or his stomach. The fantasies lasted only as long as she could hold them, and they gave her no satisfaction, because the possibility of his pain did nothing for her. This was something she had talked about with Melissa, over and again, on their long walks, as Rhianne's calves grew tight and her lungs larger, her thighs stronger. 'Not everyone would agree,' Melissa would say, hesitant, 'your father, for example.'

But Rhianne was clear. The thought of Callum in pain was like a sweet, sugary drink. It was a momentary distraction, a momentary pleasure, which was quickly superseded by the fact of loss that she felt, still, even now. Except it wasn't real grief – and Rhianne knew grief – because there was no substance to it. Quantifiably, there was nothing that had been lost, except for the possibility of a love that had never fully arrived. If she thought clearly about her life with Callum, she thought in terms of chemistry, addiction. The heart-shredding exhaustion of being drawn into something that looked so much like love, that so quickly transmuted. This, she had tried to explain to Dominic, Melissa sitting close, and Rhianne had felt her breath shorten as she spoke. 'He didn't, you know,' Dominic had said, voice unsteady, 'hurt you?'

'What do you mean?'

'Physically hurt you.'

'No,' Rhianne said. 'It wasn't like that.'

An obfuscation, but one that felt irrelevant to her. It wasn't so much his touch that had hurt her but its withdrawal, right at the times when she had needed it most. It was this, and it was all the life that had been forestalled while, waiting, she had forgotten herself. She studied her father's face, the roughness of his skin, the fear, and the relief, and she decided that she would go no further. She decided, squeezing his hand more tightly, that she did not want to cause him pain if she did not have to. 'I think,' she said, 'it just wasn't very healthy. Unbalanced.'

'Unhealthy.' Dominic nodded. This he could understand. 'That's no good.'

He held her tighter.

She hadn't been back to the hotel. Brendan, though, had come to the house, handed to Melissa a thick, wadded folder. Blue, like the kind Rhianne would have used to bring home her schoolwork, his handwriting across the front: her name. She didn't take it with her to London. She and Jess sat beneath the Bowling print. Long nights, mornings together. Repair.

The windows of the pub had misted with the heat of the afternoon. Rhianne waited.

The door opened again. Two women, contoured, skin bare.

A year now. A year of daily distance. A year of existence, beyond his sphere. The studio in King's Cross was large and light-filled, and she was left alone to work. A new painting. A photograph her father had given her. Josephine, on the other side of a student room, standing next to a record player. She was wearing an oversized cotton dress with thick tights and a blanket around her shoulders. One hand resting on the record player, the other holding a Heineken, the light catching her three-banded ring. The room was busy, full of people, but she was the only one looking at the camera: straight across the room, at the person taking the photograph. It was dark, and the flash was on, and her eyes were red where the light hit them.

The bar was getting busier. She checked her phone. There hadn't been a message: she would have to wait a little longer. There was a part of her that wanted to leave. The game had started. Across from her, two men sitting side by side, one on his phone, the other watching the football. They must be late twenties, a little older than Rhianne. One of them, blue-eyed, glancing in her direction. She took a sip of her drink, the synthetic warmth of alcohol sitting at the top of her stomach. She checked the time. Ten minutes more.

This morning, she'd been walking along Dalston Lane, and she'd seen the shape of his shoulders moving through a busy pedestrian crowd. He'd crossed the lights on red, darting through traffic, towards the entrance to the overground, and she'd seen him – felt him – move into her awareness, and her, in his presence, immediately alight, the time between them, and all of that distance, concertinaed. She watched him sling his jacket over his shoulder, his T-shirt bright, and, involuntarily, she felt her pace quicken, her breath turning shallow. She was getting the overground. It was ten to twelve, the start of the afternoon shift. He'd be getting the same train as her, south, to the restaurant.

In that moment, all of the logic of their separation fell away, and she was oriented to his movements, just as she always had been, as if nothing had changed, and now she was following, half walking, running up the ramp to the barrier, tapping her card, and now she was tripping down the steps, towards where there were two trains, stationed. It took her seconds, more time than she had, to discern which of the trains he would be taking. South, to Haggerston. The train leaving in two minutes. She stood outside the doors. And there, as she stood, was a second in which she collected herself. How easy it would be, stepping forwards, to be pulled straight back into his embrace. How warm it would be, how much like home. And then, without warning, but also without doubt, how alone.

The alarm began to sound. Rhianne did not move. She stayed where she was, there, on the platform. Perhaps she wanted him still. Loved him, even. But that was not enough, not if it was a love that voided her, drained her. So, she stayed still. And she watched as the doors slid shut, as her reflection arrived there in the glass. She watched as the train pulled away.

The doors opened again. This time Rhianne stood, pushing her drink to the side, stepped forwards. The bar was full now and the floor was sticky. There was the roar of a goal nearly scored. Jess put her arms around her, and she felt all of it – the rush of desire, the fear of loss; reconciliation – falling away, subsumed in the clarity of their embrace. 'Outside?' said Jess. They moved through the knot of people, back out of the doors, out into the last of the evening. The sky was wide, and it was filled with colour.

About the Author

Rosie Price is the author of the highly acclaimed debut *What Red Was*, an *Observer* New Voices selection. *The Orange Room* is her second novel. She lives in London.